FOOTSTEPS
in the SKY

FOOTSTEPS
in the SKY

GREG KEYES

OPEN ROAD

INTEGRATED MEDIA

NEW YORK

Cover design by Kat Lee

978-1-4976-9991-5

Published in 2015 by Open Road Integrated Media, Inc.
345 Hudson Street
New York, NY 10014
www.openroadmedia.com

DEDICATED TO TRACEY ABLA

FOOTSTEPS
in the SKY

In the world below this one, the people were unhappy. There was much corruption, and two-hearts were everywhere. The elders met in the kivas, discussing where else they might live.

"We have heard footsteps in the sky," one of them said. "Someone must be there. Perhaps we can live there."

So they sent several birds up, but all failed to find the source of the footsteps. At last they made a bird of their own, out of clay, and they sent him up. This was the catbird.

Catbird found the hole in the sky and above it a grey, featureless land. He found great fires burning, and in the light and heat of these fires grew fields of corn, squash, and melons. Catbird found a stone house and a person sleeping. Catbird waited patiently until the person woke up. This person was like a skeleton; his eyes were sunken deep into their sockets, he had no hair. He wore four strands of turquoise and four strands of bone. His voice was like the bone, dry and harsh.

"Why are you here? What is your business?" the person asked.

"I have come," said Catbird, "to find the person who makes the footsteps we hear in the sky."

"Those belong to me, Masaw," said the person. "Those footsteps are mine. Do you not fear me?"

"Ah, no," the Catbird replied. "I have just recently been created. I have not learned yet to fear. But I come to ask if the people below can live here, with you. They wish to escape the evil that infests the lower world."

Masaw swept his thin, skeletal hands around him. His voice was a grating whisper.

"You see what is here. A grey world, barely formed, with no

light. I must build fires to grow my crops. Your people would have to work very hard to live here. But there is land and water. If the people below are willing—willing to live in such a hard place, to work to make it different—then they are welcome to come."

That is what the god Masaw told Catbird, and that is what Catbird told the people below.

—From the Hopi Origin Legend

PROLOGUE

2421 A.D.

KACHINA

I. FARMER

There is mercy only in sleep. The years splinter on our titanium spines, the tiny evils of hydrogen atoms chew at us gleefully. Within, capricious quanta betray us, take our minds and memories into chaos.

Awake, we can feel this. Asleep—we just wake up a little less. Stupider.

I felt my new stupidity as we fell towards the orange light. Already I could make out the inner system dross; gas giants useful only for fuel, the sparkling belt of hydrogen and water crystals we pulled out from them so long ago. I knew assorted spheres and chunks of atmosphereless slag spun lazily below as well, though they were still too small to see. Nor could I yet see the farm.

I remembered it though. Even if I didn't—if entropy had robbed me of that, too—I would have known it. The three of us have six farms to take care of, and they all look the same.

The three of us. If I was stupid, how were the others?

Not too well.

Odatatek was beyond rational thought. Her spine still carried autonomic messages, and siblinged to us, she still functioned. She could even get through fairly simple logic problems, but cognition was lost to her.

Would that it were beyond me.

Hatedotik could still think, but what she thought worried me. She conceived of herself as a simple mechanical piston, in-and-out, ceaseless. There were no questions left in her, only a scorching certitude.

I grieved for them both, and for myself. We were all mad.

And, mad, we went to do our job.

Deep inside—in a place where I fancy myself a living thing—I created a place of gaseous oxygen and liquid water and began growing a little brother. By the time we reached the farm, he would be adult.

And down we went.

II. PELA

Pulverized stone crunched beneath Pela's thick-soled boots as she wound her way up the steep, charcoal slope. She leaned into her footprints, intent on making every ounce of her fifty-four kilos somehow work for her, though physics and plain common sense insisted that leaning forward did not help one move up.

Then again, if she leaned back, she would tumble down 200 meters of basalt rasp. She continued to lean.

At the top, Pela took a grateful breath, felt the blood throbbing in her legs and arms. With a well-earned sigh, she gingerly sat down, rocking her butt back and forth in the dense dust at the bluff's edge until her seat was comfortable. She eased out her canteen and savored a single mouthful of distilled water, still cool from the morning, felt the grit in her teeth from the climb. Her gaze walked out on yellow morning light, over the lazy, yawning valley below.

The blue snake of the Palulukang River wound confidently through the belly of the land, as if he had done the work, carved through the layers of stone, opened a wide, fertile bottom from the highlands to the dark, distant sea. But the river was young. Stronger, harsher forces than water had shaped the land here, and water only sought downhill. Still, Palulukang looked like he belonged.

Not so the misty green stain, darkest near the river but nevertheless filling the entire valley. Not from up here, at least, where it could be seen for what it was; a tiny oasis of verdure in a desert of black and red stone and the dark blue moss that dug so ferociously at it. But one day . . .

One day, the whole Fifth World would grow green.

The evidence was around her. Already the tenacious taproot dandelions were fighting the native plants for supremacy, here near the edge. Born up by thermals, the tough seeds found welcome in the nearly sterile soil, pushing their deep, spear-like roots into the rock below, drawing sustenance from the depths and exhaling oxygen into the earth. These were now in bloom, hand-sized yellow flowers bourn on thick, meaty stalks bigger around than her thumb. When they died they would quickly rot, courtesy of the specialized bacteria that lived symbiotically within them. They would add to the meager fund of organic matter on the plateau until organisms with richer appetites could supplant them.

She noted absently that the fire clover she had sown last trip was making a good start as well.

Yes, today the valley, tomorrow the plateau. Her plateau. She would live to see grass and trees up here, if Masaw so willed.

Pela had mixed feelings about that. There was a reason she took these trips on foot. She loved to wander the outback, as austere and melancholy as it was. The black and red plain stretched level and far, blotched with the persistent cyan mosses, skirt trees, weirdness and—most of all—promise of mystery. Her people would kill one beauty to make another.

She shouldered her pack, stood, put her back to the civilized world. Today she would go to the black giants she could see on the horizon, probably camp there tonight. The ancient volcanic cores were still home to many of the more complex native plants, including whiskyberry. It would be good to find some whiskyberry.

And, maybe this time, some sign of the Kachina.

That thought always brought an odd mixture of awe, betrayal, and skepticism. As a little girl, the Kachina spirits had been very real to her; they danced into town during the ceremonies, brought her presents, punished her when she was bad. They watched from overhead, too, warned the People when a fierce wind or rain was nigh, when the volcanoes to the south were belching. She adored them and feared them, the colorful dancers, the stars in the sky that moved faster than the wheel of night.

She would never forget when she became a woman, and the truth stood naked before her. The fierce Whipping Kachina—the punisher who had made her burn with shame and fear—bereft of his horrific mask, he was her mother's brother. As were the others, all of them. Cousins, grandparents—older friends. Lies on two legs, and everyone older than her was involved.

The Kachina in the sky were lies, too. Made of metal and silicon, they were satellites that orbited the Fifth World unceasingly. But made by people, just like the masks.

Oh, it had been explained to her that these people and these machines were merely the conduits for the real Kachina, powerful and distant amongst the stars. But the feeling of betrayed wonder had ruined them for Pela. The more she learned, the more she doubted, and when she went down into Salt to go to school, she met lowlanders who didn't even pretend to believe in the powerful, beneficent spirits.

Father Sun was quickening the horizon gold and purple before Pela reached the black columns. Hurrying, lest she be caught without light, she scrambled up a way she knew, gaining elevation over the darkling plain. Before the blazing in the sky quieted she had her view, renewed her faith. Savored belief again, though it was a meal flavored with the ash of skepticism.

There, beyond the basalt titans, coming night filled a vast bowl with shadow. This crater had birthed the billion billion tons of ash and crushed rock that covered the plain, which even now choked the River during floods, fifty thousand years after her savage labor. A piece of the sky bigger than all of the mesa city had struck there, filled the heavens with dirt. And not just in this place; at school she had learned that there were sixty such impact craters on the planet's surface, and evidence was good that they had all been made simultaneously.

Pela unpacked her tent and began setting it up in the little cove she had used before. Her thick, hard hands worked quickly, surely, but her thoughts were on the stars.

There was other evidence. For five billion years, the Fifth World had been a place unfit for human life. The atmosphere had been an oven of carbon dioxide, the surface a layer cake of lava flows and metamorphic rock. Then the monsters had fallen from space. Not much later—the geologists said a thousand years—there was oxygen and water. And life. Single celled at first, but within another thousand years a hundred species of plants and small animals to live in the newly-created soil.

The universe did not work so, on its own. For fifty thousand years someone had labored to make the Fifth World ready for the Hopitu-Shinumu, the Well-Behaved People.

Somewhere, beyond the masks, beyond the satellites, perhaps beyond the winking stars themselves, the Kachina lived. And some day they would return.

And so, she thought, truth nested within truth, revealed as a lie only until one knew more.

Shadow spilled from the bowl and fell in a swift sheet from the east. Pela set up her alcohol stove, for heat rather than to cook on. She was just considering whether to sleep or watch the stars when she remembered the whiskyberry bush that grew just beyond the jutting stone to her left. She flicked on her torch and walked over to find it.

Whiskyberries were always in bloom and they always had fruit. She smiled at the stubborn plant, its barrel-body, flowers and fruit protruding like pink and black knobs. She pulled a handful of the nodules and bit one open. The taste was sharp, smoky, and its fire ran up her nose before her tongue was even aware of it.

As she bit the second, the juice from the first quietly incandesced in her belly.

Better not to eat too many, she considered. But she loved whiskyberries. Other of the native plants produced purer alcohol, but they had no flavor.

Alcohol had been the main problem with the planet. Free oxygen was available, yes, but almost no nitrogen and alcohol fumes so thick that no mammal could live in it. The native animals—or the worms that passed as animals—metabolized the alcohol. There had even been little Dragonfly things that sucked in fumes like ramjets as they whirred along. Pela had never seen most of these. They had died early in the terraforming process, eliminated by soldier viruses built from their own cells. But a few—like the plants that produced fuel for bikes, cars, hovercraft, and heat—were saved. And a few that had more entertaining virtues.

Like whiskyberry. Pela sucked two more and smiled a silly smile up at the heavens. The stars remained pretty but assumed the peculiar flatness that came with intoxication.

Night painted her dark brush-strokes across the sky, and the flat stars brightened. Pela squinted once more, standing despite wobbly, uncooperative knees to see the landscape vanish. Her land, come to her from her mother and from her mother's mother. Everything she could see was her responsibility, her charge. It wasn't fertile and wet, like the river valley; no one envied her yet.

But they would envy her daughter, if she ever had one. Oh, yes, Pela would see to that. Despite her qualms, this desert would bloom with grain, run lousy with rabbit, deer, and coyote. Cornbrakes would drink the thin streams that stuttered down the slopes to the valley. Her daughter would have respect, not just as a member of the Sand clan, but as Pela's daughter.

If, of course, she ever had a daughter.

And so Pela did just what she had been avoiding. She thought about Tuve.

"Piss on you," she muttered, and bit savagely into another whiskyberry. She knew she wasn't the nicest looking woman on the mesa. But she wasn't ugly. There were men who found her broad mouth and wide dark eyes sensuous. They told her so. And if her thick, strong body wasn't that of a young girl, it was that of a woman who would not break—or even bend—in the throes of passion. Tuve knew that, first hand.

Maybe he was playing games with her. Tuve was a child that way. Maybe he wanted to see how much she wanted him.

Let him see. She could stay up here a long time before she cooled off. Long enough for him to realize that a little girl like Sia could not do much for him, not in the Fifth World.

She caught a flare of light in the heavens. A meteor? It was big. It flashed brighter, seemed to fairly explode, and vanished, leaving a magenta and blue tracer in her eyeballs. Pela caught her breath, her drunken heart pounding madly in her chest. Her thought had been a jolt of pure terror. Another world shaker, like the one that made the great craters. . . . Her imagination painted the brilliant flash, the breath of wind that would engulf her like molten lead.

Silly drunk, she thought, and bit into another berry.

And so when the shadow blotted the stars, when four steel legs chuffed into the gravelly soil, Pela lay curled on her side, snoring faintly.

III. FARMER

By the time the little brother was actually dead, I knew what had killed it. The atmospheric chemistry was wrong.

I felt remorse for dooming the little brother, though I had naturally grown him without much of a brain to spare him fear. He wasn't even needed; spectral and reactive analysis revealed almost immediately that the air was too rich in oxygen, to low in saturated alcohol vapor and carbon dioxide. The little brother starved, his enrichment gills fluttering in vain.

I assured myself that I couldn't have known; the atmospheric problems might have been very subtle, might have required an autopsy to understand. I could not have counted on the difficulty being of such a very coarse nature.

<You see? This farm is atatetak. Worthless.>

That wasn't my thought. I could tell because it was slightly blue-shifted. Also, as distance and time had decomposed us, each in our own way, we had become different in our communication styles. We were now more like three separate beings than parts of any whole. No, that thought belonged to my sister, Hatedotik.

<The atmosphere is atatetak, I agree. But there is life down there.>

<Mutated. Worthless. We must sterilize and re-seed.> Hatedotik sounded as certain as binary code. She was. Things were or weren't for her now. Only I retained the judgment our Makers think so important. Only I retained etadotetak, the emotion of self-protection that we extend to others at our own expense. Etadotetak had grown our Makers strong, allowed them to cooperate as no other species on their homeworld could. Taken them into space, where they could create planets safer than the one that had budded them.

And though I knew that Hatedotik was right, I had Etadotetak for the life forms down there.

<But look,> I argued. <See those patches of heat, along the

coast, up that inland valley? See the neutrino flow from those two sources? There is life down there like the Makers, with atomic generators, with industries. Perhaps it is the Makers.>

<The little brother died,> Hatedotik replied, unequivocally.

I was beginning to wish that we weren't so closely linked. She had access to any data I gathered, and that might no longer be beneficial.

<Yes, but the planet of our Makers has circuited its sun one hundred and two thousand times since we last saw one of them. How might they have changed in that time?>

<I don't understand you. I only know what our mission is. We change planets as our Makers specified we should. This planet has departed from that plan, despite the program we instituted the last time we were here. Therefore we should re-seed.>

<That would mean destroying the life that exists down there.>

<We have destroyed elahudotatek before. That is of no concern.>

<Spongy secretions. Single cells born aloft. We have destroyed such. But this elahudotatek—if it is that, and not our Makers—this alien life can build fusion engines.>

<Resolution!> Hatedotik demanded, and I felt automatic mechanisms locking the three of us together. Hatedotik was certain, I was uncertain, and Odatatek had no opinion whatsoever. But she could break the tie. It depended upon what criteria remained in her disintegrating mind. Right now, she was absorbing the data, evaluating our opposed stances, seeking resolution.

She could not find it amongst the few sparks still winking along her backbonebrain.

<More data,> she begged.

So.

And as if in response, something moved towards the lander. I saw it clearly, and wished desperately that my siblings could not. It looked very little like a Maker.

The thing was a cylinder balanced improbably on only two legs.

What I took to be the sensory organs were on a spherical protrusion at the top of its strange body, clustered together rather than strung along its backbone. I wondered if its brain might be in the sphere—odd, but if the sense organs were there, it would be most logical. It had two limbs and very fine hands—not like the Makers', but obviously functional and versatile. It held a tool in one of them.

Was this what had built the fusion reactors?

Odatatek had still not decided. Her criteria must not be based upon whether or not the life seemed alien, then.

Perhaps there remained in her a tiny shred of Etadotetak. That would be interesting. If I could prove that the life down there was worthy of sacrificing a prime planet for the Makers, I could win this adjudication. And there might be one very good way of gathering more data toward that end.

I was surprised that I thought of it, though I had all of the equipment. There was no need to fabricate anything. And I could use self-contained systems; the data would not be freely accessible to the others until I made it so.

All I needed was a tissue sample. The creature obliged by stepping closer, hand extended.

IV. HOKU

Hoku snarled, snapped his words off at Juaren as if they were bullets. "You may consider yourself terminated, Itupko Juaren. How in the hell could you have missed two starships, each a kilometer long? Shit, they must be visible to the naked eye!"

"Three ships, Ibaba. The polar sky Kachina just found another," Red Jimmie interjected.

Juaren's narrow mouth chewed silently for a moment, as if seeking to fill itself with explanations. Perspiration stood out on his dark brow. "Ibaba Hoku," he finally got out. "Hoku. I wasn't looking for them. Space is vast. It can easily hide three objects of that size."

"We live on a planet with multiple astroblems five kilometers and more across, and you don't keep better watch for falling rocks? How will we explain this to the councilors? To the Tech Society?" To Her? He added silently.

Hoku bit off his last word and flattened his lips into a severe line. His nearly square face made any scowl seem like an ogre mask; now it was grotesque with tension and fury.

But not fear. Hoku had not clawed his way up from a landless clan to his exalted position because he was afraid. It would take more than the first non-human starships ever encountered to make him fear. He was worried, but not about the aliens. Rather, he was concerned that as mother-father of this research station, he would be held responsible for Juaren's negligence. He would have to straighten that out, even if the boy was a clan relative. Fuck that, anyway. Hoku was no mesa-trash, paralyzed by clan and family. He flung himself out of his chair and pushed past his two co-workers into the corridor. The pale yellow lighting strips flared on to limn his progress. Thirteen paces exactly brought him to his door, and he counted each one off, an exercise to calm himself. The door opened at his rap and odor signature and closed behind him on vocal command.

The room did not slow him down. Spare, furnished only with a small table, couch, and sleeping mat, the floor was mostly bare, a place to exercise in private. Now he paced quickly across it to his destination, the outside door across the room.

The portal whisked open and a sea-breeze caught him immediately, wrapped up his anger in a sheet of cool salt-tang. The sea was beveled grey steel, white frosted on the spines of its shallow waves. Along the eastern horizon lay a lens of pale aquamarine, the eye of dawn barely slitted. Stars still glistened overhead, but their twinklings were numbered by the lifting shadow in the east. The old men up on the mesas would call this Qoiyangyesva, the first light that human beings ever saw, the grey dawn. They would be preparing to sing a welcome to the Sun Father.

Hoku sneered at such superstition, but not at the beauty itself. He breathed deeply of the cool air, felt calm settle across his shoulders like a mantle. When the muscles of his neck were unbound, he went to his terminal and softly commanded it to link him with the central office in Salt. He brushed his hand over the short, jet bristles on his head.

The cube woke to life, and a woman's features formed in it, seamed by time, eroded by care. But those grey eyes were bright with understanding. Age had sharpened them while blurring her face.

"Mother-Father," he acknowledged.

"Report, Hoku. What's going on over there? We've already found one of your damned ships."

"Yes Mother-Fa. . . ."

"Spare me that crap. The assholes who settled this planet may have condemned us to clutter our speech with silly honorifics, but we don't have to indulge their corpses. Or their non-existent ghosts. Just tell me what's going on."

Hoku nodded. "Three ships now, and that's probably it."

"And the probe, or whatever the hell the ships dropped on us?"

"Close to the mesa country, out on the big plateau. My men are fueling a truck now. I'll be on my way in ten minutes."

She nodded, but did not speak. She was waiting for something. He gave it to her.

"I'm sorry to report that Juaren Sewuptewa must be suspended from duty. I have tried to shield him, for he is my mother's-sister's-boy. But his overindulgence in alcohol and subsequent neglect of duty has endangered the entire colony. I submit my resignation for failing to report him."

Hoku felt his heart hammering. The eerie grey eyes regarded him from the screen, iron screws turning into his soul.

"No," she finally said. "I have come to expect this kind of silly clan sentimentality from most of my people. I am glad to see you rise above it, if perhaps too late. Another useless legacy of our founding generation. No. We will find a place for your cousin where he can do no harm. And you . . . we shall see."

Her eyes were scalpels and Hoku felt his heart flayed open. She saw everything inside of him. She saw the lie about Juaren, who never drank. She saw how he was prepared to suffer a bit of her ire—even a temporary demotion for coddling his relatives—as long as it meant he would stay on the ladder that lead to the Tech Society Kiva. She saw it all . . . and approved.

"Yes, Mother-Fa . . . yes. I will supervise the expedition, now." He stood and prepared to close contact.

"Listen," The woman said, and the single word stopped him, stopped every thought in his head. "Do you know how important this is?"

"I think so," he replied.

She shook her head. "You have to know it. In your bones. The Reed picked our ancestors to settle here because they were idealists at best, fanatics at worst. Willing to undergo any privation to have a world of their own, to build their vision of paradise. Their payment to the Reed was to tend the terraforming projects. Our payment, Hoku. And they reward this, in turn, with scraps of obsolete technology."

Hoku did not point out that she was stating what every school child knew, or that she was leaving out the glowing aura that was supposed to surround their part in making a home of this world. He understood that she was coming to something that people did *not* talk about . . . she was merely going by a familiar path.

"You can see, can't you?" She continued. "You are a bright boy, Hoku. You understand that the Reed is lying to us. The expense to them of terraforming this world must be immense, more than any of us can dream. They are not doing this to help a bunch of crazy Terrans re-create a mythical past. No. You know what they call us?

Sodbusters. We will work for generations to make this planet bloom, and then the real colony ships will arrive with millions of soft Terrans. And Reed warships to make sure we step aside and let them have our planet. Our planet, Hoku. The ancestors were fools—criminals, even, to condemn their children to this impoverished life—but they worked and died here, as we will work and die. We have earned more than some tiny portion of this planet. We have earned it all.

"Those ships up there. They must be very powerful indeed. If we understood them—if we were allied with them—if we controlled them—then this planet might remain in the proper hands. The hands that built it. Remember that out in the desert, Hoku. Remember that when it comes time to bleed and sacrifice."

Hoku found that he had been holding his breath, as the power of her words punched into him. He was later to see that moment as one that changed his life. He had no faith in family, in clans . . . but the planet itself. . . .

No outworlder deserved to live here. If his . . . people . . . could control power that could move kilometer-long ships between the stars, drop asteroids large enough to create seas, bring life and oxygen to a sterile planet with a reducing atmosphere in only a thousand years or so . . . that kind of power might just make the Reed rethink their contract with the colonists.

Travel between the stars took many years, and the woman was old. She was looking down the road, to a successor and his successor. Someone strong enough to put what must be done over silly sentimentality, over fictional family ties. Yes, indeed, someone just like himself.

Hoku stopped at his closet to take out a jacket: it would be cold where he was going. Too bad about Juaren; he wouldn't starve, but his promising career as an astronomer was over. There could be only limited access to the sky Kachina and the land-bound telescopes, and many clamored for it.

Hoku stopped for an instant to close his outside door. The dawn had become Palatala, a rim of fire on the far edge of the sea, a cinnamon cloud expanding above it to lighten the eastern quarter. Hoku allowed himself a brief grin, so boyish that for an instant he really looked his twenty years. Then he snapped down his determined mask and strode off towards his own coming dawn.

I. TRAITOR

The door closed fast, creating a moment of silence, a sacred space where only mind moved. Not for long: there was much to do. Nevertheless, when everyone else was panicking, stillness—and the rationality it might bring—was an advantage.

How long had this planet been home? Five Terran years. Five years since the circuit ship had passed close enough to leave behind a landing craft. A craft now hidden deep, deep in the ocean. Five years on a planet which offered, on the one hand, a pack of pseudo-savages intentionally living at the edge of habitable lands, and on the other a bitter, driven lot who knew their days of petty power were limited. Five wearing, acrid years.

Fingers danced, an identification code which had never existed as input sputtered into a crystalline brain, unlocked faded secrets.

No one knew, that was certain. Even on a planet whose population did not exceed a hundred thousand, it was possible to appear from nowhere, if one were clever with people and machines. If one were an orphan, the child of clanless loners who lived on the sea. There had been such a couple, such a child. A predecessor, making way for his replacement.

The alien ships. Who could have predicted that? But they could not fall into colonist hands. The Vilmir Foundation—or the Reed as they so charmingly called it here—would either have them or destroy them. The terraforming technology those ships carried was far, far ahead of anything human beings had developed. In point of fact, nine of the ten settled worlds had apparently already been terraformed by whoever these aliens were: nine planets with the same kind of atmospheric chemistry and plants that were demonstrably related. Nine planets with the same—non-Terran—genetic code.

And the tenth was Earth.

In orbit, a computer, cold for five years, awoke. A flexor shifted, aimed the lens of a powerful laser towards a dim yellow star. It stuttered with a tongue of light.

Afterwards, there was no trace that the message had been sent. Now there was another job. The team from the Paso observatory would certainly be first to the alien's landing sight. What could be learned there would be. That was in the job description.

The pension had better be worth it.

VI. PELA

Pela opened her eyes, fearing they would reveal the nightmare still livid behind her lids. But what she saw was blue sky and a man's face.

"She's awake," the man called. His accent was funny, some kind of lowlander dialect.

"Keep her there," a different man answered. "We'll need to ask her some questions".

Pela sat up quickly. The vestiges of a hangover and a stabbing pain in her arm made her wish she hadn't.

"Take it easy," the man said. He had a round, kind face, not quite handsome. His voice sounded nervous.

"Oh, shit," Pela gasped. "Shit. The Kachina . . . ."

It was there, where she had seen it . . . this morning? A blackened cylinder resting on four legs. Nearby an enormous flag—a parachute, she supposed—lay flat on the ground, fluttering slightly in the awakening breeze.

"How did you get this mark on your arm, Isiwa?"

Younger sister, he called her. He was trying to be nice.

"It touched me," she replied, staring at the bandage that the man must have put on her arm. The bandage and the soil near her were soaked with blood. "The Kachina touched me."

"Oh. Stay here."

The man strode off towards the other three, two men and a woman, all lowlanders by their dress. They were all wearing guns. Off to the north she could see their transportation, a bronze-colored hovercraft.

The man talked quietly with the others, who continued to cast glances in her direction. The he returned to her, just as she was groggily getting to her feet.

"This is a new model," the man explained apologetically. "We don't know what went wrong or why it hurt you. Hoku—our mother-father over there—wants to take you back to Salt for an examination. Would that be okay?"

Pela was abruptly aware that she was wearing only her thin cotton shorts. She had just crawled out of her thermal bag to piss when she saw the Kachina. The man was doing his best to avert his eyes from her breasts and doing a progressively worse job.

"I need my clothes", she mumbled.

"Of course. Where are they?"

Pela gestured vaguely towards the rising basalt behind her. He nodded and trotted off in that direction. He stopped after a few steps.

"My name is Jimmie," he said.

"Pela," she returned. "Thanks, Jimmie." The sound of his boots on the cindery earth diminished behind her.

The Kachina, made by the lowlanders? That was possible, but she didn't think so. But they wanted her to think that, didn't they? So she would, for her own safety. But Pela knew truth, knew it in her heart. The Kachina were no longer lost among the stars. They had returned to the Fifth World, to see what the Hopitu-Shinumu had done with it.

She hoped they would be pleased.

INTERIM

2429 A.D.

Alvar Washington closed the gap between himself and the Vilmir complex in a series of jarring, painful steps. He regretted the previous night's excesses bitterly, but regretted even more missing his last medical exam. If he had that the little drunk-doctors in his bloodstream had died quietly sometime last month, he would have had them replaced, or had a little less of the cheap turpentine that passed for whisky here.

Would that that were his only regret. Alvar squinted off at the distance and tried to imagine that the ugly crinkled mountains there were the Sangre de Cristos, that the sky was the right color of blue rather than a purplish pastel, even that the awful taste in his mouth was that of a certain dark Santa Fe beer. A pleasure to be hung over on that.

Unfortunately his imagination had always been less than vivid. He supposed that if it had been more colorful he would have stayed on Earth, lived the outworld life vicariously rather than opting for the reality, a reality which consisted mostly of boredom, bad coffee, bad booze, and ugly surroundings. Maybe one day this planet would be a paradise—maybe even in the lifetime of the major stockholders. But he would never see it: unlike the executives, he did not have access to the medicines that could extend life well into the triple digits.

He had opted to walk to his meeting in the hopes that exercise would clear his head. It was helping, though sweat still seemed to ooze from his pores like syrup and his stomach threatened to expel an unconsumed breakfast.

He reached his destination, a building easily as ugly as the terrain. It was constructed of native stone—which meant basalt or some close cousin. It was grey-black, anyhow, polished smooth and slicked with a silicon compound in the optimistic hope that it would resemble marble. It did not. The architecture was equally ill-advised, a revival of that insipid style known as Neo-Meshika——the ugliest aspects of classical Greek architecture heavily ornamented with bas-relief feathered snakes, tlalocs, and Atlantean figures of Meso-American provenience. On Earth, it had flourished briefly in the last century and then been mercifully forgotten. Here, naturally, it was the acme of high design.

Shaking his head , Alvar stumbled past an otherwise Doric column from which peered stylized, grinning skulls. The door checked his I.D., odor, and retina prints before admitting him.

The inside of the building was as clean and modern as the outside was archaic and grotesque. Alvar made his way to the elevator terminals, where a young woman in a fashionably crumpled black-and-gold shirt and shorts motioned him on. She examined him appraisingly—his athletic meter and a half frame, sienna skin and broad, handsome features. When she met his bloodshot eyes, however, she registered what could only be disgust and perhaps a little pity.

She thinks I'm a plaguer, he realized. He tried to smile and correct her impression with a few coherent words, but at that moment his car arrived. With a mental shrug he stepped in. What did he care what she thought? If he was right about this meeting, he would never see her again.

The old man was indeed that; Alvar recognized this fact immediately. Though Vilmir's hair was still chestnut brown, though his skin was as smooth and perfect as a twenty year old's, the signs were obvious to the practiced eye. Re-grown skin always had a sort of papery look to it, and it was always uniform, without the slight color variations that marked the run of humanity. His teeth were too white and too short; he must have recently had new buds implanted, so that they weren't fully grown. Most of all there was the way Vilmir bore himself, the way he used his black eyes and smoothly tapered fingers. An insect clothed in human form could not have seemed more alien, precise, considered in its movements.

There were logical clues as well. No twenty-year old would hold such an important position as this man; there was no one on the Foundation board under the age of eighty, and Egypt Vilmir was the majority stockholder. He was two hundred if he was a zygote.

"Mr. Washington," Vilmir acknowledged, and with a slight motion of his hand indicated that Alvar should sit upon one of the cushions that lay in a precise semicircle around his own raised couch. The room was furnished in a vaguely Arabic fashion. Muted earth tone carpets and tapestries patterned with abstract curvilinear motifs were illuminated by two shafts of greenish light falling through tinted skylights a hundred feet above them. Holographic birds filled that lofty space, distorting and changing form as they described complex patterns around one another. Truly, thought Alvar, a palace fit for a king.

But Vilmir was no mere king: he was chief executive of the Vilmir Foundation. That made him more akin to an emperor.

"Normally, Mr. Washington, I don't speak to my agents, but this is a special case. There is no time to lose, so I will be brief." His voice was smooth and pleasant, not at all like Alvar imagined an emperor's should be.

"I would first like to state that I do not enjoy seeing my employees in your present state. When you leave here, you will go immediately to the clinic and have your shots updated. You will not miss them again."

He paused for the barest instant to let that sink in, and Alvar nodded. The old man continued.

"As you may have surmised, you will soon be visiting one of our projects. This will not be a routine check, and it will not be for the purposes of renewing an agent. Something important, unexpected, and pressing has occurred that demands our immediate attention."

Vilmir paused, and Alvar saw something very human flicker in his eyes, an eagerness—a hunger, even.

"Mr. Washington, you should be aware that terraforming is a long, arduous process. It takes several centuries to make even a prime planet into a self-sustaining environment for large numbers of people. And there are very few prime planets. If we had to terraform Venus, for instance—that would take many thousands of years. We have been very fortunate to discover a number of planets which are already rather similar to Earth in atmospheric chemistry. This did not happen by chance, of course. None of these planets were actually habitable by human beings when we discovered them, and all of them had precisely the same things wrong with them. Can you comment on that?"

Alvar was taken aback. He nearly stuttered, in fact, something that he hadn't done since childhood.

"Ah . . . yes. The supposition is that some unknown race began forming those planets for their own reasons and then mysteriously stopped. Very fortunate for us."

"Indeed. They had superior technology, these aliens, though we must infer that. They could change planets like Venus into worlds with free oxygen and life in under a thousand years. It would take us three times as long. What they left us can be suited to our chemistries with relatively little modification, although the expense is enormous and the payoff long in coming."

What do you care? Alvar thought. However long it takes to pay off, you will probably live to benefit. While I decompose on some godforsaken colony.

"Mr. Washington, up until now, we have assumed that the original engineers who modified these planets somehow died off. We have been proven wrong. They have returned."

Alvar did not expect the bolt of adrenaline that surged up through his queasy stomach and thudding headache. His mouth actually dropped open as Vilmir briefly described the three enormous ships that were currently in orbit around the colony known as "Fifth World".

"At least they were seven years ago," the old man amended. "When our agent sent the message. You will go there with a contingent of colonial peacekeepers and determine what to do. Are you listening, Mr. Washington?"

"Yes. Yes. But why me? I'm no expert on these matters."

"In point of fact, you are no expert on anything. But we cannot know what will have occurred in the twenty years between the aliens' arrival and your own. The colonists may have come to some understanding with them. This cannot happen; either the aliens deal with us or they deal with no one. You, Sey'er Washington, were originally chosen to replace our current agent there, because with some training you can pass as a native. The colonists have accurate genetic records of all of their founding generation. A simple DNA check would show most outworlders to be just that. You, however, are descended from some of the same ancestors as the colonists, and the differing elements in your genetic makeup are not eclectic enough to be noticed. You can thus investigate upon the planet itself with some chance of success."

"The Hopi?" Alvar blurted, before he thought better. The reference to the "Fifth World" had rung a little bell in his head, but his fascination with the idea of the alien ships had muted it.

"Exactly so. Though most of them had little "real" Hopi blood."

Alvar remembered the Hopi. His mother had spoken of them mockingly. A bunch of crazy idealists who believed themselves to be the inheritors of an ancient Native North American religion. There had been a prophecy, made as early as the twentieth century, that the Hopi people would scatter and then become revitalized, establish a "Fifth World". It was supposed to be on earth, but with the perfection of the Drigg's Interstellar Fusion Drive, that prophecy had been re-interpreted.

And he was supposed to impersonate one of these fanatics? Because he had some of the old pueblo blood?

"Sey'er, I don't know if I can live up to your expectations. I know nothing about the old pueblo lifestyle. I don't speak old English, either. That was still the major language of West America when they left two hundred years ago."

Vilmir smiled wanly. "They don't speak it either. They insisted on speaking Hopi. Revived it from the dead."

"Even worse!"

"Mr. Washington, I have your contract, and you have no choice. There will be plenty of time to learn the native language shipboard. You have been very well paid up until now, and we have gotten no return for our money. This is where we get it. And, really, I think you will find our compensation reasonable. Hazard pay includes extended medical benefits."

For "extended medical benefits" read "extended lifespan", Alvar realized, suddenly more interested than ever. That he had considered only in his most optimistic dreams. He was a poor boy from the windowless, inner core of the Santa Fe Arcology. Only a series of lucky breaks had gotten him out of those rat holes and onto a starship. Was the Virgin about to smile on him again? Surprising, if so, considering his opinion of most virgins.

"Go down to the briefing tables," the old man went on. "You will see Doctor Tembo. He will begin your course of training and introduce you to your co-commander and crew." Vilmir motioned once again with his hand, a movement of less than a centimeter. It was the clearest dismissal Alvar had ever seen.

• • •

"Vilmir spoke to you himself. Very impressive."

Jenemon Tembo was short and round. He had mild blue eyes, an impressive nose, and skin the color of coffee with cream.

"I was impressed."

Tembo nodded, and his eyes took on a narrower focus, as if his mind had suddenly flipped to another topic. It had.

"Sey'er Washington, you are not carrying a plague, I trust?"

Alvar shook his head ruefully. "No. I'm hung over. I let my drunk doctors expire, probably for the same reason that taking a plague isn't my style. The idea of those little bugs in my blood isn't comfortable."

"You're an anachronist," Tembo observed, condescendingly. "Drunk doctors are perfectly safe. You're right about plagues, though. Since they are illicitly designed, they are often badly designed. And they mutate. I'm sure you heard about Singapore."

"No. I just got off ship a few months ago. Missed twelve years of history, and I haven't even started catching up."

"No? It seems that a bacteria tailored to carry hallucinogenic alkaloids mutated into something poisonous. Killed twenty million people."

"Jesus! No, I missed that all right."

Tembo didn't answer: he spread his hands flat on the fiberwood table and glanced up at the door. Alvar followed his gaze.

"Alvar Washington, this is Teng Shu, a captain in the colonial peacekeepers."

"Good to meet you, Sey'er Washington," said Teng Shu.

Teng stood fully a hundred and eighty centimeters tall, just below his own one-eighty-three. Her hair, bound in a tight queue, was black glass fiber. By contrast, her skin was the whitest he had ever seen. Brown but nearly yellow eyes bounded by slight epicanthic folds regarded him with the same unwavering severity. This austere strength was reflected in her clothing; a chocolate brown shirt and pants. The only unmuted item of her outfit was a silver belt buckle shaped like an ancient Chinese ideogram that Alvar did not recognize.

Teng's handshake was very strong. Her loose clothes concealed a fit figure, but Alvar guessed it was more than fit. The handshake revealed calluses as hard as hullmetal on her hands. He had heard of the peacekeepers and their reinforced physiologies. Was she one such?

Alvar did not doubt it in the least. Prickles ran along his spine. Teng could kill him with her bare hands in an instant. She probably had orders to do so, under the right circumstances.

"Very pleased to meet you, I'm sure," he said, bowing.

This was one woman he would not even try to seduce.

Teng screeched and bared her teeth. She bent and nipped him lightly on the neck, then allowed her full lips to mold there. Then her harsh breath exploded against his carotid. She flung herself back with a wild cry, and they both whirled crazily across the cabin, joined by the frantic motion of their pelvises. Her heels dug painfully into his calves, legs clamping his thighs like steel bands. She caught his arms and held them hard against his sides as the two of them bumped with painful force into a bulkhead. Alvar was absolutely immobilized; pinned like a wrestler by a superior opponent. Though it scared him, the fear was melted, fused into the white heat building in him. When he exploded, she nearly crushed him, grinding her pelvis into him with manic force. Then, just as he was beginning to fear for his life, she released him. They drifted gradually apart, enormous beads of sweat forming on their bodies.

"You're beautiful," he said after a moment, surveying her languid white form.

"You too," she said, smiling a little sarcastically. She reached out for him, caught his ankle, began to explore his leg with her tongue. Alvar twisted around to her back—a contortion impossible under gravity—and began probing and stroking with the tips of his fingers.

"We have to accelerate soon," he said. "No more free-fall for a long time."

"We should make the best of it then," she replied.

They continued touching and kissing. The first time, there had been no time for learning: now he intended to absorb everything about her body he could. And thus he discovered a secret.

The second time was gentler, though he felt a distance in her that he suspected sex would never close. She reveled in his body, but his eyes did not interest her. At climax she kept her own tightly shut. When they were done, he asked her about the small round scars on her buttocks and around her crotch.

"Cigarette burns," she said, and her face hardened up.

"How?"

"Not your business, sailor. Get that straight. You're the only man awake on this trip, and you look pretty good. Furthermore, I like you. I'm going to fuck you. But we aren't lovers in any greater sense than that."

Alvar nodded. He could accept that well enough. And they were going to be together a long time. No use in starting out arguing. Things were going fine.

"You're the boss," he said.

"Yes," she agreed. "Yes, I am."

CHAPTER ONE

2442 A.D.

SandGreyGirl finished washing her mother's hair, her narrow face clenched around the tears it hid.

What killed you, Pela? She asked in the black shadow of her mind. What ended my mother's life?

She stepped back, relieved to let her cousins close in and do the rest. They tied prayer feathers to Pela's hands and hair, gifts for the ancestors. No doubt some of the ancestors—the ones from the Fourth World, Earth—would be confused by the feathers. There were, as yet, no real birds other than turkeys on the Fifth World. The feathers were grown in sacred culture tanks.

The white cotton mask they placed on Pela's face was real. Pela had grown the cotton herself. Now it would be the cloud which hid her face when she came back to bring rain to her people.

SandGreyGirl was beginning to feel sick. She stepped out of the little apartment she shared with her mother for some air, aware even as she did so that the others would talk, call her a bad daughter.

But they already did that, didn't they?

She let her gaze drift across the box-hive of native stone dwellings and poured concrete facilities that were Tuwanasavi, the town of her birth. Of her mother's death. Father Sun was resting in his noon-time house, and his light inked doorways and windows in sharp relief. Beyond the edge of the mesa, the land stretched off, hazy and unreal, a cloud tinted grey and green.

"Sand."

She didn't turn at the voice. Her father was the last person she wanted to see right now.

"Sand, I'm sorry. There was nothing any of us could do."

Sand bit down on her lip, resisted the urge to spin around and howl at him, scream like the cyclone winds that rushed up the valley in spring. Instead, she slipped her words into him softly, each a tiny dagger.

"You could have taken her to the lowlands. Whatever she had, they could have cured it."

"You know the elders wouldn't have agreed to that."

"The elders can't stop a Dragonfly from slipping off into the air. I could have taken her. If you had called me."

He had no answer for that, and she expected none. She heard his feet shuffle uncertainly.

"She didn't want you to see her die," he said at last.

Sand finally turned to face him, and she fixed her eyes on his own until he looked away. His round face, as always, bore that pitiful expression that she so despised. It was both apologetic and sneaky. Daughters and fathers were rarely close amongst the Hopitu-Shinumu, but her feelings for him were deep and fetid.

"Why do you hate me so?" he asked.

"You shouldn't have to wonder that," she replied.

Under her hot stare he wilted further and finally retreated towards the room where his wife waited, dead.

The sun moved on, rested for the moment. Sand paced across the roof of the main house, arguing bitterly with the image of her father that she kept in her mind. With her other relatives—with herself.

After a time, the clan chief came to get her.

"It's nearly time," he said.

Yuyahoeva was an old man, at least fifty. His face was like the tortured, frozen rock of a lava flow. Sand gathered her resolve to confront him.

"I want an autopsy, *Ina'a.*"

Yuyahoeva's stone face trembled, as if it were about to become live magma. But he mastered himself. Anger was an evil thing to show. And yet, as had she with her father, he made his feelings clear in whispered, stinging words.

"You little two-heart. How can you suggest that? Your mother was a good woman. She will not be cut up by those lowland butchers."

"I want to know what killed her."

He regarded her as he might regard a clot of night soil on his shoe.

"Don't you know, after all this time, that what you want is not important? Your schooling with the lowlanders has spoiled you." The word he used for "spoiled" implied decay, corruption.

"She was my mother."

He dismissed that with a sharp chop of his palm. "She did not belong to you. She would understand that. She belonged to all of us. And there will be no more talk of autopsy. If there is, you will be banned from your kiva. Do you understand?"

Sand faced him for an instant longer, her breath harsh and salt threatening to sting her eyes. Then she turned away.

"She was murdered, I think. Somebody killed her." An unwanted note of pleading crept into her voice.

"She was sick," the old man replied, more softly.

"Sick with no disease we have ever known. Diseases such as they can create in the lowlands."

"The lowlanders are all two-hearts," he replied. "But they do not live here. They do not single out individual Hopi to torment."

"Some do," she muttered, casting a meaningful glance at the room where her father was helping to dress her mother's corpse in bridal finery.

"Enough of this, I tell you," Yuyahoeva snapped. "Come and help to carry your mother's body."

Sand glared at him again, and then reluctantly nodded. The shadows were lengthening.

Later, with her mother in the earth facing the sunrise, Sand became a Dragonfly and went to bury yet one more thing.

She could make the change quickly now. When she first became a member of the Dragonfly Society—three years ago—it took half an hour of chanting, wearing the full garb and mask of the Dragonfly Kachina to unlock the inner space where her own Dragonfly slept. Now it took a mere moment; a breath of air, her mind sinking down, crystallizing, becoming simple and strong. When she mounted the Dragonfly itself, crouched behind the windshield at the fore of its long silver body, she was already a part of it. When the underjets popped and then roared to life, she saw the pathway in the air open before her like a rainbow.

Airborne, she let the wings fold out, gossamer and unbreakable. She kicked on the afterjets and the world became a tunnel, wrapped around her. The mesa city was gone, melting into the shadows of fast-approaching night. Pela nosed east, and the quavering black shadow of the Dragonfly ran ahead of her, seemed to slide up the steep valley wall like a predacious jet amoeba, devouring meters and kilometers with unassuagable hunger. The lip of the canyon rushed down to meet the shadow, and Sand smiled as her afterjets brushed the black stone and gravel with clear heat, reveling in the absolute speed of her reflexes, the almost audible calculations in her head, the sense of seeing everything and nothing all at once.

"You will not see a stone or a tree or your own all-important thoughts," Her teacher had told her, in the quiet of the kiva. "You will hear and see and smell the world as a single thing. Or you will die."

Now the completeness that was the world was a thing of coal

and rust, blood colored oil on a pool of night, the moon a cobalt blue marble rolling on the north-east horizon. Deep inside of Sand-GreyGirl, a skeleton sorrow danced, but it was a distant grief. As the Dragonfly Kachina she was above all human cares.

Black ridges pushed up through the skin of the earth like the sharp edges of broken bones. The basalt towers waxed in her vision, devouring the sky, the wholeness of the earth, so that the Dragonfly began to leave her. The machine she straddled became just that—a hovercraft, long and thin—large enough to carry two people but perfect for one. She retracted the wings and cut the underjets on full, to break her fall, and now Masaw came dancing out of her, the death god, filling the shadows with grief and dread.

Too bad she couldn't always be the Kachina, with its shiny steel heart.

Sand stepped wide, avoiding the hot sand beneath her jets. The metal of the Dragonfly began to tick and ping as it cooled in the chill night air.

"Well, here I am," Sand remarked, as much to herself as to any spirits who might be listening. She patted the sealed pocket at her hip to reassure herself that her little burden was, in fact, there.

Her mother called this place, "Where the Kachina Touched Me". Sand had been here with her a few times, but her mother came here every month, a pilgrimage that she missed only the last time, as her body wasted with lightning speed, as her eyes clouded and ceased to understand light. Sand made this last pilgrimage for her, to bury her sacred things in the place most sacred to her. Somewhere here, in the heart of her land.

My land now, Sand thought miserably.

But where was that? These cliffs were large. Sand carefully paced across the black soil, searching for the spot, the very place her mother had seen the Kachina itself. That was easily done—her mother had shown it to her on each trip they made together—but there was nothing to signify a special place. Sand knew what she should find: a small shrine, a few prayer-sticks keeping vigil, something like that. Where?

The little bundle in her pocket seemed to be getting heavier. Sand thought back to when she was a child: her mother's story of the Kachina from the stars frightened her, fascinated her. The immense black stone had seemed poised to fall upon her, crush out her tiny life, but Pela was always unafraid. She was always able to soothe Sand, show her the beauty even in fear.

Some of those memories—the ones of their camping trips together—were the best. At fifteen, her mother had given her her first whiskyberry here, and the two of them had gotten drunk, drunk and very silly. It was that night that Pela confided some things about Jimmie, her husband—SandGreyGirl's father. Things Sand could neither forget nor forgive. It was that night that she had fallen in love with her mother.

Sand smeared the tears across her face, let a single, wracking sob tear loose from her chest. She could use some of those whiskyberries right now.

Sand knew, then, and she picked her way up the broken stone until she came into the little dark cove where she and her mother camped that night. She crossed beyond a certain big stone and saw the whiskyberry plant, their plant. Its stubby body offered her five or six ripe fruit, but Sand regretfully ignored them. She flipped on her torch and carefully scanned around. She smiled wanly at the little cornbrake her mother had begun before Sand was born, hugging the damper sand near the black stone. Some of it was tasseled, almost ready to produce the little blue cobs that her people so cherished. Each year the roots of the corn spread a little farther, and each year more stalks came up to savor the moisture that collected here. It was tenacious, like her mother had been, stunted by the desert but still bearing fruit. Sand pushed carefully through, unwilling to damage a single stalk. What she was searching for should be behind, some-where. . . .

There. Long ago, gas had slowly forced its way up through cool-ing magma. It had formed a bubble and then been frozen there when the molten rock cooled, until the corrosive forces of the winds had eaten through the stone itself. The hollow that remained was a semi-circular cavity, mostly filled with sand. The torch revealed four small prayer sticks there, colors dimmed by time.

Hello, mother, Sand thought, and began to cry again.

The moon had made his short arc across the north and set before Sand gathered the courage to do what she must. With a surprisingly steady hand, she pulled the little bundle of amulets and items that her mother had cherished. Near the little pahos, the prayer sticks, she brushed a depression on the sand.

"I will bury them here, mother, and then close up the opening. You will still know where to find them." If what the old people say is true. If she really leaves her grave in four days and comes here to reclaim her things.

And as she doubted, her fingers encountered something buried in the coarse grit.

Sand hesitated. What had her mother buried here? She gritted her teeth, summoned all of her skepticism about ghosts and spirits to armor herself with. These are just things, she thought. But this inner assurance seemed lost in a shadowy realm, a dark house popu-lated by the dancing forms of the Kachina and the souls of the dead. Nevertheless, she resumed her digging.

The object she dug out of the black powder was a book. Sand lifted it gingerly, reverently. The nearly flat, translucent rectangle was smooth and cool in her hands. She stared at it. Only one word was visible, so dim that it was obvious that the book had long been away from the revitalizing strength of the sun.

Laughs-with-me, it said.

That was her name, the name Pela had given her that night she had first been drunk.

Sand touched the contact that would wake the book up. A tiny message appeared, as dim as the first.

"Key necessary".

Sand nodded. Carefully, so carefully, she unrolled the little bundle she had brought to bury. Two little amulets, carved of the black stone of these very cliffs. A small silver star that a man named Tuvenga had given her long ago. The magical odds and ends of a too-short life.

And there was a little coded bar, twisted into the shape of a ring. Sand put the ring on and touched the book again. This time, the pale writing filled the cover of the box.

"Sand, my daughter. There are some things you must know, now. . . ."

Sand thumbed the box off. The letters were too pale, and she was too tired. The morning would bring them both more energy.

She checked carefully in the sand around the pahos and found nothing else. She buried her mother's magic things and blocked up the tiny cave with stones. Afterwards, Sand sat looking at the pile of rocks for a moment that seemed to become the whole night.

Finally, she trudged reluctantly back down to the Dragonfly and opened up the cargo hatch. She took out an alcohol stove and a wire-mesh bowl that fitted over its burners. She set the stove up with the mesh bowl, kindled the stove, and filled the bowl with the densest rocks she could find.

Another trip to the hovercraft brought her back with four long, flexible shafts and a sheet of polymer cloth three meters on each side. Sand thrust the sharp ends of the shafts into the ground so that they arched up towards the sky. When all four were planted, she had the skeleton of a dome with the rapidly heating rocks in the center. Finally, she pulled the cloth over the dome and weighed it down on the edges with rocks. Her sweatlodge was finished. She placed a small bag inside, where the heat was already beginning to grow fierce. Then Sand stripped off her tough flight suit, a one-piece garment of reinforced Densedren. The plateau breeze prickled bumps on her exposed skin as she also removed her cotton shorts and shirt. She tried not to hurry, to maintain the dignity of the ceremony. Thus she stood for a moment, her lean body fully exposed to the sucking breath of the sky, as if to express her disdain for it. She took down the elaborate braided rolls ⌐n either side of her head that signified her unmarried status, letting her dark brown hair fall thickly to her waist. Then Sand bent down and entered the sweat house.

It took only instants for her chilled pores to open up. She rocked back and forth in the furnace heat, and sweat soon slicked her body completely. I am like my ancestors, the fish she hummed to herself, recalling her clan's version of the origin. Fire seemed to walk back and forth across her dark skin, searching for a way in.

And found its egress through her nostrils, as her lungs seemed to expand with live flame.

Sand opened up the bag and pulled forth a small swatch of green branches and a thick, resinous piñon cone. Reverently, she placed the juniper branches on the now-glowing red stones. She placed the piñon cone beside it. Both of these things were rare and precious; as sacred plants, both piñon and juniper had been brought from Earth, but required much care.

They began to smoke, and the thick resinous odor of them filled the sweatlodge. The smoke covered her and filled her up, and now she was a fish in the dark depths of a juniper sea. The smoke scrubbed her, lifting away the touch of her mother's corpse, the cold plastic feeling of it. The smoke was fragrant purity, and the breath of a ghost could not long withstand it.

Goodbye, Sand told the smoke. *Goodbye, mother.*

She began to sing and did not stop until the cloth of the lodge was soaked with the earliest light of dawn.

CHAPTER TWO

"Nu'qa nauti'ta sen tumala' taniqa'e," Alvar Washington told himself for the third time, a look of intense concentration on his face. Teng had just entered. She glanced at him with a dour expression.

"You say the nicest things," she observed, leaning against the bulkhead, arms folded loosely beneath her breasts.

"Don't I," he acknowledged. "Shiau Shi: Teacher off."

The image of himself across the table flickered out of existence.

"So that's who you've been spending all of your time with," Teng murmured. "I should have known. You're the most natural narcissist I've ever met."

Alvar grinned and brushed back his long, thick hair. "Facial expressions are language too," he told her. "Might as well learn from the face I'll be using."

"Might as well," Teng agreed. "Wanna fuck?"

Alvar twisted in his seat to face her. "You could try seducing me," he said. "You know, subtly?"

"I could," she agreed. "On the other hand, I don't feel like bullshitting right now."

"That's better," Alvar returned. "Who can resist that kind of approach?"

Teng shot him a look wet with poison. She smiled without humor, her yellow eyes narrowed to slits.

"In two weeks, I'll being reviving some of the peacekeepers. Thank Durga."

"In two weeks I'll be fucking women made out of skin," Alvar shot back.

Teng took a step forward, and for the second time in his life, Alvar truly believed he was about to die. The first time, as a child, he had been playing in the desert outside of Santa Fe. He had fallen down and found himself eye-to-eye with a coiled rattlesnake. Then, as now, he kept absolutely still, waiting for the danger to pass, fearing that it would not.

But it did, as it had then. Teng took the step back, and the rattlesnake look melted briefly into something else before she turned on her heel and left him alone.

Alvar let out his breath, slowly. When he had met Teng, three years ago, he had guessed immediately that she was enhanced. But for three years he had been caressing that hard, slim body. He knew it better than any he had ever known, with the possible exception of his own. But contrary to what Teng had accused him of, Alvar was no narcissist. He like his body well enough, enjoyed pleasuring it with hot baths, good meals, fine whisky. But he loved Teng's body, even if he didn't love her. And so he knew, knew about the thick plates of plastimuscle that lay beneath her flat stomach, over her kidneys, beneath those high, sharp breasts. He had read everything he could about enhancement from the ship's library, about how they had engineered her own cells and created fibers that could stop bullets. Her vital organs were surrounded and cushioned by thick, spongy structures; her bones were very unlikely to break under anything approaching normal circumstances. She probably had extra organs, too—small, perfect backups for her primary systems.

She was all flesh, Teng was, but it was marvelous flesh. Flesh that had killed over a dozen soldiers in the Kenya massacre, maybe more elsewhere.

Alvar had watched her train, too, practice kicks and punches that were so fast and graceful they scarcely seemed deadly.

Just now, she had nearly killed him, he was certain of that.

Possibly, he deserved it. He had never made reference to her . . . state . . . before. He did not know what circumstances of her life had brought it about; the promise of distance she had made their first time together had been kept, for the most part.

But it was that most part that kept him guessing. They had talked, long and earnestly. They had played chess and riddle games. She outmatched him spectacularly in handball, usually lost when they played cards. And of course, there was lovemaking. In some ways, the latter was the least intimate thing they did together. And yet, Alvar reflected, one could not make love to the same person so many times without at least beginning to think you were in love with them.

Strike that. It was just him that had that problem.

He called his image back into existence.

"Hello," he said, in the pseudo-Hopi he had been studying, consciously and unconsciously.

"Hello," the image told him, in the same language. "What shall we talk about today?"

"Tell me about the Hopi. The real ones."

His image shrugged, pursed its lips in the "Hopi" expression of thoughtfulness.

"They were a pueblo-dwelling people of the southwestern part of North America, now the Western States of America. They probably had a long unwritten history, suggested by various archaeological traditions that are known generally as Anasazi. They first became a part of written history when Spanish conquistadors entered the region in the sixteenth century. They retained a remarkably cohesive social structure in the face of European expansion and conquest, to a limited extent even to the present day. Their religion was complex and never fully understood at any one time by outsiders. With a few notable exceptions, it remained fundamentally an oral tradition to the Hopi themselves."

"Right. Tell me about the most notable exception. The one the colonists of Fifth World predicated their society upon."

"You tell me," the image replied, with his own smug grin.

Alvar had learned things in a certain order. First the language and general cultural things like kinship; then the history of the colonists and their ideological foundations. This "conversation" was to be a sort of review, one that he badly needed. He nodded at himself.

"Fair enough. About 2025, four Hopi elders shared a vision about their people, one in which their culture and religion declined and vanished utterly. They therefore set out to record everything they remembered about the Hopi lifestyle."

"Hold it," his reflection told him. "They weren't all Hopi elders."

"Oh. Right. One was Zuni and another was Tewa, from around my old home town. But the other two were Hopi elders."

"And they were a minority in their community. Most of the Hopi believed that it was better for their culture to die than to record it on film, tape, or even paper."

Alvar glared at his image. "True enough. But that part isn't in the stories they tell on the Fifth World, is it? In their version, it was those four who were truly Hopi, and their peers who were kahopi—the bad guys."

Mirror-Alvar shrugged and motioned for him to continue. He did so.

"These four recorded all of the ceremonies, legends, and so on for posterity, and they agreed among themselves to call this lifestyle "Hopi", despite its varied origins. Hopitu-Shinumu, really, which means "The Well-Behaved People". I guess what they recorded was a sort of amalgam of pueblo lore, though, probably with some European and Asian stuff worked in."

His double grinned thinly. "Now you've strayed off of the official version."

"Fair enough. But that's about it, except for the prophecy. They predicted that one day the Hopi people would be reborn through the record that they had left, and that they would leave the Fourth World for the Fifth, a world created for them by the Kachina."

"Which Kachina?"

"Ah. . . shit, there are hundreds of them. Ah . . . Blue Star?"

"Right. And a Kachina is. . . ."

"An ancestor-cloud spirit. They live in the mountains or the sky for half the year, but for the other half they live amongst the Hopi in human form. Special impersonators wear masks and outfits. Everybody thinks that whoever wears the mask is sort of possessed by the Kachina it represents."

"Possessed," said the image, frowning, "is a crude word. They know that the person in question is still who he always was—at least they do as adults. Children don't understand that the Kachina are being impersonated by human beings. In any event, the adults believe that the person is a conduit for the spiritual presence of the real Kachina."

"I know all of that, smartass. Shiau Shi: Teacher off." The other Alvar vanished quietly. The real one stood up abruptly.

"What a load of crap. Goddamit! And I have to live with these savages?"

Nobody answered his rhetorical question. He would have screamed at them if they had.

He found Teng working out. She was sheathed in sweat, almost literally, since their deceleration had dropped to just below half a gravity and the salty water had more viscous cling. When he stepped up to the door, she was finishing a perplexing series of low punches and twisty-looking blocks. She concluded with a lunging punch into her makiwara, a flexible fiberwood board a meter and a half high, its thickness tapering from three centimeters at the base to less than half a centimeter at the top. It was about twenty centimeters wide. When her fist struck it, the board snapped back with a sound like something breaking, but the makiwara remained where it was. The knuckles of both of Teng's hands were bloody, and that was quite a feat, considering the thick calluses on them.

She stepped away from the board and faced him, her feet a shoulder-width apart, hands limp at her side. Though she looked relaxed, Alvar knew that she was not, but could move in any direction, instantly.

She didn't say anything. She just looked at him, breathing a little harder than normal.

"I'm glad that wasn't me," he said, and meant it.

"I don't have time for your shit, Alvar. Two weeks, and we come up against the first aliens anybody's ever seen, and a bunch of colonial freaks thrown into the bargain. I have a lot to do, and it starts with me getting back in top form."

"You are in top form," Alvar sighed. "And even if you weren't, it's not likely you'll be doing any hand-to-hand fighting. Most probably you'll be launching missiles. Even more likely, this is all the fucking hallucination of some fucking stupid agent whose been out here way to long. And even if those ships were ever here, they may not be now. It's been twenty years, Teng."

Teng walked towards him in a peculiar, stiff-legged way. When she got reached him, she bowed low, bending at the waist, arms straight at her sides.

"Ah, battlemaster," she said, slightly sing-song. "So good of you to impart your wisdom. But—" She straightened up, so that her eyes were straight in line with his. A few strands of her blacker-than-black hair had strayed from the confines of her queue. "But. I know what I am doing. Despite my . . . modifications . . . I require exercise and practice to keep my brain coordinated with my body. It doesn't matter whether I have to use my body to fight or not. My mind won't work fast enough if I get sloppy. Now. That said, I don't expect to have to see your fucking face around me until we need to make our course changes. Clear?"

Her thick lips were trembling, and her normally ivory face had a rosy tint. But her eyes, almond shaped, amber . . . they were sharp, steady glass.

Alvar raised his hand up cautiously.

"Teng, I'm going to do this very slowly, because I don't want you to kill me. Okay? Very slowly."

He reached up with glacial slowness and touched her cheek with his thumb. He brushed her lips with it, stroked all of his fingers along her jaw. Her face did not change in expression. Alvar leaned forward, until their lips were just touching, and she did not move a millimeter. Her mouth was dry, hot, salty. He did not kiss her. Instead, he whispered, with the faintest sound his voice could command.

"I'm sorry, Teng," he said. "I'm very, very sorry."

An eon passed like that, their breath mingling. Then Teng withdrew her lips, tilting her chin down. She rested her forehead against his. Another eon passed before they even considered moving.

"Well there goes your theory, Sey'er Washington," Teng called from the observatory station.

"How's that?"

"A week or so ago you predicted that there weren't any aliens. You were wrong, as usual."

Alvar walked over to her side, carefully controlling each step. The engines were barely burning, now, and his weight was almost non-existent. Teng was pointing to a screen bearing a computer-enhanced composite built from various data. Optical, radar, gravitometric, neutrino. It revealed a planet, mostly blue, draped in a white lace lingerie of clouds. One small moon was indicated, perhaps a third the size of Luna. Besides this, there were two bright points in high orbit.

"Those are the ships," she said. "Very hot. Fusion power of a very fine sort, much better than our own."

"Ah. Their drives aren't pointed this way, are they?"

Teng gave him her best "just shut up, stupid," look and continued.

"The other one is in a polar orbit past the horizon, so we can't see it. They are real, Alvar."

Alvar let that sink in. He had been trying to avoid senseless speculation on the subject of non-human intelligence, but of course his mind had not cooperated. Nevertheless, despite long hours of supposition, he had never convinced himself that he, Alvar Washington, was going to meet aliens. There they were, though.

"How big, Teng?"

"*Shiau Shi*: increase enhancement and apparent size of the neutrino source in equatorial orbit."

The computer complied, replacing the planetary view with a featureless cylinder, constricted in the middle so that it resembled an hourglass.

"That's pretty speculative," Teng told him. "There might be any number of details missing. It could even be two discreet sections bound together by struts. But it's certainly more than a kilometer long."

"And there are three. Let's hope they aren't warships."

Teng nodded thoughtfully. "I can't even guess what weaponry they might have, but they would have to be pretty impressive to match ours."

"Come on, Teng. I'm no tactician, as you've pointed out before, but even I know how hastily this expedition was cobbled together. Our armaments—whatever they are—must be makeshift, as well. In any case, a three-to-one advantage would be tough no matter what we're sporting. And if they have better fusion and Terraforming technology and than we do, what makes you think they don't have better weapons?"

"I don't think that. I assume they are better armed than we. Still, cobbled together or not, we could take any other three ships I can think of. We may not survive ourselves, but we would have a chance of taking them out."

"That does not reassure me," Alvar commented, dryly.

"I didn't expect it too, sailor. Don't worry; I'd rather not die myself. If they are warships, and if they are hostile, we'll probably cut and run, leaving everything that explodes, fizzes, or zaps in our wake."

"And if they're not warships and not hostile?"

"We'll deal with that when the time comes."

"What about the natives? Can they mount any appreciable resistance?"

"Nope. There isn't enough firepower on the planet to scratch us, even if they've been working at it for twenty years. Hopefully, too, they won't know we're coming. Our braking burn won't have been visible except to the most sophisticated telescopes until we were well into the system, and since we had to come in in a wide parabola anyway—one wide enough to turn into an orbit without fuss or muss—I've been trying to keep us on the other side of the sun from them. We weren't eclipsed the whole way, but damned near it, and it's just not likely that they saw us then. Now we've broken our fall, just moving in for the kill, so again, we aren't shining the flashlight in their face."

"So much caution for a bunch of primitivist colonists?"

Teng snorted. "No. I don't want the aliens to know we're coming either."

"We can see them," Alvar pointed out.

"We are looking, and know where to look," she rejoined. "The worst case scenario is that the aliens have developed strong ties with the colonists and that they are both watching for us."

"Once we're in orbit, how can they miss?"

"You'd be surprised. Even the space around a planet is pretty big. I think we can hide behind that moon."

Alvar nodded grimly.

"Ah well. 'Today is a good day to die'."

"What?" she turned away from the monitor, her heart shaped face bearing a puzzled expression.

Alvar smiled. "Right continent, wrong tribe. Some of the plains Indians of North America used to say that, not the Hopi. 'Today is a good day to die'. They mostly did, too, poor fuckers. Did you know that there was a whole movement that believed they were immune to bullets? The Ghost Dancers."

Teng had a fierce little grin on her face. "I like that. That's beautiful."

Alvar glanced back at the speculative ship and shrugged. They sat in silence for awhile.

Teng broke it. "We go to free-fall soon, she whispered, reaching over to take his hand.

"We'd better make the best of it then," Alvar answered, echoing her own words of three years ago. He reached with his other hand to massage her neck. The muscles were as hard as steel cords.

She nodded, and they left the station together.

CHAPTER THREE

Morning opened up, a door into azure, gilt along its eastern frame. Sand let her voice sag back down into her chest, and her head went light as she rose stiffly from the rock she was sitting on. A wind stirred little dust devils across the vast flat that seemed to whirl out from around her, as if she stood in the center of a spinning disk that grew ever greater in circumference from the force of its rotation. Leaving her, smaller and smaller, in the middle. Her strength to defy was gone, but a strange flat calm had replaced it, a feeling of profound endurance, and for this reason, despite the deep chill in the air, she met the sun's gaze as naked as that first sun her mother had held her up to twenty years ago. But enough was enough, and when a few wet-looking clouds appeared in the middle distance, Sand slipped back into her cotton underclothes and densedren jumper. She sat back down and starting putting her hair up in braids, blinking her eyes against the gritty tickle of a night without sleep. Unbroken by dreams, the images of the last two days raced in her mind, fast runners who finished neck-and-neck in her present and then rushed back to begin again. The news over the radio, as she flew above the world streaming a thousand kilos of fire clover seed in her wake. Her mother's quiet, gaunt face, so unlike its living twin. The deep pit, Pela curled down there like an infant, cotton-clouded face nodding eastward. . . .

Sand thought that she should sleep, now. But first, she would look at her mother's book, see what words had been hidden out here for her to find. As she picked it up, Thunder cracked in the sky, cloth ripping far away.

Father Sun had given the book new life, even as he fed heat to the greedy black rocks beneath her. The night's cold was scrambling away from those rocks, seeking a home in the sky. It brushed the few, small clouds like fingers along a man's naked flank, and they trembled, just as lightly. Sand keyed the book on with the ring.

"My daughter. . . ."

Sand frowned and looked up. The thunder had not ceased; its distant crackle was sustaining, building. And there, high against the blue, was the lightning. Lightning like an arrow, straight, slim, bright. She had seen such lightning, once, when she was at school in the lowlands, and the Tech Society had sent a Kachina into polar orbit on a hydrogen torch.

And yet, this torch was coming down.

Mother?

Sand was immediately ashamed of the thought. Even if what everyone believed was true, her mother would be in the underworld with Masaw for four days before she went into the sky. No, this was something else. A starship from the Reed? They came every few decades, bringing luxuries and farm equipment. But a starship would land out near the sea, where fuel was plentiful. What then?

But she already knew. Sand had never believed her mother to be crazy. If her "Kachina" had been some sort of deluded mystical experience, she would have told everyone, not just her daughter. But she had kept the secret close, very close. Pela had believed that the thing that wounded her was from the stars, from the race that began transforming the Fifth World millennia ago. That she saw in them the distant Kachina of her people was the product of her own interpretation. Sand herself had always believed in the ancient aliens. Who did not? The evidence was too clear. They had touched her mother, and now they were returning.

And there were no coincidences under the roof of the Fifth World. Somehow, that streak in the sky had caused her mother's death.

Sand did not bother to pack up the sweat lodge. She left it there for the wind to have. She raced across the crunching stones, stopped only long enough to grab her boots. She popped open the windshield of the Dragonfly and tossed them into the back seat, bounded into the cockpit. She thumbed on the pre-starter and waited impatiently while the jacket around the engines warmed itself and began circulating the alcohol that was both fuel and coolant. She closed her eyes, willing the Dragonfly to settle into her, but for the first time in many months, it did not come instantly. With an angry snarl, she reached into the compartment below her seat and drew out the mask. Sand held it up for a moment, observed the square simplicity of it, the delicate wings etched below the semi-circular ears, the multifaceted eyes. Then she put it on.

For just an instant, she felt claustrophobic, trapped in the smoky smell of her own hair. Then the eyes of the mask seemed to open, and her human concerns thinned away.

Dragonfly, I am. Gift of the ancients, keeper of waters, bright wings in the sky.

Sand kicked on the underjets, heard a single ping of protest from the rear of the vehicle, and then the flat earth rushed away from her. The Dragonfly rocked and nearly rolled over before she stabilized it. She would not use the gyros, not now. That was for lowlanders, for the fearful. For flying when bored and half-asleep. She was none of those, and she would suffer no interference from such mechanisms. Sand lit the afterjets and tore a hole in the air. She put out her wings and pointed her nose at the dwindling light in the distance, now almost on the horizon.

Dragonfly ate the kilometers in great gulps, but the scenery beneath her hardly changed. This upland was immense, one of the largest on the planet. Once it had been a welling of molten stone puddled thickly like blood and then congealing that way, a scab on the planet's skin four hundred kilometers in diameter. Younger volcanoes had burrowed up through it since, leaving the columns of basalt like those at her mother's place: several such grew and retreated in her heightened vision. Acidic rains had etched it, here and there, worm tracks that sought their own, melded into serpents, carried water that tasted of iron down to the lowlands.

The fiery streak was gone, replaced by a tiny blue hemisphere. Sand could see it wobble a little in the mid-altitude winds. She could see, too, where it was going to come to earth.

Thumbprint of the Kachina, they called it, but Sand had another name for the immense crater. Mother's Prayer.

Invisible fingers twisted the Dragonfly about, and Sand's gut clenched at an empty, falling feeling. The sky flashed over her crazily, and then the earth, which no longer seemed to know its proper place. Sand grinned fiercely behind her mask and wagged the stick forward and then to the side. The world learned her lesson, became down with a vengeance, and the Dragonfly hurtled gleefully to pierce the dark plain with her silvery nose.

Sand yanked the stick back, and the semi-flexible wings popped as they caught the crest of a thermal. Sand opened the underjets for good measure. The plain was an impossibly swift river of stone ten meters below her when the Dragonfly began to climb again. Adrenaline sang in her blood, a tune of joy and fear.

This was why she was a member of the Dragonfly Society. This was why the threat of being cut off from her kiva was a thing she feared.

A single pass over Kachina's Thumbprint showed her the settled cloth hemisphere and the steel spore it had born softly to earth. Sand cut the afterjets, let the Dragonfly drop in a lazy spiral. Five meters from the ground she pulled up the nose, stalled out, and cut on the underjets. Dragonfly settled down, an insect in an immense bowl. Slowly, Sand took off her mask and confronted the mystery with her own naked face.

The "Kachina" was much as her mother had described it. A burnt steel cylinder four meters tall, nearly that in diameter. It squatted on four braced legs. A bundle of cables emerged from some unseen place on its top, and they trailed away to the parachute. Squinting, she noticed the bottom seemed clean and smooth, though of course the angle allowed her only a narrow glimpse of it. Did it have engines? If it did, they must be very small. That spear of light in the sky must have been a rocket of some sort. Why hadn't the Kachina landed on it?

Sand had a sudden awful thought. Perhaps its engines were nuclear. Then the Kachina might not have landed on them for fear of contaminating its touchdown point. But perhaps it was still too hot for human beings. . . .

The Dragonfly had an adequate radiation counter. Sand voice-activated it and was rewarded with a negative reading. She shrugged. Perhaps it had jettisoned its engine before deploying the parachute, never intending to return to the sky.

Lifting up the windshield, she stepped cautiously out onto the loose sand of the crater floor, dust blasted from solid stone thousands of years before. Most of the soil in the lowlands owed its origins to this crater and its sisters across the planet.

The spirit-like detachment of the Dragonfly was gone. Sand stood for endless moments, breathing in short gulps, just looking at the thing. It was nothing spectacular, really. Nothing about its outward appearance could not have been the result of Tech Society engineering. And yet her mother had been certain—absolutely certain—that no human being had made the one she had seen. Sand felt that same terrible certainty. This little craft was from very, very far away. Farther than old Earth, even, and that was far indeed.

"I'm not coming any closer!" she suddenly found herself shouting at the thing. "You won't sting me as you did my mother!"

In the following silence, she felt stupid, and more than stupid, embarrassed. This thing, whatever it was, was no Kachina, no ancestor-spirit of her people. It was a machine of some kind, no matter how far it had come. She had seen pictures of the Reed starships, and they were very large. They had to be to carry living things through the vast light-years of nothing. This thing could hold no living creature.

As she reached this conclusion, the cylinder reached another. An unseen seam parted, a section of the thing's outer hull slid away. This left a small doorway just over a meter in height. Sand scrambled back, banged into the Dragonfly. The only thought in her head was to fly, fly until the night swallowed her, until she reached the end of the world. But she could not, would not take her gaze away from that open doorway, and so her movements to raise up the windshield of the craft were fumbling and ineffective. Something blue bumped and rustled inside of the Kachina; she could hear each movement with perfect clarity, as if the crater were a huge mirror, focusing sound in upon her.

The blue thing stepped up and poked its head into the light.

Sand stopped fumbling at the windscreen. She was looking at her mother.

CHAPTER FOUR

Hoku tapped a well-groomed fingernail against the delicate porcelain cup, savored the essence of the steam that drifted up from it. He lifted the cup and sipped, inhaling at the same time, so that the combination of pungent halia and vinegary apple cider filled his entire head. Hoku closed his eyes, wishing he could drink it all. Halia, the ginger liqueur that so few could stomach, was a rare and precious thing, and the cider just less so. Still, he needed his head clear. The taste was enough to evoke a mood, to calm him. A walk by the sea or through the tamarisk grove near the river would have done the same, but he had time for neither at the moment, any more than he had time to become leisurely drunk. He set the cup back down, content to let it spend its flavor into the air of his office.

So much to do, and only moments to do it in.

"Kewalacheoma," he said, speaking to the dark cube on his desk. It fluoresced and presented him with an image of the Biology chief of the Tech Society. She was a young woman with round features and eyes a little too close together for his taste. Her hair, normally black, had been rendered somehow dark red since he saw her last.

"Mother-Father," she responded.

Hoku liked the sound of that. Ten years had brought him to the top of his world, ten years of pain, betrayal, and suspicion. Though he had abolished the use of kin terms like "ibaba" as modes of address and the use of "mother-father" for lesser command positions, he disagreed with his illustrious predecessor on this particular point. Reserving the honorific for himself stressed the new order of things, that he, Hoku, was the last word in all matters. The council, while still existent, had little power, with the heads of the troublesome clans and society leaders bent to his will or replaced by those who were. Besides, after all of these years, he deserved the title, especially considering the truth of it. His people were like children, cowering before the Ogre Kachina of tradition, and he was both their mother and their father, liberating them. Even as he thought this, he scowled at his own metaphor. Kachina.

Hoku realized that Kewalacheoma was still waiting expectantly. Hoku snapped his teeth together behind his sealed lips. He was getting old.

"Kewa, I request to see the alien. It's been fifteen years, and I need a briefing."

The biologist nodded without expression and said something quietly to her computer. That would be the next thing, Hoku promised silently: to take the file autonomy from the societies and supply himself with direct and unquestioned access to all information. Not that he didn't have that now, but it still rankled him to have to ask for it. Still, there was already opposition to his reforms; best not go too far too fast.

The image of Kewa was replaced by a scene that he had no need to see, imprinted as it was on the cells of his brain. The cylinder craft as they cut it open; the thing that fell out.

There were few animals on the Fifth World, and Hoku had little reference for comparison. Curled in death, it had reminded Hoku most of some sea creature, a mangled crab or shrimp. Yet its thick grey skin bore no real resemblance to an exoskeleton. Perhaps it was the way its head, so narrow and pointed in the front, bulged and flared into a thick collar and then folded forwards, a structure that formed something like a shell surrounding a hole that funneled down into the skull. Or the rounded, dark bumps there that the biologists assured him were eyes—these also reminded Hoku of a crustacean. But none of the Earthlife in the seas of the Fifth World had three more eyes along their "backbones". The head hid a mouth beneath it, a horrible hole replete with wormy cilia. The rest of the alien was also like a worm, save for the legs and arms which emerged from the precise center line of its dorsal side and then twisted out so that they could function in pairs. There were three rear sets of legs, shorter towards the back so that in life it would have stood sharply sloping, head up. Just beneath the head, a fourth pair of limbs emerged, triple jointed, and terminating in seven-digit monstrosities that looked horribly like human hands.

"Tell me about this thing," he said, quietly.

Kewa's voice emerged, ghostly and unseen.

"There's a lot we don't know. It breathed oxygen, after a fashion, both through small nostrils above the mouth and through that funnel in its head. We think the funnel evolved from a sort of super-charger, designed to ingest atmospheric alcohol and create positive pressure in its circulatory system. The heart is a long, tubular muscle underneath the spine. It acted like a sort of linear accelerator, contracting in waves and forcing blood from one end to the other. It doesn't have lungs, as such; air was passed through successively smaller networks of vesicles and then injected into the heart."

The cube showed him the dissected corpse, the long yellow muscle she was referring to.

"The heart was protected by a bony cylinder lying just above it, and we think this housed the brain. It's more like a very thick spinal cord, and there are various sense organs attached along it, though we aren't sure what they all do. The strange thing is that there was much more empty space in the casing than nerve material. That doesn't appear to be natural, but we can't explain it. Our guess is that this individual had an atypically small brain, but that doesn't make much sense."

Hoku smirked sardonically. "That's because you aren't a politician. They obviously sent this thing down to see if the atmosphere was tenable. They sacrificed it. Would you volunteer for such a mission if in possession of all of your faculties?"

"Mother-Father, there is no evidence of surgery," Kewa replied.

"Assuming you know what surgery would look like in such a beast. But perhaps you are right—perhaps it was grown or raised with only a minimal brain."

There was a pause, and then Kewa stammered: "Th-that's horrible."

Hoku shrugged. "Judge them if you wish. It is not my concern. What I want to know is this: how intelligent would a fully functioning alien be?"

Kewa answered quickly, with a hint of indignation. "Impossible to tell. We don't even know how its "neurons"—if that's what they are—functioned. No, I could not hazard even a guess."

"Why are its limbs arranged so?" he asked, avoiding frustration by changing the topic.

"The backbone is its central functional support. We believe that this creature evolved from animals with simple linear symmetry. The appearance that it is bilateral in nature—like we are—is illusory. Each pair of limbs emerges from the backbone, one behind the other. Only their peculiar articulation allows them to function perpendicular to the creature's axis."

"You're saying that its ancestors would have had eight limbs arranged one behind the other."

"Yes. Much like the worms indigenous to this planet. The two are clearly related."

"This creature could have lived on this planet as our ancestors found it."

"Undoubtedly," Kewa affirmed, for once very sure of herself.

Hoku tapped his cup again. He had, of course, suspected that for fifteen years, but the Tech Society had known for sure all along. Clearly, they were due a come-uppance. But not now, not now.

All of his assumptions had just been validated. The original masters of the planet had certainly come back to claim it. And yet, they had an odd sense of propriety. For twenty Standard Terran Years they had rested in their high orbits, uncommunicative and apparently inactive. Until now, at least.

"Kewa," he said. "Copy this to my personal files, please."

The monster dissolved and was replaced by Kewa's frowning features. "Mother-Father," she began, "that is not in keeping with. . . ."

"Kewa," Hoku interrupted softly. "This is very important. A short time ago, a craft of some sort emerged from one of the orbiting ships. Do you understand? Another one of them—perhaps more than one—is coming down here. Now I want you to make all information regarding this creature available to my personal staff. This does not represent a precedent, but a singular occurrence. Good?"

Kewa regarded him for a long moment.

"This could be rendered moot," she finally suggested, "If I were a member of the immediate contact team."

So. Hoku steepled his fingers before his face to hide his expression.

"Kewa, loyalty is my chief concern, now. Loyalty and security. As a member of the Tech Society, you have other allegiances."

"Allegiance comes in layers, Mother-Father, each layer subordinate to the one above it. I can see my duties in this light quite clearly."

Hoku uttered a calculated chuckle, devoid of any real humor. "You really want to meet one of these monsters, don't you?"

"That's very true."

Hoku inclined his head. "Come up to my offices. And I still want those files. Don't try to barter with them; you've convinced me."

"Thank you, Mother-Father." Kewa vanished, leaving the cube a sullen, lightless brown.

Hoku shook his head in self-admiration. Let Kewa think this subversion of the biology chief was her victory rather than his own plan. People who thought they were making their own clever decisions were better help than those who felt coerced. That much he had learned from the Old Woman, when she was manipulating him so.

Hoku was still musing over this, planning his next, careful steps, when the cube pinged for his attention.

"Go ahead," he said.

"Mother-Father. The craft has entered the atmosphere and begun its descent. The flyers are on standby, ready to go."

"Have you calculated its trajectory?"

"It will land on the plateau, not far from where the last one did, unless it deviates significantly."

Hoku was already out of his chair, reaching for his coat.

"I'm on my way. Check the weapons once more and get me a sidearm. Also, Kewalacheoma Hoye will be joining us. See that she is properly outfitted but not armed."

"Yes, Mother Father. Which craft should she ride in?"

"Put her in mine. And Kaya—keep an eye on the mesas. I don't want any of the traditionals nosing around. I have gone to great lengths to keep this from them."

"Okay."

Very great lengths indeed, he thought, and then put that out of his mind. For the second time in his life, Hoku went to greet the unknown. He reveled in it.

CHAPTER FIVE

"No," was all that Sand could manage.

"No" meant a lot of things. No, there could not be something alive in the tiny ship. No, it could not be her dead mother. No, she couldn't be losing her mind. No, the world could not be this different from what she thought it was. No, no, no.

It also meant no, get away from me, let me think, damn it. But the ghost—or Kachina spirit—of her mother kept coming towards her, slowly, tentatively. But she was coming, dressed in an ugly robe of blue material (the same material as the parachute, one lonely, reasoning part of her mind noted for later reference). And her mother looked young, stripped of hard years.

"No!" Sand gasped again, and then she ran. She ran as if her own spine were the enemy, feet thuttering at the dusty crater floor. There was nothing in her brain to prevent this, nothing between her fear and her feet.

Breathless moments and maybe half a kilometer later, she tripped on a cyan barrel, some relative of the whiskyberry. Her knees and palms slapped against the earth, but she scrambled back up despite the bruising impact. Sand ran twenty more paces before she turned around. The Dragonfly sat still in the distance, a silver toy. Near it was the alien craft. A small blue figure stood, looking in her direction.

SandGreyGirl, get hold of your thoughts! She sat down, panting, eyes fixed on the distant figure.

Not her mother. That "woman" could be a million things, but not her mother. A planet somewhere where everyone looked like stocky Hopi women? No. A ghost or a Kachina? If the traditionalists were right, they would not come in space ships. They would not wear bad imitations of Hopi clothing. A two-heart?

Sand had to consider that last one, since her fine and beautiful world was now broken. She hadn't believed in witches before, especially shape-shifting ones. Did she now?

But again, why would a two-heart need a spaceship?

But it was not her mother. She believed that. She could not, would not, accept such a possibility.

Sand sat, watching. The figure seemed to be wandering around, looking at the landscape, at the Dragonfly.

The Dragonfly! Sand came to her feet. This thing—whatever it might really be—had come before and stung her mother. It knew her mother, knew what she looked like. Knew what she looked twenty years ago. And that's how it looked now, the way her mother had, one child and four handfuls of years ago.

"Damn you—get away from there," she screamed, and broke into a run once again, this time towards the creature.

Fine, she thought, as her legs pumped her along. They know what mother looked like. This could be a hologram, a robot, something else. They want to appear human, and mom was their model.

But part of Sand believed in ghosts. This part controlled her breathing, her bowels, large portions of her spine and brain, and to some extent, her feet.

Ghosts don't need spaceships, she reminded herself, seven times and then seven times again. That brought her back to the Dragonfly. Back to the mother-thing.

Thing was a wonderful word, Sand thought. It could abstract fear or focus it, depending upon your state of mind.

Sand looked, long and hard, the light of her new skepticism shining brightly on the familiar face. She expected that light to melt those features away, reveal something hideous and alien, but it did not. Pela's face remained her face, though Sand was struck once again by how young it was. How much it was like her own, both broad ovals, though Pela's tended towards round and Sand's was more elongate. They both had the same almond shaped eyes, just touched at the corners by a hint of epicanthic fold. Pela's orbs were black, however, while Sand's held her father's grey. Their mouths were most similar; wide and full, both of them, able to lift into smiles of stunning beauty or fold into awesome, froglike frowns. They differed more in body, Pela generally thicker through the hips, waist and thighs, her shoulders a touch broader, too. It was like looking at one's sister; their apparent age was the same.

"I know you aren't my mother," Sand remarked, aware of the hideous, uncontrolled sound of her own voice, jerking and quivering like a wrestling match between crying and hysterical laughter.

The Pela-thing looked at her closely.

"I am not your mother," the thing agreed—with Pela's voice. And yet, finally, it wasn't Pela's voice. It had the same resonance and timber, but there was nothing else—neither inflection, modulation, nor tone—that reminded Sand of Pela.

"Then what the fuck are you?" This was upsetting Sand more, not less, though she couldn't quite see why. She couldn't quite see anything.

"I'm . . . I don't have a name. Not one that I can say."

The thing spoke with a lowland accent, used lowland slang and contractions. Pela had always spoken with the conservative mesa speech, even when she was drunk, despite a year or two down there, by the sea.

"You look like my mother. Why?"

The woman's face twitched, as if trying to express something, but it never settled on anything Sand could identify as joy, puzzlement, or concentration. If it weren't so utterly bizarre as to be frightening, it might have been funny.

"I don't have all the words I need to explain that. I grew this body according to a plan I copied some time ago. Was this your mother?"

Sand just stared. It could be done. Almost anyone could do it. It wasn't magic, but technology that was centuries old. No ghost, no Kachina.

"What do you want?" She whispered, an obvious question, but obvious for an excellent reason.

"I need to talk to some of you, that's all. I need to know more than I can learn from your communications network."

"Talk, then. I'm listening."

"Yes. But first, I need for you to tell me something. Do I frighten you?"

"You scare me shitless."

"Are the other people on their way here likely to be as frightened? How can I ease their fears?"

"What others?" Sand snapped, but even as she did so, she remembered the thing's ship, howling through the atmosphere like ball lightning with thunder to match. She also recalled her mother's story of the Tech Society people who had come so quickly to where her Kachina landed.

"From the industrial settlements by the ocean," Pela-thing said. "Several atmospheric jets started towards here when I was making my descent."

Sand bit her lip. She didn't have much time, but her decision was already made. The Tech Society knew a lot more about this situation than anyone else, and they had been hiding that knowledge for twenty years. They wouldn't do that unless there was power in that knowledge, in these things that came from space. And though she often sympathized with Tech Society aims, she wasn't yet ready to let them have something powerful, not until she understood, really understood. And she would not give them her mother, or any facsimile thereof.

There was one more, very selfish thing. Sand now knew, very broadly, why her mother had died. The coincidence was too great that the only mesa woman to have seen the earlier Kachina should die just before the second one landed. And any mesa trash—like herself—who ended up knowing too much for her own good was damn likely to be talking personally to Masaw themselves.

Sand was sure she already qualified for that conversation.

"Get in the Dragonfly," she said, decision finally giving her control of her voice.

"What?"

"Those who are coming will kill you. We have no time for me to explain this. There are two seats in this craft. You sit in the back one."

"Why would they want to kill me?"

"Come on!" Sand shrieked the last word, and the Pela-thing shrank back, almost like a little child, face pulled away in a parody of terror.

"I didn't like that," it said, quietly.

For a moment, Sand felt her heart catch and her eyes mist up. Her mother. . . . Shit, it was her mother, in a way.

"I'm sorry," Sand replied. "But you have to listen to me."

The woman nodded. "Show me where to sit."

Sand motioned towards the seat, which the woman tried to climb into clumsily. Sand had to guide her with a hand on her arm. The arm was warm, solid. Not a ghost, not a Kachina—and yet both, Sand began to believe. From the stars and her mother as well, spirit and ancestor made flesh.

But this was the time to fly, not to get mystical. Sand jerked down the windshield and lit the jets, heard the woman behind her gasp as acceleration crushed them both back into their couches. She would fly low, mere meters off of the ground, that the horizon might swallow them more quickly. The Dragonfly took her with joy.

For the second time I suffered the pain of acceleration. I, who fly with a barely tame star in my belly.

I won't dwell on this; my brethren cannot comprehend it and Makers and Human Beings understand it all too well. The word for "pain" has always been in my vocabulary—the Makers know fifty-nine varieties of pain. I have always assumed that the alarm and even fear I have felt when something was terribly wrong with some part of me is analogous. It is not. Pain is a watery thing that confuses rather than denotes its cause. It altered my consciousness in such a way that I will never be the same—or even similar—to the way I was. Corporeality was a sickness for me, full of mirage and confusion. Since the human structure began growing in my womb I had been altering it, guiding it, so that its brain would be a replica of my own. That was, of course, impossible. I would have had much more luck with a little brother, whose brain would sensibly lie in a clean column along its spine, so like the way I am built myself. It took much trial and error, much patience, to imprint my tohodanet, that frail essence of consciousness—on such an alien organ. I did not dare to disconnect the many glands which affect the brain, since I never really understood them. If only there had been a little more time—but I saw the burn of the starship coming, though it tried to hide behind the sun. I knew the time to act was come and perhaps even gone. Though I had learned a lot from the body itself, from living in it, and by being very clever I hid it all from my sisters. If I presented my evidence, and it was not enough, they would stop me from any further experimentation.

I said I would not dwell on this, but glands are strange, stranger than the mere misfunctioning I am used to. They cause me to think in ways I despise. As we flew across the desert at what seemed a dangerously low altitude, they poked and prodded at my sanity, offered to relieve me of it.

"Strap in," she said, or at least I believe she said. Her language was the one I had studied for many turns of the planet around the sun, and still much of the process behind it was difficult to grasp. It was more like the language of the Makers than my own flitting thought and communication, but just barely so. Regardless, though I understood her words, the meaning of them together lacked sense.

"That webbing," she said, after I did not reply. "Pull it down across your chest and fasten it to those nodes on either side of you."

I did so, but I was puzzled. I said so.

"In case we crash. The web will keep you from bouncing around in the cockpit."

"Why should we crash?" I inquired. "Surely this craft is built to fly efficiently."

As I said, their language is strange, and strangest are the many positions of the facial muscles, the meaning that they denote. But when she pulled her lips away from her teeth, I did not like it. Not at all.

CHAPTER SIX

The Vilmir Foundation ship Mixcoatl peeked from behind the rugged face of the moon with disembodied eyes. Alvar and Teng scrunched over the terminal, intent on what it saw.

"Do they know we're here?" Alvar asked.

Teng shrugged. "They haven't responded to us in any way, whether you mean the colonists or the aliens."

Alvar nodded, wondering why he asked. Teng would alert him if something important were happening. He assumed.

The image of the alien ship was the focus of Teng's attention. It looked like a stylized dumbbell, without much in the way of detailed features. Either end of the dumbbell was pierced by a dark orifice. There were a number of other, much smaller apertures arranged around the rims of the flared sections as well, little black portholes.

"Any guesses as to what we have here?" Alvar asked.

Teng answered him dreamily, as if most of her mind were thinking of something else.

"Only the obvious. One or both of those big holes indicates the drive. The little ones could be attitude jets, or gun ports, or both. I think the flared ends store fuel and I have some evidence that they may contain magnetic field generators."

"For . . ." Alvar began.

"I don't know. It could be a lot of things. Maybe they create a fusion bottle outside of the ship, though I'm not sure that can be done. I'm no engineer."

"Could it be a ramjet?"

"I don't see how. If you throw out a magnetic funnel big enough to collect sufficient interstellar hydrogen to fuel a ship, the resulting drag against those atoms is too great to allow you to build up much velocity."

"Maybe they have an improved design."

"Maybe," she answered dubiously. "But if they could dispense with the inertia of hydrogen molecules, I don't think they would need a fusion drive at all. But you may be right, in a way. They could use a ramscoop to slow down after turnaround and refuel in the bargain. Especially if they nudged close to some of the gas giants . . . hell, strike that. They probably came around the sun, like we did. They could really pack in the fuel there."

"If they intend to leave. If they don't have some kind of drive we've never even thought of."

"True," Teng deferred. "But for now we have to work from analogy. To guess at what potential threats we're faced with."

"Go on."

"A ramscoop generator is a formidable weapon, defensive or offensive. It could cripple our systems, disrupt any smart weapons and most dumb ones. It wouldn't affect our laser, but it could sure as hell confuse our targeter. Could kill us, too."

"Oh, you just thought you'd throw that in, eh?" Alvar said. "It might kill us."

"It gets worse. If they use lasers to pump the fusion drive— and if the actual fusion takes place outside of the ship—then the lasers themselves have to be taken into account. And of course, the drive—a big nuclear blowtorch. All of that without even considering any specialized weapons systems we don't know about."

"And the good news is, there are only three of them," Alvar said, sarcastically.

Teng pursed her lips. "Uh-huh."

"What about communication? Can we talk to them?"

"We'll try that eventually," said Teng. "I don't want to do that until we've separated the landing drum from the drive section. Until we're on the planet, really. Then if they attack, we can work the weapons by remote, especially if the peacekeepers are killed."

"I didn't think we were going to land yet."

"Plans have changed. I have some intelligence from the surface."

Alvar stepped back, scowling. "What? I thought you said no one had noticed us."

"I said the colonists weren't behaving as if they had. But I have made contact with our agent. The one who sent the original communication twenty years ago."

"Jesus. Why didn't you tell me this?"

"I just did."

"I mean earlier."

Teng smiled. "Need to know basis, my trusty steed."

"Do they know?" Alvar jerked his thumb at the bulkhead, vaguely indicating the awakened peacekeepers, wherever they were on the ship.

"They will when I tell them. Are you jealous?"

Alvar fumed silently, chewing and swallowing a number of unpleasant responses. He finally let the matter pass without further comment, though he vowed to remember—not out of pique, but because he should never forget that no matter how he felt about Teng—or she about him, for that matter—there would never be much trust between them.

"When do we go down?" he asked, finally.

"Don't you want to know what the agent said?" Teng asked.

Alvar stared, chagrined that his anger had overwhelmed his curiosity. And curiosity was a survival skill. "Okay. Please," he muttered.

"'Barbell II', over there just dropped a second probe down to the planet. Launched it several days ago, before we even got here."

"A second probe? Then they know we're here."

"What?" Teng turned to stare at him dead on, her earlier vague look replaced by hawk-like intensity.

"Where's your natural paranoia, Teng? Two probes in twenty years? Shit yes they know we're here. And they're up to something."

Teng bit into her underlip and nodded.

"I'm slipping."

"Maybe it's the smell of testosterone," Alvar suggested, as a footstep sifted in from the corridor behind them. He turned to see Jones Cortez enter the cabin. Jones was a big man, black as carbon, with glittering diamond eyes. Jones scared the hell out of Alvar, though no more so than Teng did. But Alvar knew Teng. Jones was an unknown quantity.

"The landing drum is ready," he remarked.

Alvar marked that. Jones, at least, knew they were planning to land.

"Fine," Teng noted, avoiding Alvar's troubled gaze. "You, Rafin, and Vraslav will go down with us. The rest will stay here, under Becka. Go see it done."

"Done," said Jones, and padded off, catlike.

Alvar took Teng roughly by the arm, something he would have never done in a saner moment.

"What else aren't you telling me?" He hissed.

Teng looked down at his hand clutching her arm.

"Move that," she said, in the merest whisper. Alvar let go slowly, color draining from his face, but he repeated himself.

"What else?"

Teng's face softened a fraction. She reached over and stroked his trembling hand.

"There are two big factions on the planet. The traditionalists and the coastal people. Both are generally unfriendly towards the Vilmir Foundation, but the coast people play along with us to get their supplies every decade or two. The traditionals don't even know that the ships are up here; only a few highly placed people among the progressives know. They snatched the last landing craft the aliens sent down, and they know about this one too. We have to get down there and beat them to it."

Alvar acknowledged that with a brief snap of his jaw. "Sounds simple enough."

"It's not. First, we don't know whether or not the progressives have managed to communicate with the aliens yet, although our agent has a good inside position and says they haven't. Second. . . ."

"Yes?"

"We're already too late. It touched down hours ago."

"Shit."

"You bet," Teng replied, sourly.

CHAPTER SEVEN

Hoku glanced around the crater floor in disgust.

"Don't anybody touch anything else," he commanded danger-ously. "Don't even walk."

The rest of the party froze in place, acquiescent to his demand. Far away, a black horizon was sweeping towards them, bringing rain and probably tornadoes.

"Check it out, Homikniwa."

The slender, dark man nodded fierce agreement and picked his way across the sand, studying the many marks upon it. Homikniwa had the way of the pueblos about him, in his gait, in his knowledge of the land, but no one dared to call him mesa trash or question his loyalty. Or his tracking skills.

"There was a Dragonfly here, an old one from the pueblos. The underjets don't burn evenly," he indicated the blacker-than normal patch of sand.

"A woman came in the Dragonfly, just one, but two got in when it left." He looked up thoughtfully and added, "They were about the same size."

"There was a woman already here?" Hoku interjected.

"I say women, but they could both be small men. Hard to say."

"Where did the other woman come from?"

Kewa, the biologist, indicated a trail of footprints that came from the north. "Maybe she walked in?"

The tracker shook his head. "No, two sets of tracks there, one going out one coming back. Same person, running like hell on the way out. See? she stepped on her own tracks on the way back. Anyway, this is the woman who came in the Dragonfly, not the mystery woman."

"What are you saying?"

"Pretty simple. The second woman came out of the lander. Something with a woman's feet, anyway."

"Impossible!" Kewa snapped, oblivious to the fact that Hoku was opening his mouth to remark something similar. "Impossible that it was a human being."

"Nevertheless," remarked Hoku, so dryly that it was clearly a reprimand, "The evidence speaks for itself. Even I can see that. What does your sniffer say?"

"May I walk out there now?" asked Kewa, stiffly.

"You may."

The biologist unhooked the flexible hose from the black box she wore on her belt. She walked around the clearing, eventually approached the lander itself. She hesitated at the opening, then seemed to steel herself and duck inside. She emerged, moments later, a look of profound dissonance on her face.

"Human," she muttered. "Human. And female, as Homikniwa says."

"What does this mean?"

"Fuck if I know, Mother-Father."

Hoku frowned, as if plowing his brow with furrows could grow new ideas in his brain. He walked, slowly, over to the alien ship.

It was very small inside. There was a sort of reclining chair that looked blown or cast from some foamy substance. There were a few plastic tubes extruded from the wall; one dripped what was undoubtedly water and the other was smeared with a sticky substance that smelled a little like honey. More or less identical to the earlier lander, the one back in the Tech Society labs. The central difference was the chair; the other had been nearly unrecognizable as such due to the alien's queer shape. This one was suited to the contours of a human being.

"What is going on here?" Hoku asked the ship.

He stepped back out and found the team staring at him, lost. Expecting him to lead them. He must show no fear, no indecision.

"Kachina," he heard Kewa whisper, and that was too much.

Hoku strode angrily forward, almost running. At the last instant, the blank look in Kewa's eyes was washed with a film of panic, but by then Hoku had his whipper out. He tapped the thin, hard rod against her shoulder and she screamed, toppled over as her legs spasmed. Hoku regarded her writhing form for an instant, his breath harsh and rasping, before he turned to the others.

"No one, No one is to say that. Are we superstitious mesa trash? No. There is an explanation for everything, and every explanation is in our hands if we handle the facts carefully enough. Do you hear me? I will not surround myself with mystics and fools!"

They were watching him, each desperately trying not to watch Kewa thrashing on the crater floor. He held each of their gazes, let them drink from his strength, before he motioned to one of the warriors.

"You may help her," he said. The young woman stepped forward and bent down to the unfortunate biologist.

Hoku paced out into the desert, motioning for Homikniwa to follow him. Fifty paces out they stopped. The approaching wall of rain and dust was nearer. Webs of lightning spun themselves and blew away, and a wet wind ran in front, bringing them the acrid, exciting scent of wet cinders.

"The pueblos have her, whatever she is. A Dragonfly Society woman. Find out who."

"Why not just go take her?"

"The time isn't right. We can win a fight against the pueblos, but not easily, not quickly. We have our resources there. We will use them."

Homikniwa looked off into the coming maelstrom.

"Perhaps the pueblos have their resources amongst us. Perhaps they have used them."

"Meaning?"

"The mesas are easily as far from here as the coast. How did a Dragonfly happen to be right here, at the proper time? The seeding projects are hundreds of kilometers away."

"They could not have known."

"But they did." The tracker's black eyes were narrow behind lids slitted against the wind, his beak of a nose already tasting the rain. "Mother-Father, you always underestimate the Old People. You don't understand them."

"Are you confessing to something, my friend?"

"You know better than that. My loyalties don't lie with the pueblos or with the coast. They lie with you."

"I am the coast."

"Maybe."

Hoku clenched his hands into fists, a paroxysm of frustration threatening his control. In the end, he clapped Homikniwa on the shoulder.

"Let's get away from here," he said, wearily. "We have things to do."

CHAPTER EIGHT

Sand and the ghost of her mother settled onto the blackened stone with the grace of a feather. Around them, the pueblo swept out and away, cubic shapes bunched and crowded onto the natural crescent of the mesa-top. A few heads turned to look at them—people drying laundry on the roofs of their houses or shelling corn into five-liter buckets or doing any of a thousand small chores that consumed the lives of the People. The glances were brief and unexcited: people were used to the strange comings and goings of the Dragonfly Kachina and thus paid Sand and her companion little mind. Sand popped the windshield, and the two of them stepped out onto the landing pad—a natural formation, just a raised part of the same flat stone table that half of the pueblo was built upon, and that in turn one of many shelves of striated rock that made up the structure of the mesas.

Of course the Hopi had chosen to live on the mesas, rather than in the fertile, rich lands along the coast. After more than a century, the pueblos were still at the edge of the terraformed world, though trees now grew even on the plateau. But on the coasts and in the lower river valley, there were forests, wetlands that chirped and buzzed with insect life, seas full of plankton, shrimp, and crabs. People lived down there, but they were not the traditional Hopitu-Shinumu.

The Old People said the mesas had been chosen and modified by the Hero Twins as the dwellings for the Hopi. Otherwise, in a world that had only known liquid water for a few hundred millennia, how could there be cliffs of eroded sandstone? Cliffs that so resembled their old homes in the Fourth World. Sand knew better; that the layers reflected an ancient sea of vast sand dunes, deposited and shifted over millions of years by the brief, corrosive winds of a world without water or even free oxygen. The dunes, layered one upon the other, had become stone and then cracked here and there, when the restless earth beneath them moved, perhaps tired of their weight. New sandstorms armed with a billion corundum teeth channeled into those cracks, and then, finally, the rains came. They lasted for centuries. It was rain of a particularly acidic nature, since the atmosphere was relieving itself of the strata of sulfuric clouds that laced it. The windworn channels were exploited by the new water-spirits and widened into vast but shallow canyons. Further south, the shape of the rift-valley the dunes had originally filled was now virtually free of its sedimentary coat, for the stone was always crumbly and brittle. In the uplands, however, rain now seldom came, and for whatever reason, the stone here was better cemented, less susceptible to the ravages of a kinder water.

At least, that was what the Tech Society people said. Sand had wondered about it more than once. Could a single flood, however great—even one that lasted for a hundred years—have wrought such changes on the land?

Whatever, the stone was solid beneath her feet, and beneath those of the ghost who came behind her, wearing Sand's own Kachina mask. The mesa cared little about her opinion of its origins.

"Come on," Sand hissed, and the ghost complied. Their feet rasped across the small, windswept court, past potted cacti, juniper, the sharp resin scent of sage. Her mother's apartment door was closed but not locked. Sand ushered the ghost inside, followed, closed the door and locked it with a double code.

"You can take off the mask now," she said, secretly wishing it could stay on. How would this thing react to seeing her mother's house? Sand's house now.

The house was immaculate. Pela had been a neat person, and her end had come quickly enough that the house hadn't become disordered. Then, too, Sand's cousins and aunts may have been here, after the funeral, cleaning up the place and perhaps "liberating" a few memorabilia.

Pela's face appeared as the woman lifted the mask from her head. She gazed curiously around the small, functional apartment. The floor was the same stone as that outside, but smoothed and polished, covered sparely with the mediocre rugs Sand's father wove. A work area contained a small cube, several book wafers, a loom. Two futons lay on raised slabs—one of these had been where Pela had lain, just a day before, dressed in her funeral finery. Some cushions surrounded a small table. A dry goods pantry, water basin, and a small irradiant oven comprised the kitchen; Sand and Pela both did their cooking at the clan stove-house. In the kitchen a narrow door concealed a lavatory; otherwise the walls were covered by shelves filled with all kinds of knickknacks—pots, figurines, jars of tobacco, herbs. Dried corn and squash hung from the ceiling in netted baskets.

Sand watched the ghost look around, registering no decipherable emotions.

"Listen," Sand began. "I will get us some water, and then you will tell me what you're doing here." Why you have my mother's face.

Sand walked to the tap by the microwave and measured out two tumblers of distilled water and carried them to where the ghost stood. She handed her one of them. Sand sat on the edge of one of the beds and motioned for the other woman to do the same. The water tasted good, tickling cool with a hint of copper tang.

"Now, tell me, or I'll call those who can make you talk."

The woman sipped the water carefully, imitating Sand. Nevertheless, she spilled some down her chin and brushed at it spasmodically.

"So strange," she said.

Sand waited.

"This body is not what I am, of course," The ghost began, after a moment. "I am, really a . . . 'farmer' might be your best word. Somebody who makes things grow. I make planets grow."

"You create planets?"

"No. I seed them. I work on them, and then I leave. When I come back, a work on them some more. Then I leave again."

"Why?"

"So the people who created me will have planets where they can live."

Sand smiled a little sarcastically. "You must be very old."

The ghost cocked her head oddly, a jerking motion. It took Sand an instant to realize that the woman was trying to nod her head yes.

"When I first came to this planet," The ghost went on, "It had a dense reducing atmosphere. The only native life were single-cell organisms in the high clouds."

Sand set her tumbler down on the table. Why was she feeling sick? Was the room receding, the sound of her own voice becoming hollow and distant, like an echo? The ghost drank more of the water, spilled a little more.

A two-heart, Sand thought, with chill calm. She will kill me, now, take my form, walk among the people. Two-hearts have been with us since the First World, so the legends say. We thought we left them on earth, back in the Fourth World, just as the ancients believed they had left them in the Third World. But we can't escape them. They came up the Reed, just as we did. They are the part of the way things are.

To her credit, Sand realized that she was going mad. Her mother was sitting there. A two-heart was sitting there. A Kachina was sitting there, the creator of the world. Sand felt something trickling on her chin and realized that it was the confluence of two salty streams, running down from each eye. Desperate, she sought escape in the Dragonfly, but it was no use; the calm of the insect would not fill her, and though the mask was just within reach, she would have to confront the thing to get it. Sand's breath came in short gasps, and the world erupted with spots of fuzzy darkness.

Thing, thing. Sand had a chance, one chance, and she took it, stepping out on a lame foot, but still capable of running.

"I. . . ." she began, and realized that her voice was going to fail her. She sucked in air, but the breath broke in a shuddering sob. She had no center, no focus for her thoughts. Yet she had a plan, if she could only breathe.

The breath came. "I'm going to give you a name. Something to call you by," she said. The ghost squinted its eyes.

"A name?" the ghost asked.

"Your name is Tuchvala."

"Okay," said the ghost. "When you call me this name, I know you mean me."

"Say it!" Sand hissed fiercely. "Say your name!"

"My name is Tuchvala," said the ghost, and was a ghost no more. The change was not visible to the naked eye, though Sand might have glimpsed a wavering, a subtle shift in its features. But as the ghost became Tuchvala, her power blew away like smoke from a dying flame. The stolen name of Sand's mother vanished, never again to be a part of the body that sat in front of her. So, too, did the power of the two-heart, and perhaps even of the Kachina. Whatever power those names had were replaced by that of Tuchvala, the spittle that Spider Grandmother made the first people out of. This person was Tuchvala, the half-formed substance of life, a becoming-person. A thing from another star, perhaps, but human now.

And that, Sand could deal with. Her breathing slowed. She

had won. Her thoughts would stay straight now, unbent by other-worldly charms.

Idiot, said a tiny part of her mind, the part that had taken a course in psychology at the lowland school. But Sand had learned what her mother had learned long years before, that reality and truth have many layers. She could sort it out later, the nonsense from the real. Now she had to learn what Tuchvala had come to tell her.

"Tuchvala, how can you be so old?" She asked, this time with no trace of sarcasm.

"I am a very complex device," Tuchvala said. "A created thing. My thoughts are patterned on those of the Makers, a race not unlike your own. In turn I patterned the thoughts of this brain—the one in this body—on my own tohodanet." The last word came out as a series of hisses and clicks.

"Your soul? Is that what you mean?"

"I don't think so. Your people use two words that together come close to what I'm talking about. The tohodanet is the part of you that sees itself again and again. It is a pattern, an ambiance, rather than a single thing in the brain. It is very difficult to re-create, especially in an alien. To my knowledge, it has never been done before. Frankly, it is possible that I am insane. In the lander, I maintained contact with my original tohodanet—which orbits above—checked my response against hers, but it is still difficult to know. Do I seem strange to you?"

"Strange?" Sand muttered. "I would say so. Crazy? I'm no judge. Can you prove what you are saying?"

Tuchvala considered. "Are you aware of the three starships orbiting this planet?"

"I think I would say no," Sand replied, skeptically.

"Then it will be difficult to prove anything to you. But they are there. I and my three sisters have been parked above this planet for twenty local years."

"Doing what? For what reason?"

"I've been growing this body."

"That doesn't answer my question."

Tuchvala sighed, her first truly human mannerism, one she must have learned from Sand.

"If you planted a million square kilometers of taproot dandelion at great expense. . . ."

"How do you know so much about what we do?" Sand demanded.

"I've been watching and listening to you for twenty years," Tuchvala reminded her.

"Go on, then."

"If you planted this crop and then returned to find that something had killed it all—say an ashfall from a volcano—what would you do?"

Sand shrugged. "Re-plant somewhere else. There's plenty of planet."

Tuchvala continued. "But suppose that there were only a few places to plant. Just a few small hectares on a barren, sterile world? And suppose that instead of a natural disaster, your crop was destroyed by vandals? What would you do then?"

"I don't like where this conversation is going," Sand said. "You're saying we spoiled your terraforming project."

"We weren't terraforming. We had no intention of making this planet like Terra. That's what you are doing."

"Semantics. You started this planet out and left it. We came along and thought it looked too good to be true and fucked everything up."

"From our point of view, yes."

"What will you do about this?"

"That's what I'm trying to decide," Tuchvala replied.

"What can you do?" Sand protested. "I mean, speaking for the human race, I apologize, but we're already here."

Tuchvala nodded, this time with a little more ease. "True. But we could start over. Sterilize the planet and re-seed."

"Sterilize. . . ." Sand stood up, quite slowly. "I think I should kill you," she said.

"And I think that that would seal your fate," Tuchvala replied. "I'm basically on your side. It's one of my sisters you need to worry about. She would have sterilized you long ago, if given the chance. I'm doing this to try to prove that you are similar enough to the Makers to merit our losing this planet."

"You're our judge."

"No. I'm an observer, a kind of scientist. But I'm biased. I want to convince my sisters to spare you."

"Why?"

"That would take a long time to explain. It involves concepts that I have no way to frame for you yet. You have to be patient."

"Tuchvala, you're asking me to accept an awful lot on your word. I saw you drop out of the sky, but that doesn't prove you're some ancient planet-farmer. The Tech Society could have cloned my mother pretty easily. This could be some bizarre stunt of theirs. I've never heard of these ships you're talking about, and in twenty years I think somebody here would have noticed them. Even if everything else you say is true, I have no reason to trust that you have our welfare at heart—on the contrary, you're right: if I'd been working on terraforming some planet for a hundred thousand years or so and some alien squatters messed it up, I'd be damned tempted to wipe them out and start over, or at least demand that they leave. Have I left anything out? Probably."

Tuchvala regarded her with an imitation of Sand's own thoughtful gaze. "I can't reassure you about most of that. But the ships are there, and your people know about them. They have been broadcasting messages at us for twenty years. They also came and took away the first landing craft, little brother and all."

"Little brother?"

"I have stored all of the genetic information necessary to replicate most life forms from the Makers' homeworld, including the Makers themselves. I grew a male of the species to test the atmosphere with. He died, and a number of your people came and took him away."

"My mother was there," Sand whispered.

"Your mother was the first being to approach the lander. I sampled and replicated her genetic pattern. It should not have harmed her."

"No, it shouldn't have," Sand replied. And it didn't. But that was when she met my father. He was with those bastards from the coast. That eventually harmed her a lot.

Maybe it even killed her.

"Well, Tuchvala," Sand asked quietly. "What now? How do you go about proving to your sisters that we're worthy of life?"

"I . . . don't know. I think I may have known when I started this out, but I have certain problems."

"Problems?"

"I am very old, even by my standards. One of my sisters is nearly mindless, and the other is . . . malfunctioning at best. I think I flattered myself when I believed I was the sanest of them. Perhaps I thought that just being down here, living life the way you do, would furnish concrete evidence that you are sentient, worthy heirs to the Maker's planet. Maybe I had a more specific agenda."

"You communicate with your—with the ships in orbit?"

"No, not without the communications terminal in the lander. I can broadcast my findings to the ships from any form of laser or radio-wave transmitter, however. The proper code will reveal my identity."

Sand sank back into the cushion, picked up the half-empty tumbler and began turning it in her hands.

"This is beautiful, Tuchvala. Even if I believe you, you have no idea what we should do. At least there's no rush, I suppose. If we can hide you from the Tech Society for a while, and surely they aren't expecting a human woman. Especially since they already know what your "Makers" look like."

"Will this be difficult?"

"Shouldn't be. They don't dare come here and look; it would be a declaration of war. What will be harder to explain is why my dead mother is living with me. The council of elders will probably have something to say about that. So them we have to tell, at least if we're going to hide you here."

Tuchvala nodded again, and seemed more or less human doing so. "I have to correct you on one thing, however," she said.

"What's that?"

"You are wrong about there being no rush. I came down now, rather than later, because a starship entered this system."

"Another one of you?" Sand asked.

"No. The drive is much less efficient than ours. I can only assume that it was one of yours. If it does anything——anything interpretable as an attack, all three of us will synchronize into a defensive mode. The decision regarding this planet will then become certain; hostile life can never be regarded with etadotetak." Another hissing-spitting word.

"What's that?"

"It would take a while to explain. It's one of those concepts I was telling you about. But it is etadotetak that will save your people, if anything does."

Sand set the tumbler down, paced across the room.

"Tuchvala, I need some time to think about this. Not much time. Meanwhile—stay in this room. Don't leave and don't open the door."

Tuchvala began to respond, but at that moment, the cube pinged and began to glow cedar-branch green.

"Lay on the floor, Tuchvala. Now."

The woman did so, though with some hesitation. Sand clucked twice, her mother's old signal for contact.

Sand gritted her teeth in distaste as her father's face appeared in the cube. His mostly-grey hair was disheveled, as if he had just awakened, his watery eyes bloodshot.

"Sand. Sand, how are you doing?" The question was as strained as the man's smile, clearly a rushed attempt at pleasantries.

"I'm fine. What can I do for you?"

"Ah . . . Sand, I know you don't care much for me. I can't really blame you, considering. I don't want to beg you, but without Pela, you're all I have left. Sand, I need you. And I need to talk to you."

Sand sighed, felt ready tears, but they did not come. Her power over the newly named Tuchvala was power over her own emotions, too, and she was in control. Had to be, or madness would slip up on her like a witch in the night.

"We'll talk, father. But not now."

"No! Sand, we have to talk now. This is important, really important. I'm coming over there. I just wanted to make sure you were back."

That wouldn't do. "No. I don't want you over here right now. I can't stand it. I'll meet you somewhere."

"Come here then."

Sand heaved a vast sigh, and shot her father an ambiguous expression of rebellion and acquiescence.

"I'm on my way. Just stay there."

"Hurry, Sand. This is important."

"Right."

The cube lost its cyan glow, left Sand chewing her lip.

"Shit," she remarked, turning to face Tuchvala. She panicked briefly until she remembered to look down. Tuchvala was lying there earnestly, face pressed flat against the stone as if the planet were under acceleration.

"Tuchvala, you can get up now."

"Good," Tuchvala said. She levered up to her knees and then rose rather gracefully. Despite her new-found confidence, Sand felt a tiny pang as she remembered Pela rising so, after morning exercises. The same unusual grace in a body that seemed unsuited for it. But this was Tuchvala, not her mother.

"Tuchvala, I have to go out and meet someone. Right now, I don't think anyone else should know of your existence. Don't forget that you resemble a woman who died only yesterday. People will think that odd, to say the least. I'm going to code the door shut with the strongest commands I can, so you won't be able to leave even if you want, and no one short of a sanctified council member will be able to enter without my permission. You saw me work the water tap, I assume, and I'll bring us something to eat on the way back. Look in the pantry if you get hungry before that; there should be some bread in it."

Tuchvala nodded her head. She learned fast. She smiled, and that was not nearly as convincing.

"What about elimination? Shitting, I think you call it?"

Even under the circumstances, Sand felt a smile twitch at the corners of her mouth. She crossed over to the kitchen and pressed a small turtle painted on the wall there. The narrow door sighed open. Sand pushed wider to reveal a small lavatory.

"You sit on that," she said, indicating the toilet. "When you're done, pull the ribbon that dangles down in front. The toilet will—ah,—clean you. When it chimes, you can get up."

"That's pretty complicated for simple elimination," Tuchvala observed.

Sand agreed and closed the door.

"I'll be back soon," she said. "Don't answer the door, and if the cube pings or comes on, hide in the bathroom."

"The what?"

"The room I just showed you," Sand clarified.

"Okay."

Sand nodded and went to the front door. She voiced her commands low, hoping that Tuchvala could not hear, and when it opened, she went on out, allowing it to close behind her. She checked it to make sure it was secure.

Tawa, the sun, was looking at her from the west, and she realized her battle for sanity must have lasted longer than she thought. The crisp air and the warm bronze light made that contest seem far away, and an unaccountable happiness struggled to express itself within her. All of her life had seemed like Qoiyangyesva, the moment before creation, the faint grey before real light flooded the heavens with morning. The morning of her mother's death, it had seemed that the real light would never come, that her life would never truly begin. But now a motion was expressing itself across the Fifth World, and she sensed that it would not soon end, but would gather force. The face of the Fifth World was changing, and she would be in the whirling nadir of the storm that changed it. It might kill her, it might change her. That was okay, as long as she was there.

CHAPTER NINE

Sand picked her way through the chaotic jumble of houses, winding through the narrow spaces between them, walking across the flat roofs of first-story buildings. Rooms and houses in the pueblo were added by accretion when they were needed, rarely from any well-considered plan. Once Sand had believed this to be sloppy, and when she went to school on the coast, she was impressed by the well-ordered streets that separated the modern, concrete structures. Homesickness had finally changed her mind, though, and when she returned it was to welcome the unstructured nature of her native city.

She passed two little boys trying unsuccessfully to keep a home-made shuttle-cock in the air with their palms. They could exchange it between themselves for perhaps three blows before their youthful lack of coordination allowed the synthetic-feather and cork construction to fall onto the roof of their house. This didn't seem to upset them, however; they picked the shuttle-cock up try after try. Sand flashed them a brief smile and they waved before starting their game again. Six rooftops away, her cousin Kayahongva waved from where he sat at his loom, having moved it outside to enjoy the sun.

Soon she left the houses of her own immediate clan, and the pueblo took on a different texture. Sand had never been able to pinpoint precisely what it was that differed from one clan area to

another. It couldn't be the actual houses, all either built square from
native stone or blown from concrete. The strings of red pepper,
corn, and winter squash that hung drying on the rooftops were no
different, and the smells of mingled tobacco, yeast from baking
bread, and subtle human odors were the same in this or any pueblo.
Perhaps it was just a different ordering of space, or her own knowledge of the clans and her relationship to the people in them. Where
she walked now, men would see her as a potential lover or even a
wife. Mothers would see her in terms of wealth—what could she
provide their little boys with if she married them?

To Sand, this was something of a nuisance. Sex was fun enough,
if the man weren't taking himself too seriously, but that was rare,
and most had ulterior motives; her membership in the Dragonfly
Society made her a good catch, and her lineage was pretty well con-
nected. More often than not, Sand preferred woman both as friends
and as occasional sexual partners. They were less cloying and posses-
sive of her than men were—they couldn't marry her and share her
property—and they tended to be better at the kinds of things which
gave her the most pleasure.

Sand did not intend to marry, that was certain. What was hers
was hers, and she would not share it with some man who was, as
likely as not, apt to turn into a complete bastard in short order.

She walked on past the last of the real clan houses and into the
jumbled hodgepodge of single buildings that marked the western
edge of the mesa. The stone here was broken and uneven, scarcely
fit to build good houses on. For that reason, the houses there tended
to be the ugliest sort of concrete blobs. Those who lived in them
were as unfit for the rest of the pueblo as their homes. Kahopi lived
there: Castoffs from the clans, foreigners from the coast, criminals,
and of course, her father, Red Jimmie Tuvenga.

He was sitting outside, waiting for her, smoking a cornhusk cigarette. When he saw her coming, he stood up from his stone stool,

dropped the cigarette stub and squashed it with his foot. A thin blue wisp nevertheless continued to rise from the smudge, distinguishing it slightly from the thousand-or-so similar stains that dirtied the stone near Jimmie's door. He smiled at her wanly, moved as if to hug her when she came near, but dropped his arms with an embarrassed flush when she stepped back.

"I'm here," she said.

"Thank, you Sand. Thanks for coming."

"What was so important?"

"Walk with me a little ways."

"I don't see anything wrong with talking right here."

"There is though. You have to believe me."

Now that she was closer, she could smell his sour stink, accompanied by the sharp odor of alcohol. This was no surprise; she had seen him drink fuel before, when more palatable stuff wasn't available. Still, he claimed to have stopped drinking a year or so before. Pela, to Sand's chagrin, had even been considering letting him move back in with them. Sand knew that her mother had begun sleeping with him again. What Pela saw in this wretch, despite all he had done, had never made sense to Sand in the slightest.

"You're drunk," she growled.

"Not drunk, just drinking. I stopped drinking for Pela, remember? Now. . . ."

Silly drunk tears started from his eyes, and Sand suddenly wanted more than anything to leave this man, to get away from him. Her earlier elation had become a source of irritation—a bliss denied her by her present circumstances.

"What did you want?" she repeated, firmly.

"Walk," he snuffled, and motioned for her to follow.

They moved silently, out past the last of the outcast houses, down the broken frets of stone that led to the edge of the mesa. Sand found herself hoping that they would go very near, near enough to for her father to reel drunkenly out into space and put a man-shaped dent in the corn crop three hundred meters below. Yet her father's steps seemed very sure, surer even than her own.

"I wanted to get away from the house," he muttered after awhile. "People can hear us there."

"What people?"

"Just people," he said. "Dangerous people."

A thin prickle of unease raced up Sand's spine. What was this about? Jimmie occupied a strange position in the pueblos. He was originally from the coast, and thus clanless. He had renounced his old ties with the Tech Society twenty years before, when he married Pela and brought his much-needed skills to the mesas. Whatever Sand might think of her father, he was an adept mechanical designer. The traditionals had no real dislike of technology—as long as it was technology that they themselves could build and maintain. They would not become dependent on trade with the coast—and absolutely had no use for trade with offworlders. They saw the lowland reliance on such imported kahopi technology as a dangerous addiction. Red Jimmie had a skill for finding ways to simplify design so that machines like the Dragonfly—though less complex and "smart" than lowland vehicles—could nevertheless be built and maintained solely by Pueblo technology and hands. Over the years, this had made him influential in the council, even though he had no real clan outside of his marriage to Pela. He was a brilliant man, and people listened to him. Of course, this also meant he had enemies, including Sand herself, who spoke against him at each opportunity. So who did her father fear, right now?

"You know," Jimmie began, almost to himself, "I always wanted to be good for Pela. I always wanted to care for her like a husband should."

"You had a funny way of doing that."

Something flared in Jimmie's eyes, something that Sand had never seen before. She had witnessed him raging mad, and she was all-too familiar with his more characteristic apologetic whining. Now she saw something unnamable, but hard—harder than she thought anything in her father's soft body could be.

"You don't know me, girl. You don't know much at all. I did the best I could, and your mother knew that. She was a person of great understanding——unlike her daughter."

"Well, we both know where my flawed genes came from," Sand spat at him hotly.

Jimmie snapped his teeth shut over some response and rolled his head loosely on his neck. He peered up at the gradually dimming sky, and fresh tears caught the darkness of it.

"Sand, I'm trying to save your life. Don't make me regret it."

"What the fuck are you talking about, save my life?"

"You don't want to know."

"No, that's where you're wrong, old man. You have just ten seconds to tell me what's going on."

Jimmie sat silently, hugging himself. Sand snorted in disgust.

"Goodbye," she said.

She had only gone a few steps when he called after her.

"Wait," he said, and it sounded like a command rather than a request. Sand turned angrily. Her father held a sinister-looking tube that Sand recognized as a wasp—the weapons lowland policemen used to subdue criminals.

"What is this?" she demanded, more surprised than afraid.

"Just sit down. In a few minutes, it'll be over, and then we can figure out how to save your life. I really want to, you see."

"Then put down that pistol."

"This won't kill you, but it will hurt very badly. I want to spare you that, too, but I'd rather see you hurt than dead. Now. Sit. Down."

Sand fought back a surge of panic and anger. She had no doubt that this involved Tuchvala; she did not believe in coincidence. She carefully squatted on the rotten sandstone.

"Can't you tell me what's going on, father?"

The gun barrel didn't waver. Sand wondered what its range was. Wasps were like whipper sticks; they affected the pain center of the brain directly. Unlike whipper sticks, they could do this at a distance. But that distance couldn't be too great.

Jimmie pursed his lips. "I think you know. Who else but you would have been out over the plateau in a Dragonfly last night? I assume your mother must have somehow left you a message. I tried my best to clear anything like that from the information systems. Pela doomed herself, but she didn't have to take you with her."

Sand surged to her feet. "So she was murdered. And you knew. Who did it, you bastard? Who killed my mother?"

"Sand, you don't want to know these things. You can't know, not now. The less you know, the greater your chance of survival, do you understand? It's going to be very hard keeping you alive as it is, but I'm determined to do my best. In a few months, a year . . . it won't matter anymore. I have to take care of you until then."

"Like you took care of mom? Great. No thanks. I'm a big girl, Jimmie."

"So was Pela. I'm not losing you too."

"You never had me. And what does he want?"

Remarkably, he looked, jerked the gun barrel around too, and Sand was instantly in motion. Her slim legs launched her up the stone shelves, and she hit the higher ground running. She heard a grunted exclamation behind her, took three, maybe four more steps before her skin, teeth, her very bones turned into magma, searing, awful pain that tore an inhuman scream from her lips. The pain stopped in the same instant as the scream, and though she faltered, she didn't stop running. Vaguely she comprehended that this shouldn't be so: she had seen a man shot with a Wasp, and he had folded up, twitching, couldn't talk for an hour. She was either nearly out of range or the pistol wasn't very well charged. Or both. The adrenaline left in the wake of the pain was like an underjet, bearing her up over the stone like a Dragonfly. Behind her she heard her father's anguished voice cry her name, but then she was too far ahead, her blood beating any sound out of her head like a drum in a small kiva. She ran towards home, hoping desperately that she wasn't too late.

Sand had no plan, was not even sure what the danger was. The shadow of pain still hung in her brain, and the confused but clear feeling of impending doom combined with it to cloud her reason. Her senses, too, because she was halfway back home before she realized that the pueblo was dead. The rooftop doors, normally open until nearly sundown, were closed and battened. Wash waved untended in the wind. Twice, she heard children screaming beneath her feet, so hysterical that their high-pitched voices cut through the roofs of the houses. With that shuddering realization came another perception, at the edge of hearing, barely overriding the cyclone of blood roaring in her head.

Yu! Hoo! Yu! Yu!

She was a little girl again, and she had been bad. The Whipper was coming for her, across the rooftops, across the mesa. He was coming through the air itself, the most feared of all Kachina. No wonder the children were screaming.

Sand had been through too much for sheer panic to overwhelm her, but it crouched in her, a mantis ready to strike its claws into her forebrain. It took only instants to understand that the Whipper was moving, not towards her, but towards her own destination. Towards Tuchvala, of course.

The Whipper; she imagined she could hear the rattles on his legs, the rasp of air behind his black-bearded mask, his dry chuckle of appreciation at terror. He would not be moving quickly. Who would run from the Whipper? Who could?

Sand reached her house, heard the Whipper still coming, off in the distance. She gasped the unlocking codes and had to repeat the third, so short of breath was she. The door popped open at her touch. She thrust herself inside.

Tuchvala looked up with an unpracticed but recognizable gape of fear.

"We're going, now," Sand told her, brushing past into the small apartment. She ran to the kitchen, frantically hoping that her cousins hadn't found the one thing she needed now, most of all. They hadn't—it was still there, hidden in the compartment behind the water tap. Sand checked it once, the smooth, black object. Then she rushed back to the door and locked it securely.

"What? What is this?" Tuchvala asked.

"Just follow me, Tuchvala. Just shut up and follow me."

Sand slapped the rear wall of the room, and it slid aside to reveal a window half a meter square. Sand backed up, ran, and leapt, kicking the window with both feet. The resulting recoil spilled her heavily onto the floor, but the window responded by giving somewhat beneath her attack. Sand jumped up and pounded on it with both hands, and on the third strike, the whole pane burst out of its fitting with a high-pitched thwimp. It clattered to the stone outside. Sand poked her head through, not quite cautiously, motioned for Tuchvala to follow her. Sand desperately surveyed the surrounding houses and rooftops as the other woman crawled clumsily out of the open window. She could no longer hear the Whipper at all, and she knew that he was supposed to be able to move without the slightest sound if he wanted. Was he at her door?

Tuchvala was through, and Sand pointed out their route across the uneven layers of houses. Tuchvala nodded, and together they started running. Beyond, in the east, the sky was thickening with dark color, and in the north Moon was peeking over Yellow Corn Mountain. They ran through the cooling air, silent save for the sound of their feet.

Sand felt a tingle on her spine that was not natural, and Tuchvala stumbled. Sand turned and brought the slim black barrel of the crab gun up. He was there, just stepped from behind a house; mostly black, horns arcing up on either side of his massive head, black beard falling stiffly to mid-chest. He held his long, blade-like whip in one hand and a wasp in the other.

Sand fired instantly; she had used the crab-gun often when she was in school, hunting the pan-sized crabs that clustered on the offshore ridges. The trick was to run up on them quickly in a power boat, shoot one before they could scuttle into the water or beneath rocks, and then hope you could brake before hulling your boat on the black granite teeth that comprised the islands. A sport for the young and stupid, of little use in procuring food. And the guns themselves were illegal in the pueblos.

The gun recoiled in her hand, but the tracer from the dart and it's micro-fine trailing wire formed a bright line that ended in the Whipper's left shoulder. He was already turning with the impact when the charge caught up with him, the gun's small battery discharging all at once. Sand heard the ogre croak, but she was already running again, dropping the gun and exchanging it for a grip on Tuchvala's arm. The strange woman jerked her along for a few paces, until she got her own stride.

They jumped from a rooftop, and Sand's knees failed to take all of the impact of the three-meter leap; she felt her backbone jar sickeningly and her stomach suck in. Tuchvala actually seemed to have landed with somewhat more grace, surprisingly. They began running again, but Sand wobbled, trying to recover her wind. They had only a short distance to go, however, because Sand's goal—the Dragonfly—was only a few meters off.

They reached the craft, and Sand had the windshield up in seconds. Tuchvala was just getting in when the Whipper re-appeared.
When he saw what they were doing, he holstered the police pistol
and pulled at something dark and vaguely sword-shaped in his sash.

Sand leapt in, not bothering with the windshield, certainly not
flipping on the block warmer. It was live or die, and she did not
intend to die.

The underjets cut on with a horrible belch, like a monster's fart,
and for a horrible instant, the flame they sat upon coughed and
stalled. Sand thought she saw a flash of green flicker wide of her face
by a few meters; then the jets lit full on and acceleration crushed
the blood from her face as the Dragonfly leapt straight up, eager to
embrace the sky.

CHAPTER TEN

Hoku felt the drumming of the engine in the Bluehawk's belly. Below him, the edge of the escarpment slid down, and, as if it were a child kicking up waves in a pool, gave way to the black, folded creases of hills. Ten kilometers of washboard hurled by effortlessly beneath, and then the earth plunged again, as the broad floodplain of the Palulukang Delta flattened out before them. Hoku reveled at what he saw there; the dense, motley green. Stands of juniper, willow, cottonwood, Russian olive, and tamarisk were viridian cotton-puffs. Dark emerald strands fanned out like a lover's hair on an earthen pillow, streams and backswamps choked with cattail, horsetail, marsh grass. The long strips of levees—natural and artificial—were checkered with more clearly human product: cornfields, hectares of soybean, millet, and cotton. Here, closer to the river, a system of rice paddies. Above that, Hoku made out a silver dart, a minnow in a sea of air. It was a Dragonfly, trailing a yellow cloud of nutrient-fixing bacteria. Though the soil of the lowlands was rich, now, it still kept many of its elements locked up in igneous compounds.

Hoku frowned at the Dragonfly. Not the one they were searching for, surely. No, that one would be crouched on the edge of some mesa, thinking itself safe. Wrongly so. Hoku had influence everywhere, and he expected word on the alien—and her . . . ally? Abductor?

Hoku heard the sigh from behind him. It was Kewa. She had been huddled in on herself, wild eyed, when he last spared her a glance. Hoku did not fear her at his back; Homikniwa sat near, and while Homikniwa lived, nothing and no one could harm Hoku.

"Mother-Father . . .," Kewa began.

"Yes?" The time for remonstration was over. Hoku had a keen sense of proportion.

"Mother-Father, I apologize for my remarks earlier. I understand the danger of slipping into superstition. It is all too easy for us."

"True. Our ancestors were benign, but foolish. I've given up despising them. But this trap they built for us—this silly, made-up religion—this has held us back for too long. Nothing more important than this alien has happened since we emerged into the Fifth World. We have a moment, Kewa, just a fraction of an instant, to act. To do the right thing. If we don't, we may lose the people to ignorance. We will lose all of this." He swept his arm across the windscreen, at the green vista flowing by beneath them. They were passing over the coffee-colored Palulukang River even as he spoke. Boats, like brightly colored toys, plowed tiny "v's" on its sluggish surface.

"I don't understand."

"Kewa," Hoku said, in a somber, conspiratorial tone, "this is our only opportunity to defeat the Reed. Unless we have the power of those starships, the Reed will push our children into the wastelands so that wealthy Fourth-Worlders can squat on our gardens. We will all live like the traditionals, whether we like it or not."

"I can see that, Mother-Father, but I don't see what you can do about it, or what good the aliens can do us. We in the Tech Society have never communicated with them, have no idea what they want. Do you know something we don't, to consider making a bargain with them?"

"I do not. But look, they have fashioned an envoy in our own image. They must want to talk to us, to strike some sort of deal. If that is the case—and I believe that it is—then the deal must be made with us, not with superstitious traditionals that might act from fear and ignorance."

"What deal can the aliens strike?" asked Kewa, unwilling to relinquish her initial doubt. "They cannot live on this world, not since we have altered it. They must be angry about that, as angry as we would be if those squatters you speak of were to come and take what we labored to create."

"Who says what they can and cannot do?" Hoku replied, reasonably. "If they can take human form, they may very well be able to live here. That we could deal with, if they agreed to settle farther along the coast, or better, on the far side of the globe. We could help them. They, in turn, could help us, when the Reed starships come to steal our inheritance."

Kewa didn't look convinced, but said nothing. Hoku gave her his confident smile, but he wished he had some clear, compelling plan to share with the young biologist; perhaps then he himself would not have doubts. But what really mattered was that there was an opportunity, and that they grasp for it.

A dry chuckle from Kewa. The delta was lifting up below them, as they turned west, toward the settlement of Salt.

"Mother-Father," she said. "As much as I regret my outburst, I still wish you had been content to reprimand me with strong words."

Hoku nodded at that. "Without the religion—without the fear of the Whipper Kachina—still we have to have discipline. I'm sorry I hurt you, too. But I thought it had to be done. Prove yourself to me, Kewa, and you will be rewarded sufficiently to offset the pain you experienced."

He left the implied threat where it was, in the unspoken realm. As he was lavish with rewards, so too could he return to the role of the Whipper, if need be. Kewa might resent him; that was okay, so long as her resentment proved to be a motivation and not a hindrance. Hoku could feel Homikniwa's eyes on his back; the little puebloan knew what Kewa did not; that Hoku had acted from blind rage and fear, that the whip he laid on Kewa was a whip he laid on himself. Everyone believed in the Creator and the Kachina, deep down, even Hoku. He could only hope that his misstep with Kewa was not a crippling one. He needed her. For that reason he let her into his confidence, voiced his fears about the Reed. His worries were scarcely secret; many knew at least this much about Hoku's beliefs, his conviction that the Vilmir Foundation would one day take their land. But he was rarely candid with underlings, and he hoped she would take their conversation to heart.

The flat screen pinged for attention, and Hoku gave the voice command for contact. A familiar image flickered on it.

"Mother-Father," the image sighed. "The Whipper has been sent. I know where the alien is."

"Voice only," Hoku commanded, and the face was replaced with swirling geometric designs. "Good," continued. "Let me know when she is in custody."

"I will."

The contact broke. The Bluehawk bucked across some thermals, as one of Hoku's fears subsided. The city of Salt came in sight, and he banked to circle it once before landing. His city. His planet.

That was when the screen demanded him again. This time it was his staff foreman, Hova, with a fearful, anxious expression unconcealed.

"Mother-Father. I . . ."

The man stumbled on his own tongue, seemed to be gathering for another try.

"Go on," Hoku chided gently.

"Mother-Father, there is a Reed starship hiding behind the Moon. They just sent down a landing drum."

Hoku let that sink in, his face stone. His plans seemed to be coming apart like wet tissue, each new event more catastrophic than the last.

"A starship," he commented, at last, very carefully. It would not do to scream at his foreman.

"Yes, Mother-Father."

"It was not detected approaching?"

"Mother-Father, we still don't see it, but the landing drum is already in the upper atmosphere, so we know the starship is there."

Hoku rolled the Bluehawk out if its holding pattern. The concrete platforms of the landing stages rushed up at them.

"Assemble the warriors. Now. Fuel all the missiles."

"Already begun, Mother-Father."

Hoku nodded brusquely and severed contact, wondering how many people would have to die before this was over.

Alvar Washington gazed dumbly at his second alien world and wiped the speckled remnants of his lunch from his chin with the back of his hand. The deck of the landing drum heaved dizzily beneath his feet, and the grey horizon of the sea beckoned him to enrich it with more of his bodily fluids. He resisted, though his legs wobbled like jelly and his stomach complained bitterly.

"I've always hated the goddamn ocean," he muttered, half to himself and half to Teng. She answered him with a disdainful glance and then turned her regard off towards the thin black line she claimed was distant land. Alvar doubted it was, as he had begun to doubt everything Teng said. Indeed, he had begun to think that the concept of honest, solid land was itself a lie, something he remembered from conditioning rather than as a part of his own past. The sea, though—the sea that lurched the landing drum beneath him and stank of salt and rot——that was real enough, and as far as he was concerned, identical to any of the miserable seas of earth.

"Now what?" he asked, gripping the rail ringing the upper, flat end of what was essentially a truncated cone. He watched queasily as Teng effortlessly paced the full ten meter diameter of it.

"Now we wait a little bit, make sure the reconnaissance craft are fueled and working. Wait for our agent to give us a call."

"What if he doesn't? What if they caught him?"

"They haven't discovered our agent in over twenty years," Teng replied.

"That's because he——or she——" he added, because Teng would give him no information about the agent, and he wanted her to know that pissed him off——"was probably doing nothing suspicious. That's likely changed in the past few days." He frowned, struck by a thought. "How long is a day here, anyway?"

Teng smiled. "This planet was supposed to be your area of expertise."

Alvar nodded glumly. "I admit it. I've been so concerned with language and customs, I never even thought about things like day length. Stupid of me. But then, I'm not perfect."

"Neither am I, love," Teng said, gently. "And I like you the way you are."

"Stupid."

"If you say so. And the day here is very close to Earth normal—— about twenty-one hours. Very little axial tilt, too, so it won't vary much."

"I knew that at least," Alvar said, fighting down another bout of nausea. "No seasons."

"Good for you."

Alvar closed his eyes and wondered why his drunk doctors weren't helping at all. Alcohol affected the inner ear, and so did the goddamn ocean. Maybe there was something else he could take for this. He would ask the computer if he ever made it below again. Better yet, he could steal one of the flyers and go to dry land. He opened his eyes once more, deciding that darkness was no help at all.

A peacekeeper stuck his head up through the open hatchway. What was his name? Achmed?

"Teng-Shu. You have a message on the mat. Came in just now." Teng grinned.

"Cheer up, Alvar. We may be headed for the coast sooner than I thought."

Not soon enough, Alvar thought, staring at the broken mirror of the water and the distorted pieces of him it revealed.

CHAPTER ELEVEN

Sand had never dreamed that even the Whipper would have a sunbow, but the third flicker of green scored across her newly-expanded wing and cut it. Sand hadn't bothered to flip the gyros on, so she yanked the stick down, watched the canyons yaw up at her, as she retracted the wings. Once more green lance scythed by, and then they were below the mesa edge, beyond the Kachina's vision. Sand fought the stick and her own sudden vertigo. For a long moment the Dragonfly did not respond, but then Tawa, Father Sun, stood framed in her windshield, pursing to kiss the horizon. Sand put the wings back out and bore hard west, towards Red Corn Mountain and the Hoed-Up-Place. The Dragonfly had done well, but she saved her self-congratulations.

Sand peeked out around the edges of the imaginary Dragonfly mask that cloaked her, now that the immediate danger was behind them. The first thing she noticed was a sour, fermented sort of smell, spattered pink dots on the inside of the windshield, and a sticky dampness on the back of her neck. A glance in her mirror showed her the source, quieted a possible panic. The pink wasn't blood: it was whatever Tuchvala had last eaten. The woman-thing was wiping it from her mouth, staring miserably down at globs of it on her ugly blue imitation of a dress.

"Was that normal?" Tuchvala croaked. "Am I hurt or dying?"

Sand hissed a dry little laugh. "Just sick. Aerial cartwheels do that to most people."

"You didn't get sick."

"I'm not most people."

Tuchvala continued brushing ineffectually at the mess. "It's ridiculous. I've whipped around stars at seven gravities. How can these minute velocities upset me so?"

"Tuchvala, I think you're going to have to come to terms with something. You are not that ship, that computer in space. That may be what made you, what your mind was patterned on. But you are something different. Human beings have inner ears, and so do you. We weren't designed very well for flying, and it shows."

Tuchvala seemed to digest that a moment before answering.

"Do I seem human to you, then?"

"Human, yes. Normal, decidedly not. You can't pass for a Hopi, if that's what you want. But you can pass for human, because you are. Shit, I'm still not sure if I believe your story. You could still just as easily be from the Tech Society—or even from the Fourth World, for that matter."

"And yet . . . I assume that person with the weapons was after me."

"The Whipper? You bet. Dear old dad was trying to keep me distracted while the Whipper came to get you. Almost managed it, too."

"Why didn't you let it take me? Those are your people, aren't they?"

"They are," Sand replied, "and that first is a good question. I'm not sure I know the answer. But something seems terribly wrong, Tuchvala. If the council wanted to see you, they would have just called me, I think, or sent some old men. But they couldn't even know about you, could they? Had you—the other you in space, I mean—spoken with them?"

"I didn't talk at all, only listened. That may have been a mistake, but I couldn't risk my sister guessing what I'm about. You don't know how precariously balanced the three of us are, right on the edge of the abyss. And if we fall into night, your people may go with us." Tuchvala shook her head, a curiously mournful gesture. "It would have been better if we had gotten lost between the stars, or rounded some sun too closely, better all around. But those parts of us are built the best, with the most redundancy. When all of our sentience is gone, we will still go from star to star. Even when we have forgotten what to do, we will still go on and on. . . ."

"But you digress," Sand remarked, sharply. "Do you know how the Whipper could have known where you were? Or even that you existed? I have heard of no mysterious ships in orbit for twenty-some odd years, and I'll bet that the council hasn't either. That's the sort of thing the Tech Society would keep to itself."

And yet, there was her mother's book, the one she hadn't yet had an instant to read. Her mother had known about the ships, of that Sand was sure. Having seen the lander and been stung by it, Pela would not have rested until she understood. Even if there was danger in the knowledge; she would have been careful, quiet about what she found—but she would have found out. Stupid, like her daughter.

"You said your "dad" knew?" Tuchvala asked.

"'Dad' means father," Sand told her. "And yes, he knew. And the people coming up from the coast knew, I guess. But even if someone found the lander, how could they possibly know you have a human shape? My mother's, on Masaw's lips! Or that I had you? The Whipper went straight for my house."

"I don't know. This is all very confusing," Tuchvala complained.

"Maybe I'm being too paranoid," Sand grumbled. "If someone at the pueblo saw you, they probably thought you were a two-heart and called the Whipper for that reason. In that case, this all has nothing to do with what you really are, just what you look like. Actually, that makes a lot of sense."

But Sand's heart didn't lighten. It still didn't feel right, and that conversation with her father—his part in the whole mess—didn't fit somehow. Why would her father know? Sand tried to picture an hysterical neighbor calling the council, telling them she saw a two-heart in the form of a dead woman. Would they send a Whipper? Probably not; witches were not the area of expertise for the Whipper Kachina. And if they did send it, why would they call her father first? Her father had implied great—even mortal—danger to her if she were caught with Tuchvala, and that made even less sense. The puebloans weren't the superstitious buffoons low-landers thought they were. No one had been seriously punished for witchcraft in a hundred years—and she could easily prove her innocence. Further, Tuchvala could be just as simply be shown to be a clone of Pela. The traditionalists knew and understood bio-technology very well; they were, after all, primarily Terraformers. So what danger was her father concerned about? Did his fears lurk in a whiskyberry? That could be, too. But he had seemed very, very, earnest.

There was something she could do, before the mountains took her and Tuchvala in.

She thumbed on the flat screen and muttered her father's name and district.

For a long while, there was no answer, but just as she was considering breaking contact, the screen washed with light. Red Jimmy was faded, his eyes growing vague with alcohol. He goggled at her.

"Sand! Oh . . ." He muttered something she didn't understand. It sounded like another language.

"Sand, you stupid little bitch. Listen to me! Listen!"

He was raving, slavering almost. He had been drinking a lot.

"You'll die, unless you do what I say. Do you understand, Sand? They'll kill you, just like they killed Pela."

"Who?" Sand snapped.

Red Jimmie stared at her, and then he laughed, a painful, explosive sound. "Everybody, honey . . . there are more people trying to catch you now than you even know. Listen, listen, and don't give me any of your outraged-young-woman shit. Pela is dead. I can't hurt her anymore, no matter what I do."

"You can still hurt me," Sand shrieked, tears blurring her vision. She flipped on the gyros and quit trying to hold the Dragonfly steady manually.

"Honey," Jimmie said, pleading, tears streaming down his face, "Honey, I'm trying to do just the opposite, okay? I'm going to give you some coordinates. It's a place on the coast where I used to live. On an island, far from the lowland settlements. You'll be safe there until I can think of something."

Sand recorded the numbers he slurred.

"Go there," he said. "Sand, honey. . . ."

She broke the contact. The mountains were coming up, and she could not fly high enough to get over them. But they would be a good place to hide; a very good place. The hell with her father and his secret island. He was the last person she could trust.

But she kept the coordinates.

I didn't know what I was doing, and that worried me. At the time I marveled that worry—perhaps it was even fear—could make one feel physically ill. Just as I had never considered that the erratic flight of an air vehicle could make me sick, make me painfully eject half-digested food.

Not knowing what I was doing was worse than physical illness, however. As stupid as my sisters and I became, whatever we lost, our fundamental purpose lay along our backbonebrains, a spine of certainty. I thought when I transferred my tohodanet to the human body that absolute knowledge of purpose would come with it. It had—or at least it had seemed that way for some time. But now

I felt it unraveling, growing vague. Though I could perceive the odd creak and flexing of my spine, there was no solace, purpose, or even knowledge there. The rest of my body itched with need, and I remembered a tiny fragment of philosophy, told to me by one of the Makers, before my hull ever strained under acceleration.

Life is need. Its bones are necessity, its organs lust and longing, its skin dissatisfaction. That's why I envy you, you beautiful, sleek thing. You have intelligence without need. Need does not allow us to think, not really. You and your sisters will be truly sentient.

It was true, and I could feel the certainty of it. This body, this brain of mine, strung my thoughts and actions, not along a core of purpose, but along a wavery strand of necessity. Each moment was just a movement from urination to eating to sleep, and on and on. . . . In my great body amongst the stars, I had occasionally doubted the reality if time, despite my sensitive ability to measure it. A human being, I decided—and surely the Makers too—could scarcely doubt such a thing. Not when one had to piss, which I did. And I knew enough to not just let it go.

It's not that the body was all that new to me: I had been building my mind in it for many years. But tohodanet—that which sees itself—was new to this brain, though an alien one had struggled to form when I imposed mine. I suspected now that I had been tricked, that my tohodanet was not all that much like the one I copied it from.

But there was nothing to do about this.

I watched the back of my companion's head as she flew us into the jagged landscape she called "mountains". She acted with the kind of certitude that I once had, or seemed to. But perhaps—if I understood her needs—I would see that my old Maker was right about life. My problem was one of being torn between trying to comprehend—why were we flying from place to place, why were people trying to kill or capture me—and merely settling back to let things unfold. I was greatly attracted to the latter idea—after all, I had merely come to see, to observe. Or had I?

That's what was nagging me. There was a plan of some sort, up there in the sky. Where had it gone?

Sand ducked the Dragonfly into one of the trench-like valleys between the rolling folds of the mountains, night within a night. Radar and infrared painted her a landscape more razored and jagged than light would have, and it seemed as if they were a tiny insect whirring through a giant's garden of knives. Sand caught herself humming the Dragonfly song, a rhythmic chant with only four tones.

"What are we doing? Where are we going?" Tuchvala asked from behind her, denting the deep silence that had fallen between them since Sand's conversation with her father.

"We are hiding," Sand replied.

"From your people?"

"From everyone. I don't know. I just need time to think all of this through, to make sense of it all."

"That's both good and bad to hear," Tuchvala observed. "Good, because it makes my own confusion seem natural. Bad because I had hoped that with experience, I would understand your society. Yet even you seem uncertain of it."

"Good luck," Sand muttered, dropping the Dragonfly a fraction lower. For the moment, only the sky Kachina would be able to track them, and only then if one were directly overhead. The mountains were ample shields against prying eyes, even the ones that saw outlandish segments of the spectrum. And they weren't leaving a trail . . . were they? Sand turned her mind furiously to that, welcoming the immediate distraction from even more troubling thoughts.

Their heat trail should quickly dissipate. Any pursuer would have to right behind them to track them that way. What about a chemical trail? What did one get when one burned alcohol? Sand couldn't think; she had never wanted to be an engineer. That Dragonfly worked, and that she knew how to diagnose and affect common repairs, and that was all she really cared about.

"Tuchvala," she asked, glancing back slightly, "do you know what alcohol is?"

"My vocabulary is fairly large," Tuchvala assured her. "I know the properties of that substance."

"What traces does it leave when you burn it?"

"Water. Carbon dioxide."

Sand nodded. That shouldn't be a noticeable trail. But just in case. . . .

Sand continued a bit farther; the mountains here were very steep, but she seemed to remember a place up ahead, where the clean ripples of the mountains were disturbed by a younger upwelling of magma. Her memory was good, and soon her windshield was enhancing a confused jungle of planes and lines. Sand cut off her afterjets and coasted on her outstretched wings. The Dragonfly settled back over her, caulking the cracks in her thoughts with clarity. The injured wing had torn a little more under acceleration, but now it was performing admirably. Sand banked around the not-so-gentle curve of a thick young dome of basalt, followed the black highway of its lava flow into a twisty maze, losing altitude constantly in the dead, chill air. When she had glided for a little more than a kilometer—turning thrice—she lit the underjets for support, just nudging on the aft engines. She retracted the wings and scanned the windshield for a flat spot.

She saw one, looking like a puddle of smooth, black glass to the Dragonfly's enhanced vision, but she knew that in actuality it was probably quite rough. She brought the little craft down onto it gracefully, without the smallest bump. She took a deep breath, and reluctantly released the Dragonfly with her own exhalation.

Sand cracked the windshield and pushed it up. A rush of chill night air swept around the two women, and Sand heard Tuchvala gasp—whether with surprise, delight, or consternation, it was difficult to say. To Sand, the night air was delicious after nearly two hours of stale, hot, vomit-smell, but she also understood that very soon the night would begin to suck at them, bleed off their body heat until they were miserable. She stepped down onto the invisible stone, felt its unforgiving strength, and wondered where she could possibly have an ally. It seemed that her world had turned against her, and she expected at any moment for the landscape itself to follow suit.

"We better put up a tent, Tuchvala," Sand remarked, lighting their immediate area with a small prayer-stick-candle. It was almost better without light at all, so huge and hollow did the world seem around them. As Tuchvala joined her on the ground, Sand had a brief, chilling image of them as twins in a negative-image womb—light, rather than dark—surrounded by a measureless, hostile realm of shadow. A womb that exposed rather than nurtured them. High above, a wind shrieked through some unseen fissure, and even the stars were obscured by a shroud of low clouds.

Numbed, both physically and spiritually, Sand began showing Tuchvala how to help her erect a tent.

CHAPTER TWELVE

The Tech Society Kiva seemed to hum like a tension field, a vague, bone-sawing but unhearable vibration. It bored into Hoku's skull like a weevil, conspired with the sour, thick tea he had been drinking to keep him both awake and on the edge of a tantrum. And yet, cocooned in the anger and the frustration, Hoku felt a tiny elation. He was being challenged, the challenge of his life. He had always managed to make things fall his way, but he had been a giant amongst dwarves. He was ready to prove himself against other giants.

Hoku addressed himself to a balding, gnomelike man in a bright yellow Tech smock. He was correlating data from the Kachina satellites and two planet-bound observatories.

"What's the story, Tomas?" Carefully keeping his weariness and irritation from inflecting the question.

Tomas frowned briefly at the cube and the figures scrolling through it.

"The Reed ship is down off the coast, thirty-two kilometers north-west."

Hoku did a quick calculation in his head. "Wife-Tell-the-Sea-Point".

"Yes, thereabouts. About two kilometers off-shore. So far they haven't launched any reconnaissance craft, though I suppose we can't rule out submersibles."

Hoku stood and walked to the wall map, traced his finger along the bay that swept north-west from the bright red dot signifying Salt. Below his finger, the bunched elephant skin of the Cornbeetle Mountains puckered out at him.

"Interesting," he noted. "This is where the girl went—what was her name?"

"SandGreyGirl. Sand clan," Homikniwa offered from behind Hoku's left shoulder.

"Perhaps she goes to rendezvous with the Reed ship," Hoku speculated, his mind wheeling back for the implications of that. "That would mean she has somehow been in communication with the Reed."

"Or her mother was," Homikniwa pointed out.

"Yeeeesss," hissed Hoku. "I see the Reed's hand in this. Somehow we missed it. As closely as we watched that mesa bitch, she somehow made contact with the Vilmir Foundation. She should have been killed right away, twenty years ago."

"That wasn't your decision to make then," Homikniwa whispered, by way of consolation. "And after all, the woman was touched by the thing. The Tech Society wanted to understand that."

"Which they still don't." And yet, Hoku felt that he was near a revelation. Some obvious truth was dancing in the darkest kiva of his mind, waiting to be called into the plaza. When he concentrated on it, however, it willfully slipped away from him.

"What progress on finding the girl?" he asked, knowing what the answer would be.

"No word from our agent. She's in the mountains somewhere, hiding. We have several hours before a satellite can cover that area," Tomas told him. He had been concentrating intently on his job, no doubt trying to give the impression that he was not listening to the exchange between Hoku and Homikniwa. Still, he looked faintly troubled. People were squeamish: it was what kept most from becoming great.

"You should send your own patrol," said Homikniwa. "You should get there ahead of the pueblos, if they send a flyer."

"My thoughts exactly, my friend. The Cornbeetle Mountains are nobody's territory. I don't see how the pueblos can complain. And if they do. . . ." He let the threat die on his lips, but it remained in his bunched jaw muscles.

"What about the Reed ship?"

Hoku sighed, felt his stomach churn like crashing waves.

"I'm sure they are well armed, both here and in space. We have to be very careful with them. Even if we succeed in disabling the landing drum, we can't touch the warship itself."

"How do you know it's a warship?" Tomas interjected. Hoku smirked at him paternalistically.

"It's a warship, have no doubt. The Reed gives no quarter and asks none. They know what is at stake here."

A needle-sharp man in a red jumper walked up and waited to be noticed. When Hoku acknowledged his presence, he nodded and snapped off a few short words about the warriors being ready. Hoku thanked him and sent him on.

"Here we go again, Homikniwa," he said, and was gratified by the nearly imperceptible smile on his aid's face. He smoothed his hands against his slacks and went to put his armor back on.

Kewa, the little biologist, intercepted him.

"Mother-Father."

"You have something to tell me, Kewa?"

"I . . . I think I have a suggestion, Mother-Father."

"I'm open to suggestions."

"May we speak privately?"

After a brief hesitation, Hoku motioned her into his office and sealed the door behind them.

"What is this, Kewa?"

"I didn't want to disagree with you in front of your people."

"Very kind of you, Kewa," Hoku said, and meant it. The woman rose a bit in his estimation; she had learned her lesson. His people's confidence in him was probably already a little shaken.

"Here is my suggestion, Mother-Father—but it begins with a question."

Hoku raised his eyebrows, indicating that she should go on.

"This woman—this SandGreyGirl—why is she trying so hard to elude us?"

"I have several suspicions along those lines," Hoku answered. "She may be a traitor, like her mother."

"But you could not have suspected that to begin with. Not when you had the Whipper Kachina sent after her."

Hoku nearly gaped at her, which would have been most undignified.

"How did you know that?" he hissed, instead.

"I was there, when the man called you in the Bluehawk. You damped his image, but I still recognized him. So I did some checking. You had him send the Whipper Kachina after SandGreyGirl and our alien."

"How could I do that? The pueblo council hates me."

"You didn't go through the council, though I suspect more than one of them secretly sympathize with you, Mother-Father. You are a most capable leader."

"And you are a most capable spy," Hoku returned, feeling his eyes narrow.

Kewa drew back, looking really injured. "Mother-Father. Your only fault is that you don't trust your inferiors more. I hoped to help by. . . ."

"By tracing my communications? I must see that the Tech Society power to do that is annulled."

"Don't go too far, Mother-Father," Kewa snapped. "I'm on your side in this, but more of the Tech Society resists you than you would believe. If you abrogate our privileges too quickly, you will have a rebellion we can ill-afford right now."

Hoku glared at her, but quietly admitted she made sense.

"My only point," Kewa continued, "is just this; if you are wrong— if this girl is not an agent of the Reed—then sending the Whipper after her has naturally caused her to flee. Anyone with any brains will run if they're being chased. But this girl has nowhere to go."

"You think we may have frightened her."

"Shit, yes. The Whipper? I have nightmares still, from my mother's stories."

Hoku nodded. "You may be right," he admitted, and he felt a gate open, somewhere. It swung wide, and doubts crowded to get out. "I thought it was the smartest thing to do, especially when we realized who the girl was. The coincidence seemed too great."

"No. You hate to depend on someone else's decision. You want to do everything yourself, make every die fall the way you call it. You couldn't depend on the girl. . . ."

". . . because she is an unknown quantity, Kewa. This is too important. At best she would have gone to the pueblo council. Who knows what they would have done? Anything. Worshipped this alien, whatever it is. Perhaps seized its power for themselves. And if she is a spy—if she is going to the Reed ship—then I was fully justified. Shit, how could I know she would escape the Whipper?"

And why the fuck am I telling you this? Who are you, Kewa, that I'm parading my doubts in front of where you live?

He felt a warmth on his hand and looked down to see her touching him.

"Mother-Father. Just try. Try talking to her. You might be surprised."

Kewa turned and let herself out of his office, leaving Hoku a little confused. What if he had been wrong? Certainly he had misjudged one factor in the situation; the Reed. The appearance of their ship complicated things beyond all measure, because it was no longer a simple conflict pitting him against the traditionals. Perhaps Kewa was right. The warship's presence might be enough incentive to make even the most conservative of the pueblos councilmen listen to reason. In that case, this expedition into the mountains might be another mistake, angering the pueblos beyond rationality.

No. Because if Kewa was wrong—and why shouldn't she be?—then SandGreyGirl was headed for the Reed ship with the alien in tow. That was as parsimonious an explanation of the past day's events as any. And that simply could not happen. He had to find her. Then, maybe he would talk, as Kewa suggested. In fact, he might try talking as soon as the Kachina satellite was in position. But talk or no talk, Hoku would get what he wanted.

CHAPTER THIRTEEN

I saw space was full of shifting forms, and cursed, knowing that my mass sensor had finally broken. It was an old curse, taught me by a Maker.

I switched on the braking field, and it felt strange. A sort of contraction, a tightening. . . .

Something was amiss. The brake had triggered some problem in the fusion bottle. The reaction was out of control, hammering at the walls of the field. The sensors were malfunctioning as well, because instead of a calm, composed signal, they sent a scratchy, itchy kind of feedback.

I bled off the excess ions, felt the reaction subside to manageable levels. It was a vast relief.

Meanwhile, my sisters were screaming at me. Hatedotik was sending something unintelligible but angry, and Odatatek was repeating the same phrase, again and again. Her sentiment seemed familiar, urgent, and it made me sad, but I could not understand it.

That itching was back. Alarmed, I bled charged hydrogen into space, again felt the sensors register normal.

"Mother!" The small, slim ship that was my daughter skittered ahead. Planets lay as dense as gas molecules in front of us, and I knew she was going to die, dragged into a gravity well or vaporized by an impact. The fear was terrible. I reached out to her frantically, and she grabbed my hand, jerked me along. Someone wearing a mask pointed a rod at me, and my shoulder went numb.

"Come on, you fool," my daughter screamed. I looked back, and Hatedotik was behind us, her drive lazily turning in our direction. The braking field was already on, the numbness in my shoulder the fringes of its effect. Soon, it would wipe my mind clean. . . .

And still, the burning pressure. Maybe it wasn't the fusion bottle at all. No, the coolant system was over-pressurized. I leaked that out to the terrible stars, screamed as I fell and fell—I was always falling or climbing. My daughter grabbed my arm, yanked me along. She looked like me. So did my sisters, who were walking behind us with grim faces.

Falling. And still, something demanded to be relieved. . . .

The darkness was suddenly different. I was no longer falling. The woman I called my daughter was shaking me and calling me "Tuchvala"; I could see her by the dim glow of her torch, turned to minimum.

"I. . . ." I began, but had nothing to say.

"You were dreaming, Tuchvala, and it wasn't a good dream. You kept crying out."

"Dreaming?" That made sense, and now, so did the persistent pressure between my legs.

"I have to piss," I told her.

"Go outside, but close the tent behind you. It's cold out there," Sand told me. She showed me how to open the fabric of the tent. It was warm to the touch.

It was cold outside. Wind battered me, and I wondered if it could blow strongly enough to lift me off of the ground, rake me along those sharp rocks, make my pitiful body rupture and die. I tried to recall the range of surface wind speeds I had recorded from orbit, and though I could, found the information useless. Oh, I could recall how fast the wind was, but I had no way of calculating what that meant in terms of lift. I was stupid that way, now. Even simple calculations had been a part of subroutines that occurred below the level of my consciousness, like the autonomic systems of my human body. I understood the concept of calculation—even knew which kinds of calculations were appropriate to specific problems. But in terms of operations, I couldn't even do simple division.

A more urgent question involved the appropriate distance to travel before finally relieving my bladder. I knew that there were multiple and complex cultural parameters surrounding elimination, but the few that I was specifically aware of from my orbital monitoring seemed to have little application in my present situation.

It was cold. I didn't go far. Sand had made me strip off my clothes; she said the tentskin would keep us warmer if it could respond to our own body heat.

Here was a problem; none of the communications I monitored explained how to piss. Before, in space, I had used a modified Maker apparatus—a soft tube the coupled directly to a Maker's slightly protruding cloaca. By adding a trifling suction to the hose, I had been able to stand freely, and this seemed natural. That had been so I did not soil my relatively limited shipboard environment, but here, that was not a problem—there was a whole planet to piss upon. So where was appropriate, and how? Frozen out of further logic, I stood straddled and released the pressure. Warmth drizzled down my legs, and in alarm, I squeezed shut an unseen sphincter. Whatever I didn't know about humans, I did *know* that they scrupulously avoided contact with their own waste. If I was pissing on myself, I was doing it wrong.

I was beginning to shiver, and the warmth on my legs rapidly became a chill. I would have to think of something or ask Sand. But by asking Sand, I could break some taboo. . . .

I settled for lying down on a slightly tilted slab of stone, legs raised and spread. That worked in that I got only a little more urine on myself, but it wasn't very comfortable. I hurried back to the tent. The warmth inside felt wonderful, almost as wonderful as that final feeling of release when my bladder was empty at last. Sand was still awake, and she wrinkled her nose as I entered. I wasn't sure what this facial language signified, but she cleared it up.

"You pissed on yourself," she said.

"I had some trouble," I told her cautiously.

"You don't know how to piss?"

"Not outside, on rocks, in the cold."

She reached for something. It turned out to be a swatch of the tent fabric.

"Dry yourself off with this. It'll help clean you, too."

I rubbed myself with the warm cloth. The chill from outside clung nevertheless, and I shivered.

"What were you dreaming about?" Sand asked me.

"I don't know. Nothing. Dreams are nothing."

"What do you know about dreams, Tuchvala? You said you were a machine before."

"Not a machine, exactly. And I had dreams, even then. I shut down my consciousness between stars, but pulses from the engines still stimulated the latent circuits unpredictably. My brain is not unlike yours, a network of varying pathways. My memories are associative, like yours. Certain patterns of thought recall certain past thought and stimuli. Between the stars, I dreamed, and they were not unlike the dreams I have now. Not always, anyway. They were dimmer, less coherent, usually. I did not mistake them for reality, as I do now. Still, not that different."

Sand moved her head up and down, affirmative.

"But my people make much of dreams," she told me. "We believe that they reveal things. Tell me your dream."

I did, and she listened without speaking. When I was done, she smiled.

"Yes. That dream is full of meaning. It means you had to piss."

Then she paused and fiddled with the torch, and the light went out.

"Tuchvala. In your dream you thought of me as your daughter."

"Yes."

"You aren't my mother."

"I understand that. As I said, dreams mean nothing."

"Go back to sleep, Tuchvala. In the morning, we'll need our strength."

I lay there, silently, listened as the sound of her breathing became more regular. I did not go back to sleep. I don't know how much time had passed, but eventually, Sand began to groan and gasp in her sleep.

A bad dream? She had awakened me. I reached over and shook her gently. She moaned and curled towards me, hands greedily grasping at me. She pulled her head into my breast, reached one leg over mine. I didn't know what to do: she had not awakened. I started to push her more, but the touch of her flesh against mine was pleasant. It seemed to melt against me, bring the warmth of the tent into me. Sand ceased moaning, and I guessed that her dreams were gone. I shifted a little, put one arm beneath her head. Her breath tickled against my clavicle, and the pulse of her breathing and her heart slowed.

It felt good, and soon I was asleep. If I dreamed again, I did not remember it.

Sand's limbs felt heavy and warm, and they seemed to lack the power to move. Muzzily, she fought to make sense of her location. In a tent? The pale light seeping through the fabric indicated that it was day outside. She was spooned against another woman, but she could not imagine who it was. Who?

It came like a lightning-stroke, as such realization always does. Tuchvala.

And with that, a shattering wave of fear and worry that obliterated her morning torpor. She sat up quickly, roughly disentangling from the flexed form that so resembled her mother. And yet, in this light, naked, her unkempt hair plastered across her face, Sand realized that Tuchvala did not resemble her mother much at all. She looked more like a sister, or a cousin. All of the things that had made Pela really look like Pela were lacking in Tuchvala—that half cocked eyebrow that showed puzzlement, the round-eyed blaze of anger, the tight but beatific grin. Strange that in sleep, with no expression at all, she should resemble Pela least.

Of course. She had renamed the thing, stolen back her mother's ghost. Its essence was not Pela, and now its appearance was changing too.

Her chagrin at finding herself intertwined with Tuchvala, her relief in discovering the lessening resemblance of the alien to her mother, were all swept away by a tiny, metallic sound. She realized suddenly that it was this sound that had awakened her. It was the communication link in the Dragonfly, yammering for her attention.

That meant that there was a Kachina, somewhere above her.

Sand quickly stepped into her jumpsuit and sealed it up. Tuchvala was looking around the tent, puzzled.

"Get dressed, Tuchvala," Sand told her. "We may have to leave soon."

Sand pushed out of the tent. It was still early morning, and the sun was not visible, hidden by the stone cathedrals surrounding them. The sky was clear, though, a plate of unveined turquoise.

The Dragonfly trilled for attention once again. Sand approached the craft cautiously, scanning the surrounding rocks for anything unusual.

She shouldn't answer; it would only help them get a fix on her. But this was a new day, and certain doubts had begun to settle around her. Why was she running so hard, so fast? That was all she had done since her mother's death, and she had only the word of her father—an undependable source at best—that she was really in danger. The Whipper Kachina had tried to kill her—that she could not deny—but she had proven herself dangerous by shooting him with the crab gun. While inhabited by the Whipper Kachina, its wearer had little choice but to respond to such kahopi threats with violence. If she had not attacked it, would the Whipper have used the Sunbow? Probably not.

And if her communications board was engaged, "they" already knew something about where she was. It was time to find out who "they" were.

She pushed up the windshield and took her seat in the Dragonfly. The flat screen chimed once more, and she commanded it to display.

The square, handsome face that materialized before her was a familiar one. Hokuhemptewa was famous, even in the pueblos, but Sand had met him when she was at school in the lowlands. She remembered the uproar over his appointment as Mother-Father at Salt and his subsequent claim to sovereignty over the whole of the Fifth World. He had not pushed this claim with the pueblos, of course—the bulk of real terraforming was still in the hands of the tra-ditionals and no one could afford a shutdown due to strike or worse yet, war. Still, his imperious claims and "reforms" amongst the coastal communities had the pueblo councils in a state of constant irritation.

"Ah. SandGreyGirl," he said, his voice deep and reassuring. As if they were friends.

"Mother-Father," she said, seeing no reason to irritate him immediately.

"SandGreyGirl, you have been foolish and caused us all a lot of trouble. You now have a chance to rectify that situation."

"I don't understand you, Mother-Father. What trouble have I caused?"

The face nodded in a fatherly gesture. "You—perhaps inadver-tently—took something which belongs to the coastal communities. I think you know what I'm talking about. If you return it, there will be no penalty. This will all be deemed a misunderstanding."

He's afraid that the pueblos might be listening in, Sand realized. He doesn't want to spell out exactly what I have.

"I don't know that I have anything that belongs to you, Mother-Father."

The man's face clouded, and the righteous anger there made Sand feel ashamed. How could her feelings so easily hinge on one man's facial expressions? She hardened her stomach muscles as he continued to speak.

"Enough of this, SandGreyGirl. We know what——or rather who——you have. Your heroics are silly, unnecessary, and dangerous. As an individual, you are not equipped to handle this situation, nor do you have the moral right to try. This is a matter for the Hopi people, not some half-cocked youngster. Frankly, I'm astonished by your lack of common sense and social responsibility. You contacted neither me nor my local representatives, the clan council."

"The clan council," Sand returned, finding her voice, "is not representative of you and your policies, as I'm sure they would agree, though it is clear to me that you have a traitor working amongst them. It was you who sent the Whipper after me, I assume?"

"Religion is not my jurisdiction, granddaughter," Hoku said, stressing the kin term he himself had discouraged as a lowland form of address. "I do not command Kachina. If you fear Kachina, I suggest you come to the coast, where we have dispensed with such silly superstition."

"What do you intend to do with what you think I have?"

Hoku smiled, seemingly with great sincerity. "Such convoluted language. Child, we only want what is best for the Fifth World, can't you see that? This first contact with——" he stopped, and his face clouded briefly. He began again, speaking faster.

"Alright," he said. "No more hiding between words. SandGrey-Girl, you have abducted an ambassador from an alien race. This ambassador's mission is with the legitimate government of this planet, and that is me. Our contacting this ambassador is more necessary and urgent than I can say. SandGreyGirl, you are an inhabitant of the Fifth World, like your mother before you. Your allegiance should be to your home."

"I know where my allegiance lies," Sand growled, suddenly angry without knowing why. "What are you implying?"

"What is your destination?" The man asked, in lieu of answer.

"I don't know. I'm trying to decide."

"I don't believe you. I think you are headed for the Reed ship on the north coast. I must warn you, I will not allow you to reach it, nor will I allow you to return to the pueblos."

"What fucking Reed ship? What are you talking about?"

"If I have misjudged you, I apologize. Yet I feel I have not. I know you loved your mother, as every woman should, but you must have known that she was full of wrong-headed ideas. . . ."

"My mother? You bastard, what are you talking about?"

Hoku seemed sincerely taken aback by her outburst, and also distracted by some off-screen comment.

"Look," he said apologetically, palms up in a gesture of conciliation. "I understand you are still grieving her death. I'm sorry to have touched a sore spot. . . ."

Sand closed contact. She had put something off for far too long, and now it seemed that her survival might depend upon it. She leapt out of the Dragonfly and opened the storage hatch. There, where she had laid it the day before was the translucent charcoal rectangle of her mother's book.

She thumbed it on. Characters spidered across the page.

Sand, my daughter. There are some things you must know now.

Sand paused, scanned the sky and cliffs once more before returning to her mother's words.

"I am selfish to leave this for you. I have thought long and hard, but in the end I don't know if you will be safer knowing these things. For that reason, I avoided telling you when I was alive. Now I am dead, and the dead are selfish. We want to be remembered and we want to be avenged. More than that, I feel that someone must know what I do, and you are the only person I trust, sweet daughter. You are so very much like me, Sand.

Where to start? With the Kachina that touched me, I suppose. It took a sample of my blood and skin, Sand. The government people came from the coast, and I met your father. That part you know. They took the Kachina and never spoke of it. Moreover, they warned me not to speak of it as well.

Your father was the spy they set on me, and I always knew that. They needed to be certain that I never speculated publicly about the Kachina, or questioned what they told me about it: that it was one of their own experiments. I was clever Sand, too clever. I played along with Jimmie because he, too, was a source. Men let things slip, when they are drunk, when they are in bed. I found his access code, after a time, and very discretely, with great care, I began to probe the lowland data banks. I found things out. By that time, Jimmie and I were bound together, tied up with lies. There was a kind of love there, too, though I know you never understood it. The things he did to me, I think, were largely out of frustration. He did care for me, Sand, and yet every instant of every day he was my betrayer. That made him sick. There are other things about your father, too, some of which even I don't understand. There is a deep, deep loss inside of him——and he never belongs, no matter where he goes. The lowlands, the pueblos—all just as alien to him. He grew up nearly alone, on the sea, without clan, without the Kachina. Pity him if you can, because he will always be alone. Kahopi.

That's enough about your father. The Kachina—that's what I want you to know about. There are three starships orbiting our world, daughter. Three ships, each of which could swallow every person on this planet and still have room inside. That is where the Kachina came from. The Kachina that stung me had a passenger, too, and thus we know how very alien this race is. It is the race that made the Fifth World, Sand, and

I believe that they are the ones spoken of in the Great Prophecy—the Blue Star Kachina and his siblings. They made this world for us to live on, and now they have returned. I don't know what the lowlanders plan, but it isn't good. I hope to find out, though I have become more wary over the years, afraid to use Jimmie's code. I think he knows, by now, what I've been doing. Probably he has known for many years. I also don't think he has told anyone. The lowlanders are dangerous people, with dangerous thoughts. I think they see these ships as weapons that they can wield, somehow. They will never consult with the pueblos. My time has not come to speak, but when I do, the clan council will listen. Sand, all of that assumes I will be alive. If you are reading this now, chances are good that I never made my speech, never told the elders anything. But the Kachina have returned for all of us, daughter, not just for the people down in Salt and Paso. I trust you, your mind and heart. You are smarter than ever I was. Make of this what you can, though please understand that I will also understand if you keep silent and guard your life. But if they killed me, that might think you already know, so be careful no matter what. I love you, little girl. I treasure all of our time together, and I will bring you only gentle rains in times to come. Take those wheels down off of your head one day and make me a grandmother. In a world of pain, children can be joy. Goodbye.

Hands trembling, Sand scanned the rest of the book and found it blank. She reluctantly reached up and thumbed it off, and when she looked up, she found Tuchvala watching her. Sand felt papery, as if she were the ghost rather than the strange young woman. The breeze threatened to carry her off.

"We have to get moving, Tuchvala," she said, through a tight throat. She opened the storage hatch on the Dragonfly and removed a second jumper.

"Put this on," she told Tuchvala, who was still naked. The woman nodded without a word and began to clumsily don the garment. Sand went back to the tent and began to cast about, aimless, unsure what to do next. Had the lowlanders pinpointed her location? Could they see her even now with their orbiting eyes? But she had been right. Right to run. Those people had killed her mother, and whatever they wanted, she would not give them, ever. And her father. . . . she would see about him. Yes, she would.

It was then that Sand heard a sound that was not wind. It was a keening, metallic sound, coming from no particular direction. She virtually leapt out of the tent, becoming entangled in the flap, and when she recovered her balance, she frantically searched the skies. For a moment the sound just hung there, rising in volume but no clearer in bearing. Then metal flashed in her peripheral vision. Something like a Dragonfly roared into the little canyon.

Sand had never seen the Wings of the Whipper, but she had no difficulty recognizing them. A blunt, powerful craft, a crooked mouth was painted below the mirrored windshield. Two horns—Sand suspected they were gun mounts—projected from either side of the small cockpit. The rest of the craft—a flattened "V" shape flaring towards the afterjets—was painted black with white spots. It sat on blue underjets, five meters off of the ground. The horns winked green, and Sand hurled herself to the side. She hit the ground hard, rolled, came clumsily to her feet, and it took a moment for the change in the tableau to register. When it did, she screamed in anguish.

The Dragonfly shuddered and fell apart along a new seam between the cockpit and the engines. There was almost no sound.

The Wings of the Whipper turned so that its mouth and horns were facing her.

CHAPTER FOURTEEN

Alvar looked longingly at the solid earth below him. Three years subjective time in space, a gut-wrenching eternity bobbing in the ocean of the Fifth World, and still he did not get to set foot on land. Not that the land looked all that pleasant; broken and rocky, carpeted with something like grass or maybe clover. But it was land, goddammit.

"Soon enough, lover," Teng told him, eyes fixed on the convoluted mountains they were fast approaching.

"Soon enough for what?" Her profile was lovely, alien, and hard in the light of the strange sun. He thought that she might be some kind of cat that had somehow donned human form.

"Soon enough and you can put your delicate little feet on dirt," she answered, smiling faintly. Behind them, Jones Cortez was sounding faint, percussive notes as he loaded weapons. Chills shivered up Alvar's spine. He hated guns.

"Teng. . . ." Alvar began, and stopped. He looked back at the mountains, trying to ignore the movie his mind was directing, one in which their little reconnaissance craft blossomed against some black mountainside, a stamen of red fire waving in the wind.

"Go ahead, Alvar. I can put up the soundscreen." Suddenly the noises from behind them ceased, and the whining of the engine dropped away to nothing.

"Thanks, Teng. Your friends make me nervous."

"They're just like me, little Alvar."

"You make me nervous. Do you know what it's like making love to someone who can break you like a twig if they want?"

"I think so," Teng clipped out, and each word was a drop of liquid helium, cold enough to burn a hole through unprotected flesh.

"Sorry Teng," Alvar said, remembering the unexplained scars on his lover's body. "You know my mouth."

"It's a sweet enough mouth. It's those messages working down from your brain that are the problem," Teng retorted, but she broadened her lips just enough to disarm the insult. "What's on your mind?" she continued. "Not sweet talk, I gather."

"I'm just wondering about all of this," Alvar said, uncomfortably. Teng didn't seem to like to talk about their job, but if they were to ever have a discussion about it, now was the time.

"All of what?"

Alvar pressed his lips tight, resolved to go on with it. "These aliens. They've been here for twenty years without hurting anyone. That seems to indicate that they aren't hostile, even to squatters."

"Could be," Teng allowed cautiously. "Or it could be that we just don't understand them that well. If those ships started terraforming this world—what, half a million years ago? Twenty years might not seem like very long to them. They could just be warming up."

"You aren't seriously suggesting that these are the same ships? Nobody could live that long."

"They wouldn't have to, if they spend most of their time at near light speed, going from planet to planet. Subjectively, they might be only a few thousand years old. That's moot, though. I don't think there is anything alive on those ships. None of the tests I've run indicate that they are built to maintain an atmosphere. Those are drones, Alvar."

"Robots? Jesus, even robots, in half a million years. . . ."

"Well-built robots, surely. But Alvar—of all of the planets that this race must have terraformed—and I bet we've only found a fraction—why do you think we have never found an inhabited one?"

Alvar brushed stray hair from his face. He didn't like it long, and hoped that Fifth World fashions had changed in half a century so he could wear it short again.

"Yeah, of course I've thought about that. But maybe they are very long-term thinkers."

"Oh, they were," Teng agreed, a faint ring of admiration in her voice. "But I also think they must have over-estimated themselves. They must be extinct."

"Maybe," Alvar mused, "they were just altruistic. You know, seeding the galaxy for some religious reason? Spreading life around?"

"Like a man worried about his mortality? Fucking as many women as possible to insure his posterity? Hey, Alvar, that's good. But we have very little data on their psychology to speculate with. You could assume anything. But the most obvious reason to reform worlds is so that you can use them—because you expect to need them."

"Okay. We've gotten away from my point," Alvar said. "I'm just wondering if we're doing the right thing, coming in with guns blazing like this."

"'Today is a good day to die,'" she reminded him.

"I should never have told you that," he groaned.

"Anyway," Teng went on, "we've played this pretty cautiously. We have to, not knowing exactly what's going on."

"But right now we're going to kidnap whatever came down from those ships, right? Couldn't that be interpreted as an act of aggression? Hey. . . ." Alvar frowned at Teng. "If there isn't any atmosphere on those damn ships, what is this thing we're chasing?"

Teng's face scrunched in what looked suspiciously like a troubled expression.

"That's the crazy part," she said. "It would seem to be a human woman."

Moments ticked by as Alvar stare blankly at her. He had almost forgotten the mountains, though they reared above them like scaled and plated dinosaurs.

"Teng, you should tell me this kind of thing. I shouldn't have to cross-examine you to get it. What do you mean, a human woman?"

"The coastal government sent some people out to the landing site. They got there too late: one of the locals had already taken the occupant off in some kind of hovercraft. But the tracks coming out of the lander were human—and a sniffer caught a whiff of human woman in there, nothing else. Like the inside of a fishing boat."

"How do you know this shit? How many agents do we have down there?"

"Just one."

"But I thought the pueblos were after this whatever-it-is too. I thought our agent was in the pueblos."

"Yes, that's what I told you, and that's where it stays right now, Alvar. You'll meet this person soon enough. When you take his place."

Her words slipped into his belly like a shiv, and with it an accompanying stab of remorse and self-pity.

"Do you really want to leave me here, Teng?"

Her face remained flat. "It's my job, Alvar. It's one of the things we came here for."

"Won't work if my cover gets blown."

"Look, Alvar, it's been fun. It can still be fun, for a while, depending on how things work out. But the agent here is old, nearing the end of his usefulness. Like you—and me—our agent has a contract for life extension, and that contract is coming term. Vilmir doesn't like court hassles; he honors his contracts. That agent comes back, and you stay. Very simple."

"Right. But the old agent came here undercover, very low profile. This isn't the same situation. You and I are likely to become quite famous, if things don't go just right. My time as an agent here could be extremely limited. I got the impression that my main mission here is to pose as a native until this job is done—to interpret for you, and so on."

Teng glanced back over her shoulder. Cortez was checking a deadly-looking rifle.

"Alvar," she whispered, "I'm telling you this for your own good. This could cost me my own contract, so listen to me. I am not, under any circumstances, to bring you back from this place until your contract is up in thirty years. Do you understand? And if your cover is blown, you just become a liability."

Alvar found that he was not surprised.

"Will you kill me yourself, Teng? What about my goddamn contract?"

"It's in your contract, you moron. Didn't you read it?"

"Not the fine print I suppose," he sighed.

They turned, edged between the sharp backs of two parallel ridges. The sky was suddenly gone, and Alvar felt a terrible claustrophobia building. His throat was tight.

"I won't let anyone kill you, Alvar," Teng whispered. It was such a faint sound, he was scarcely sure she said it. He looked at her with wide eyes, and she met his glance for such a long time that he began to fear they would brush against the relentless valley walls. But when she turned back to her instruments, they hadn't wavered in their course.

"Just don't worry," she said. "I'm going to watch out for you. It's going to work out, one way or the other, and you'll be fine. Okay?"

"Okay," he said. He felt like a little boy, the first time he had been arrested by the Santa Fe cops. His mother had made him that promise and seemed to keep it, turned her sharp tongue and powerful black eyes on the constable, so that the lash of the whip had never fallen on his back. But when she got him home, he almost wished the police had whipped him, because they could never have been as thorough as she was. He had been sore for three weeks.

He wasn't a kid, and it wasn't a whipping this time. He hoped that Teng was more trustworthy than his sainted mother, god rest her.

God rest him, too.

He suddenly heard Jones and Cortez muttering behind them, and knew that the private conversation was over.

They flew on, taciturn. Stone walls went by, climbing, falling. Now the land looked familiar to Alvar, and he could have almost been back on earth, taking one of his many long camping trips in the mountains. Alvar liked mountains; they tested you; they had no forgiveness in them, and no malice either. Attributing either to them was a sign of weakness, though Alvar had seen people do it, retreating from the real world and its hard face into a dreamland where the world cared enough about human beings to kill them on purpose. Living indoors did that to people, an old man had once told him. The old man had been dying of lung and skin cancer, courtesy of the toxic air those indoor people had created to maintain their sweet illusions. Alvar wanted no part of either, had headed off-world to places where living outside could be a little healthier. That's what a younger man had thought, anyway. Lord knows what he thought now.

"There we go," Teng grinned.

"What?"

"Radio transmission. We couldn't have even picked it up if we were a kilometer east or west. Lucky."

"Then who the hell are they sending too?"

"A satellite, probably. Nothing to stop the signal from going *up*."

Teng did something to the controls, and the hoverjet began climbing, leaving the valley floor dizzyingly far below. They seemed to be blowing upwards, like leaves caught in the thermals of a forest fire. A jagged mountain hove close, raked by under them, gave a brief impression of solidity before they were out over open space again, falling. Alvar felt his stomach float up, and he had a brief fond memory of Teng wrapped around him in free fall, muscles rippling against his skin.

"There," Teng said, jarring his reverie, and the fall became a dive, an arrow plunging earthward. Alvar shut his eyes, waiting for the ride to be over.

CHAPTER FIFTEEN

Sand did the only thing that seemed even remotely sensible; she ran like hell. She went ten steps before her calf muscles knotted and rode up under her knees. Spasms rippled up her back to her neck like a massage in reverse and her fingers contracted into knobs. The earth came up and bounced off of her, rolled her over. She tried to scream, but her tongue was crawling back into her throat like a flatworm. Her forebrain saw death coming, and again she wondered what she had done that was so bad as to deserve this.

She couldn't see Tuchvala, but the Whipper's Wings settled onto the earth where she could see it without the impossible necessity of turning. She watched, vaguely aware of the drool dripping down her chin, as the windshield split open and the Whipper, still in full regalia, stepped out.

A fool to think I could escape the Whipper, she thought. One part of her knew that the Kachina was just a man—almost certainly someone she knew. On another level, she understood that he was also more than that, just as Sand was more when she became the Dragonfly. The conditioning—both biochemical and psychological—that he had undergone allowed him to fugue into a reasonable facsimile of the most dreaded of Kachina; smart, fast, unstoppable. Finally, at the deepest, most fearful level, Sand believed that this really was the

Whipper Kachina, a being born from thousands of years of fear and discipline. It was real, a manifestation of the punishing aspect of the universal power, just as Tawa the Sun was the ultimate incarnation of light and fusion. This thing, this Whipper, he was coming for her now, and protest would do no good even if she could speak. Indeed, the wasp he had just used on her might have been set to a lethal intensity; she might be dying now, though she thought she could still feel an erratic heartbeat in her chest. Sand wished she had been more devout, that she might think of the proper power to call upon for her salvation.

Mother! But her mother was not yet a Kachina; she had two days yet to remain in the ground before her spirit rose to become a cloud. No help there.

The Whipper was drawing much nearer, but he was in no hurry. His bearded, horned face turned this way and that, very slowly. He carried a sunbow, a green-black glass tube as long as an arm and a little too thick to hold in one hand. It rested on the Whipper's shoulder.

The painted smile seemed to mock Sand as he approached her. He reached into his belt and pulled out a pair of resistance cuffs. Halfway through the motion, his slow, deliberate movements erupted into a flickering blur that Sand had no hope of following. He dropped the cuffs, whirled the Sunbow from his shoulder and traced a crazy green line in the air above her head. Then he was gone, out of her range of vision.

But the sky above Sand bellowed, and exhaled a breath so hot that she felt her skin burn and the hair on her neck singe. She had the hazy impression that it was raining fire.

"Fuck!" Teng shrieked, as the green light cut across their windshield. The heavily tinted window went opaque instantly, but it spattered like water on a very hot rock. Alvar felt intense heat pass across his face. The windshield looked like marble, veined with black cracks instead of mica.

"Fuck!" Teng repeated, as the hoverjet yawed wildly. "He just got the jets! Shiau-shi! Eject us!"

Alvar opened his mouth to scream, so that the foam that instantly encased his body filled it. It hardened there, froze his frantic bleat in mid-gape. Far away, his body seemed to compress, sink down into his feet, and then he was encased in light as well as impact foam. Free fall, and then a lazy moment that seemed to go on and on. Alvar winced in anticipation of the impact: he knew the drags didn't have time to open and do any good at this height. His wince was too early: just as he relaxed it, thunder struck.

Impact foam had been designed for paratroopers; it allowed for a much greater falling velocity than a normal parachute and it also quickly dissolved on impact, so that a soldier could be up and fighting instantly. There were drawbacks to this; Alvar's first landfall on the Fifth world occurred thirty meters up a talus slope. As he rolled and bounced down the rocks like a wooden barrel, the foam broke and shucked off of him, so that for the bottom ten meters it was his own flesh and bone that absorbed the fierce pummeling. He managed—more by reflex than by design—to wrap both arms around his head, protecting it. Almost mercifully, he fetched up against a boulder large enough to arrest his roll, though it nearly cost him some ribs in the process.

Adrenaline yanked him into a crouch, despite pervasive pain. Beyond the boulder, things were still happening more quickly than mere mortals—like him—could be expected to easily comprehend.

The hoverjet was a smear of flame along the far canyon wall; smoke blacker than space was belching furiously up from the deepest, most perfect orange he had ever seen. Silhouetted against that was another craft of some sort, cut rather neatly in half. A. . . . tent? Something like a tent, anyway, and someone lying dead next to it. Crouching near the body was a monster. It was mostly black, with a huge head full of grinning teeth. Two horns branched out from that cylindrical head, and a stiff projection that looked, for all the world, like a beard depended from its scowling jaw. As Alvar watched, it whirled with superhuman speed, sidestepping a yellow flash of fire singed across its shoulder.

The fire came from Cortez: the big man was already out of his foam, firing a large, black rifle of some kind. He snapped off one more round; its trace speared straight into the monster, but the thing just kept moving. A green ribbon darted out from the heavy-looking tube it carried. It stroked Cortez lightly, feather-like—but the man's head fell off, just like that.

Jesus save me! Alvar whispered, forgetting that he was agnostic. But how could he fail to recognize El Diablo?

El Diablo turned in his direction. He must have seen me come down here, Alvar thought frantically. How did one hide from the devil? He didn't even have a rosary.

An angel answered by whispering in his ear. For one terrifying instant, this was no metaphor for Alvar; he had forgotten the transceiver on his skull. Then he recognized Teng's terse commands.

"Alvar. Don't move until I tell you. Then run as fast as you can down that slope, away from that thing. There is a side canyon just around the wall from you. Try to get in there and hide. Do you understand?"

"Yes. Where are you, Teng?"

"Never mind that. Just don't move until I tell you. As soon as he sees you, you're dead."

"Okay," Alvar said, trying to sound confident.

Alvar was trying to remember a prayer—any prayer—when a faint crack-crack floated down the canyon, an almost pitiful sound that seemed flat and silly. El Diablo reacted dramatically, however. He pivoted around about twenty degrees and green lanced out from the tube he held. Alvar could not see where the light was probing; it was farther up his own side of the canyon, beyond an obscuring bulge in the irregular stone.

"Run!", the angel on his skull hissed.

Alvar sprang up without question. His sore muscles whined in protest at their sudden flexion, and he felt slow, as if he were in one of those dreams where one can never outrun danger. The horrible fact here was that this was literally true. He was the only human being in this canyon, Teng, his protector running second, and El Diablo. . . .

Alvar reached the bottom of the slope. He could see the "side canyon" described by Teng, which was nothing more than a fissure in the upthrust stone wall. It was less than a meter wide.

Stop that! He remonstrated himself. That is not el Diablo. It is . . . . Was it the alien? It didn't look like a woman. But it reminded him of something else. He should know what the damn thing was.

He quickly saw that the fissure was going nowhere. It grew narrower, but not too narrow to negotiate: however, a rockfall had filled the far end with debris. He might just be able to get over it, but it looked pretty steep and crumbly. He looked up, frantically, at the little ribbon of sky that he could see. It was partially blocked by a chockstone, a lump of rock that had fallen and wedged itself in the crevasse. It hung about five meters above him, a blunt but effective sword of Damocles.

To his surprise, Alvar's panicked brain presented him with an idea. Chockstones were familiar enough to Alvar; rock climbing was one of his few real skills. If he were fast enough, if Teng kept that thing busy for maybe five minutes, he could give himself a fighting chance.

Here, below the lodged stone, the crevasse was still under a meter wide. Alvar put his back to the wall, lifted one foot and placed it firmly against the opposed stone wall. With a grunt, he pushed out, wedging himself by muscular effort, lifted the other foot to reinforce the labor of the first. As quickly as he dared, Alvar began working his way up the crevasse, pushing out and down with his legs and sliding his back up incrementally, then bringing his legs up, one at time, to push again. He helped himself with his arms, spreading them wing-like to either side of his body. He wished the split were a little narrower; it was better to go up in a sort of standing position, working one leg and arm against each stone face. It was easier to catch yourself if you fell. It was also much faster, if you were adept. At three meters, the ground seemed far away, and the walls might have been getting farther apart. His legs began to tremble, making him realize what a sorry shape his body had gotten into. Nevertheless, he continued to move up.

He hadn't heard from Teng since that last command. Was she dead? The black monster seemed to be at least as skilled as she was—a damned fine shot anyway. Cortez hadn't lasted long at all, and Alvar had seen the man work out.

Push, slide push. He was almost level with the chockstone, now.

Where had he seen such a monster before? His mind was beginning to sort things out. It was a man—or a human being anyway, wearing a mask.

A mask. It was a Kachina. How stupid could he be? What had he studied for three years?

But Kachina dancers were supposed to be sort of friendly and peaceful, personifications of rain and agriculture spirits doing folksy little dances in the pueblo squares. He had not pictured them waving light swords, killing professional, augmented soldiers and chasing him through Fifth World Badlands.

But there was a Kachina who punished, wasn't there? And there were also the twin war gods. They weren't Kachina, but they might have masks, too.

Some old books said that Hopi meant "peaceful people". Peaceful People my ass, Alvar thought. It was a mistranslation, anyway. Hopitu-Shinumu meant "well-behaved people", and good behavior could involve killing, under the proper circumstances.

Push, slide. A few more and he could hide on top of the chockstone. He was already sort of behind it; he could just see over it enough to make out the place where he had come in. He was pausing to get his breath for the final push when the horned, black clad figure entered the canyon, stepping lightly and holding its weapon in front of it. Alvar slowly tucked his head down; like most people, the Kachina hadn't immediately thought to look up for him. Anyway, Alvar was mostly hidden by the stone, and as the Whipper progressed in, he was eclipsed completely by it.

Unfortunately, that meant Alvar could not see the Whipper, either. He dared not move, though his legs were beginning to really ache. If one of them cramped, that would be the end of Alvar Washington and his brilliant career.

His career would end soon enough anyway, when the Kachina dancer noticed that his tracks had vanished and did look up.

"Teng?" he whispered, just barely, with his sender on. "Where are you, woman?"

There was no answer.

The Kachina was only a man. In fact, he must be some low-tech version of Teng. He shouldn't be a match for her.

But he had been more than a match for Cortez. Alvar reminded himself that Cortez had been poorly armed to fight a laser. He had been ejected with the weapon he was loading, not his weapon of choice. If he had been armed with a laser himself, the duel would have surely been more even. But what was Teng armed with? Not much, probably. She had been flying. The shots he heard were probably from some kind of side arm.

Alvar tried to control his breathing and bring his mind back into focus. It was down there below him, utterly silent. Did it have a soundscreen or could a man really walk and make that little noise? Or maybe the whumping of Alvar's heart was drowning out the shuffling footsteps. He strained his neck to peer between his own legs. His only chance would be to let himself fall on the Kachina while it was pondering his tracks ending. Before it looked up.

Alvar sighed. He would probably miss, like the Coyote in those films from his early post-atomic film class. Splat! Maybe the Kachina would spare him out of a sense of humor.

Suddenly the black, cylindrical head—with its outspread horns—was in view. As Alvar released his hold, he amended the imagined result of his fall, saw himself comically impaled on the horns, the Kachina turning its head this way and that, wondering where he was, unable to see him of course, since he was on its head. . . .

"Alvar!" someone screamed, as he fell. He heard another one of those puny cracks!. The Kachina stumbled back, and Alvar, trying to get his feet under himself, missed his enemy's torso but hit both of his arms. Alvar lashed out blindly, felt something tap his ribs. Then he was airborne again, whirling in a somersault. He landed in a pocket of hard vacuum that sucked the air right out of his lungs. His chest seemed filled with glue, as he strained to draw in breath but absolutely unable to. Nothing else hit him, so he levered up, spitting sand and blood. He had to get away.

Teng was there, somehow. The Kachina had not fallen, but it had dropped the laser. It now wielded something like a machete. Teng was busy throwing her undoubtedly empty pistol at the Kachina's face. Her opponent didn't flinch; the gun struck his mask and bounced off.

For a moment, Teng and the Kachina merely regarded one another. She looked relaxed, her hair almost playfully mussed. Her yellow eyes seemed to sparkle with what had to be glee.

Teng then darted forward, and the machete descended in a simple, oblique strike aimed at her neck and shoulder. Teng was somehow a half a meter to the right, however, spinning and sinking, one leg lashing out. She caught the Kachina right on the ankle. He was already leaning onto it to counteract the sweep, but the force of her kick staggered him, nevertheless. He turned with the blow, somehow brought the sword back around. Teng and the sword briefly shared the same space—Alvar could not see in what way—and then Teng was inside his guard. Her fist crunched dully into the Kachina's solar plexus, her other arm deflected the Kachina's second, chopping hand, and then her punching hand pistoned straight up under the hooded mask. Even Alvar, gasping as he was, heard the snap and gurgle as the Kachina rocked back on its heels and sat roughly down. To its credit, it did not grasp vainly at its crushed larynx but instead groped for a black baton in its sash. Teng was having none of that; she leapt like a dancer and stamped her heel sharply against the Kachina's breast, just over the heart. He pitched back and lay still.

She regarded her downed opponent for a long moment, chest heaving, as if a little uncertain of her work. She picked up her pistol, pushed a second magazine from her belt into it, and very carefully shot the still form three times. She returned the gun to a holster beneath her grey jacket. It—and her hand—were sticky with blood.

"Shit, Teng," Alvar gasped as he finally came to his feet. "He got you."

"Flesh wound," she said, quirking her lips sarcastically. In fact, the blade had sliced a palm-shaped depression in her shoulder, shinned across her ribs, and bitten deeply into her thigh. The entire left side of her body was soaked with crimson. It was still gouting from her thigh, but the other wounds had already ceased bleeding as some strange thing in her blood clotted quickly along the oxygen boundary. No matter what had been done to improve Teng, however, Alvar could not believe she wasn't in bad shape.

"You saved my life, Teng. Thank you."

"Told you I'd take care of you. Now come on, before those two wake up."

"Who?"

"The alien and the other woman. I saw them twitching; this thing must have stunned them."

"Oh. Very observant of you."

"It's my job," she said, and Alvar was sure he detected some bitterness. Teng stooped and picked up the laser, examined it and made a face.

"Fuck. It's keyed to some remote, probably in his brain. Useless." She bent and quickly searched the body. The mask came off easily, revealing the face of a young man, probably no older than twenty-five. His broad, handsome face was serene save for the trickles of blood from his mouth and nostrils. His eyes were half lidded, as if waking from a nap.

"Oh, shit," Alvar groaned. He staggered away from the dead Kachina, spewing his lunch onto the reddish sand. He felt Teng's eyes on him, sure that they were full of disdain. When he turned, shamefaced, to face her, however, he caught a peculiar light in her eyes. A sad kind of light.

"You're a sweet boy, Alvar," she said.

They started back towards the larger canyon, Alvar at a loss for a response. He let Teng take the lead, and he was distressed to see her legs tremble. In fact, she almost stumbled as they crossed the edge of the slope he had so ungracefully descended.

How bad are you hurt, Teng? He knew what shape he would be in with similar wounds. He knew something else, as well.

"You knew he would follow me, didn't you?"

"Yes. I only distracted him from taking a shot at you, but I knew he would follow you first."

"I was bait, then," he said, without rancor.

"Yes. It was the best way."

"But you didn't expect me to attack him myself."

"That was an attack?" she said, trying hard to be light. "I thought you just fell."

"I made you act too soon, Teng. If I hadn't tried that stupid stunt, you wouldn't have been injured. I'm sorry."

Teng leaned briefly against a large rock. She looked at him with weary eyes.

"No telling, lover. You made him drop the laser. He might have gotten me with that, which would have been much worse."

"Yeah, but if I hadn't been here at all. . . ."

"That's silly shit, Alvar. You think too much. Even when we fuck, you think to much. Just let things happen and be, okay? It's alright."

With that, her legs wobbled wildly, as if they were rubber. Under other circumstances, it would have been funny. She straightened back up and fell again.

"Shit," Teng whispered, as Alvar bent frantically over her.

"Teng, what can I do?"

"I'll be okay. Just lost a little too much blood. Get those women on that thing's ship and tie them up or something. Take my pistol. Then get me on board and let's get back to the ship. I'll just lie here for a moment."

"Teng, are you lying to me? Are you okay?"

She didn't answer. Alvar sucked in a deep breath, took her gun, and jogged off across the canyon floor, damned if he knew what he was doing.

CHAPTER SIXTEEN

Sand managed to get to her feet and stand for a brief moment before toppling for the sixth time.

Seven's the charm, she thought, grimly. The Whipper was off in the rocks, hunting whoever had been in the downed ship. That should be a break for her, but the wasp sting was wearing off slowly. Though her back and arms held only the dull ache of remembered agony, her calves and feet were still cramping, evidence to Sand that human beings should never have been bipeds; they should have stayed in the First World with fish, bugs, and lizards.

Seven was not the charm, and Sand collapsed once more before pragmatically resigning herself to crawling, inspired by her thoughts of the First World. *Climbing down the reed rather than up*, she thought. Ironic, since Tuchvala was climbing up, from whatever she was to human.

That assumed, Sand realized suddenly, that humans were always up the reed. Crawling was making her humble. The religion taught that the Hopis had climbed up through Four Worlds on Earth, right up through the sky of each on ladders or canes or whatnot. The sky of each previous world then became the floor of the next. The Fourth World—Earth—had been Masaw's world, and the Hopi lived there only by his leave. They had climbed once more, through the roof of the Fourth World, via starship and the Vilmir Foundation—which Fifth-Worlders, for obvious reasons, nicknamed the Reed. The Reed was their Masaw, now.

Hopi leaders taught that the movement from world to world was a metaphor, on one level, for evolution; that the essence of the Hopi had resided always in certain creatures, from the first, single celled creatures, and that this spirit had moved upwards towards the present state. Intellectually, Sand knew that evolution did not work in this way—that there was no up to seek, that people were anything but inevitable in the scheme of things. But if one believed in the gods—well, human beings could manipulate living substance to create whatever they want, now. Why couldn't gods?

And why was she thinking of this as she dragged herself painfully across the many-fanged canyon floor? Her mind seemed to buzz with a life of its own, demanding her attention. *You've been thinking with your legs*, she seemed to be telling herself. The Kachina took your legs for awhile. *Use your grey stuff, idiot!*

She wasn't making all that much progress towards the Whipper's ship, but soon she would try to stand again. She could humor her brain for a while longer. There had been a thought a little earlier that jogged something. About Masaw. How did the legend go? In the Third World, the ancestors of Human Beings had been plagued by two-hearts and other evil. They heard footsteps in the sky above them. They fashioned a catbird out of clay and sent it to see what was there. The footsteps came from Masaw, the master of fire. Being a thing of clay, the catbird did not fear his dreadful appearance. The catbird asked Masaw if the people could come up to live in Masaw's world. The god replied "there is nothing here, only grey mist. Nothing grows; I must build fires just to tend my crops. But you are welcome to come."

The people accepted this challenge, came to the Fourth World. In the domain of Masaw, they naturally came to know death, but they also had fire, and the power to make the world a fit place to live. The Hero twins Pokanghoya and Polongahoya changed the grey face of the Fourth World, made it fit to live in for many centuries, until the nineteenth century, when the two-hearts revealed themselves, cut the forests, filled the waters with stink that nothing could live in, tore holes in the roof of the Fourth World so that the light from Tawa became harsh. Many Hopis had eventually participated in this destruction; the two-hearts had infiltrated every race and tribe.

So once more the Hopis heard footsteps in the sky, but these footsteps were bursts of hydrogen fusion, and when they sent their catbird, he met the Reed. And what had the Reed said? "It will be a hard life, because there is nothing there. You must make this world grow, but then it will be yours."

There was the rub. The Reed was a two-heart. Was he as trust-worthy as Masaw? Certainly not.

A shadow fell across Sand, and she clenched her teeth against coming pain. It did not come. Instead, a voice that evoked more than one layer of familiarity spoke.

"Sand, are you okay?"

It was Tuchvala. Standing.

"Tuchvala. Help me up. Help me get to the Whipper's ship. We have to get out of here."

Thinking with your legs again, her brain reminded her, but she pushed that away. She rolled over onto her back. Tuchvala bent over and they locked arms at the elbows. The other woman pulled back as Sand struggled to get her feet under her. She stood, shakily, but quickly collapsed against Tuchvala. The woman slipped a shoulder under Sand's armpit and reached around her back. Pela's stocky body was good, strong, just as Sand remembered it from childhood.

"How is it that you're up so quickly?" Sand asked as they moved—much more quickly now—towards the Wings of the Whipper.

Tuchvala made a noncommittal noise that sounded rehearsed; her off-the-cuff vocalizations were still anything but. "I think I must have been farther from the wave emitter. I didn't know who was coming, but you've run from everyone so far, and it seemed a safe guess that I should run from that ship—especially after he cut yours in half."

Running, Sand's mind echoed, taunting. They had reached the hoverjet. The door was locked.

"Fuck!" Sand hissed. The Kachina would have the key.

What now?

"I've never seen one of you dead before, Sand. It made me sick, like I was sick in the flyer."

"What?"

"The Whipper. He cut someone's head off."

"Show me, Tuchvala."

Sand could have probably walked unassisted, but Tuchvala's shoulder felt good under her own; comforting. Sand saw what her companion had been talking about almost immediately. A human body was lying some twenty meters or so from the Whipper's Wings. It was in the direction of the broken Dragonfly and the burning ship—wherever the hell it was from. As they drew nearer, the body looked stranger, however; less human. It was only when she noticed that the oblong rock near it had open, glazed eyes and white teeth showing behind skinned-back lips that the whole picture came into focus.

The man was black. There had been a few people that color among the original Hopis, Sand thought, but no one living was that black. Briefly, she wondered if the sunbow could have turned him that shade, but discarded that as silly. The color looked right on him, as right as anything could look on a decapitated corpse. He was wearing an odd uniform, too, one she did not recognize as any pueblo or lowland society.

This man was not from the Fifth World.

The swirling, chaotic, saltwater thoughts in her head settled then, and clear crystals precipitated. Hoku had mentioned a Reed starship; he thought she was going to it. Somehow, the Reed had known about the Kachina orbiting above and sent a ship. The Reed, which had given the Hopi this land, and which would undoubtedly take it back when they had made it a fit place to live. That's what they whispered in the lowlands, in the school at Salt. She had believed it, but she had put that thought away, as a vague, distant danger. Hoku must take it very seriously, however. He must think that Tuchvala could offer him the power to confront the Reed. Despite his professed atheism, Hoku still believed—whether he knew it or not—that the Kachina could save them, as they had always been taught. The Vilmir Foundation must believe that, too, or they wouldn't have sent warriors to take Tuchvala themselves. This man had been a warrior, that much was clear. An ugly weapon of some sort was still clutched in one ebony hand.

This explained a lot. It probably explained how and why her mother had died. Ironic that the lowlanders were seeking the very woman they had killed. Sand did not wonder how the murder had been done: viruses tailored to kill individuals were among the easiest life that could be engineered.

Sand gingerly stepped away from Tuchvala, testing her own legs and finding them finally able. She reached down and pulled the rifle from the black man's fingers. He was reluctant to let it go; she avoided the disembodied stare a meter to her right.

"That is a weapon," Tuchvala offered. "I saw him fire it at the Whipper."

"I know."

"Put that down. Now."

Sand turned slowly to face the soft, strangely accented voice. She saw a young man—maybe a bit older than herself. He had a round face that looked Hopi, handsome in a boyish way. He had a Badger Clan look to him, but Sand had never seen him before, of that she was certain. He was dressed oddly, in loosely draped clothes that suggested a pleasant, lean body. He also wore a serious expression and held a pistol in both hands. It was pointed at Sand's chest.

"Stranger," Sand said quietly. "The Whipper is about. He killed your friend and he'll kill us, too. I need this gun."

"Put it down. The Whipper is dead."

Sand gaped at him. The man looked pleasant, but not dangerous. Not dangerous enough to defeat the Whipper. Still, he had a gun which he clearly knew how to use. Sand had not yet had a chance to figure the rifle out. She bent over and gently laid it on the ground.

"Okay. Now move away from it. You too," he said, gesturing with the weapon to include Tuchvala.

He's nervous, Sand thought. How could someone so nervous kill the Whipper?

"I don't believe you," Sand blurted, suddenly. "I don't believe you killed the Whipper."

"Good guess," the man said, the first hint of a smile twitching at his lips. "But he is dead. I'm not alone. And I can kill you."

Sand didn't think he would, be she didn't want to test that just yet. With the Whipper dead, there was no real hurry. Or was there? If the Whipper could find them, so could the lowlanders.

"You're from the Reed," she stated, flatly.

"No," he replied, glancing around nervously. "No, I'm from Parrot Island, up the coast. Cortez here was from the Reed. I'm their translator."

"A traitor, then," Sand said, trying to sound indifferent. Parrot Island? Where had she heard of that place? It sounded very familiar—a place with unpleasant associations.

"What's your clan?" she challenged.

"Why?"

"Perhaps we are related," she replied.

"Even if we were, I couldn't help you. But we aren't, I'm sure. I'm clanless."

Parrot Island. Clanless. Her fucking father was from there! She had heard him mention it, just once or twice. A small family, the last members of a dead clan, the Parrot Clan. This asshole was a relative of her father's!

And so not really a relative of hers, not in any real way.

"It must be easy for the clanless to turn traitor," she sneered.

"Must be," he replied. "Now, I want you to walk this way with me. I have a friend who needs some help—oh, Jesus."

He was staring at Tuchvala. She held a pistol much like his own, pointed at him.

"I got this from the dead man," Tuchvala informed him. "I know it works."

"I can still shoot your friend."

"You could," Tuchvala replied. "But she is the person you are seeking. The one from the sky."

The young man's eyes clouded with uncertainty. He believed her! As ridiculous as it seemed.

"Shit." He sighed and lowered the gun. "Look, I meant you no harm. I'm not very good at this."

"No, you aren't," Sand agreed, as she stepped forward and took his pistol.

"We still have to help my friend," he said, his tone pleading. "She is very badly hurt."

"No tricks," Sand said. "We both have guns now, and were very fucking tired of being chased and pushed around. I will kill you, if I must."

"What do you want? Why did you come here?" He asked.

"Later. Where is your friend?"

He led them back over the valley floor. Above, the winds had begun, sawing at the harsh stone rims above them. A half-dozen cyan barrels were opening their thick, petal-like maws towards the Sun, who was just now peaking over the walls of the canyon. The light was pale and yellow, choked by the thick clouds of smoke still billowing from the downed Reed ship. They passed the slug-like trail that Sand had left when she was crawling, and they made a slight detour to pick up the resistance cuffs the Whipper had dropped. She made the man put them on.

His friend was in bad shape, and Sand's impression was that she could not live for long. The woman was beautiful and very alien looking, as certainly an outworlder as the black man. She was half painted with blood, but her breath still whistled harshly, and her eyes, incredibly, were slitted open, feral. Here was the person who could kill a Whipper. A chill finger touched Sand's spine.

"Tuchvala, aim your gun at her. If she moves at all, shoot her."

Sand took the cuffs off of the man, and then tentatively knelt beside the woman.

"We're going to help you," she said, "But I can't trust you, what-ever you are. You killed a Whipper."

The woman lashed out at her feebly, and when Sand caught her arms there was surprising strength. The man started forward.

"Teng!" He shouted, and then something in a foreign language. Teng sounded like a name.

Sand felt a lot safer when the cuffs were on. They would tran-quilize her arms up to her shoulders, render them nerveless. She wished she had another pair for the woman's legs—which looked dangerous too.

To her surprise, she found a second pair ticked in a pouch on the woman's side. They were of Hopi make.

"Where did she get these?" she asked, directing her question to the man.

"Off of the Whipper. Don't hurt her."

"Show me the Whipper's body."

"Please, Teng needs help."

"She'll get it, in a moment. We need the key to open his ship. Or did you take that, too?"

"I don't think so. What does it look like?"

A cylinder the size of your little finger."

"We didn't find that."

"Come on then," Sand ordered, waving the gun. "Tuchvala, stay with this woman."

Resigned, the man trudged off in the direction of a pile of stone rubble, skirting around most of it. Twice, Sand saw him tense as if preparing to attack her, and twice she saw the tension melt out of him when he caught her eye.

"I've been wondering what an alien would be like," he said, as they picked their way over the cracked, weathered stone.

"Have you?"

"Yes. How is it that you look just like a human woman? I'd heard that report, but it seemed absurd. How could another world have produced such similar species?"

"You're right. It is absurd. But nature didn't produce this body; I did." Sand was warming to this game. This man was even more gullible than he looked.

They entered a narrow cleft-canyon, and Sand could see the dark form of the Whipper lying thirty meters or so up it. Fear gripped her momentarily, and she almost thought she heard the ghostly hu! hu! hu! of the Kachina's song, but it was only wind, flapping through the stone corridor.

When they reached her former antagonist, she stood as if rooted for long moments. The dread mask had been torn away, and though the face was obscured by blood, Sand had no trouble recognizing her first cousin, Chavo. If she had ever had a friend in her family, it had been Chavo. As children, they had pretended to be from different clans and talked of marriage. As teenagers, they had stopped just short of incest, his penis being the first male member she had ever touched. He had sighed and bitten his lip then, but it was hard to connect that image with this corpse. Tears started, and Sand reflected that she had cried more in these three days then she had in her entire life. Her mother and now Chavo. She could not blame him; the Whipper had been upon him, and he could not have known or cared who she was. And yet, his aim with the Sunbow had been so unerring against the Reed ship and warrior—and so poor against her own Dragonfly, when she escaped from him at the pueblo.

Here he was dead, Kachina no longer. He should be properly buried. She should tell the clan.

Sand found the key in a small pouch under the sash.

"Pick him up," she whispered to the stranger.

"What?"

"Pick him up!" She screamed.

"Wasn't he trying to kill you? That's what it looked like when we showed up. He cut your ship in half!"

"He was my cousin, you bastard!"

The man narrowed his eyes in understanding, and then they flew open wide as the understanding deepened.

"You are not the alien!"

"Wonderful. You have a brain. No, Tuchvala—the woman back with your friend—that's who you want. She bluffed you out."

"What will she do to Teng?"

"Nothing, I think. Pick up my cousin."

The man looked rebellious for an instant longer, and then he shrugged and knelt to lift Chavo cradled in his arms.

They found Tuchvala and the woman named Teng where they had left them; Teng's eyes had finally closed. The man put down Chavo's dead body and knelt next to her, his face distorted by concern or fear.

"She needs help," he snarled.

"She'll get it. Bring her along."

Sand walked ahead of him to the hoverjet. The door keyed open easily, and Sand was glad that it had no more sophisticated protection devices. Traditional Hopi distrust of technology they could not themselves maintain was responsible, and though in the past she had occasion to curse this cultural trait, for a fugitive it made life much easier. Sand located the first aid kit easily too; it was stashed in a small cabinet; the Whipper ship had a roomier cockpit than her own Dragonfly. It also had a detention compartment with static restraints. She directed the man to place Teng in it.

"Go get Chavo, now," she said. "I'll be looking after your friend."

The stranger left sullenly. Sand nodded at Tuchvala, who followed him at a safe distance with her gun.

Sand turned her attention to the woman's wounds. They looked bad; on the other hand, the blood on them had already congealed into a hard, rubbery mass. The woman was clearly augmented biologically. She was unconscious because she had lost a great deal of blood. What she needed, then, was fluid. A quick check in the kit turned up a half-liter bag of memory plasma. Sand detached the tube attached to it and placed the flared nozzle against the strange woman's arm; when it was positioned correctly over a vein, the clear plastic glowed a pale blue. Sand pressed the nozzle down and released it when she saw the skin pucker slightly. The tube was now sealed against her arm; inside, a sterile needle plunged into the thirsty vein and the clear fluid began to measure itself into her. Once in her body, the organisms suspended in the fluid would contact and imitate Teng's own red blood cells. For good measure, Sand also placed a patch of strong painkiller under her arm, both for her comfort and to prevent her from struggling should she regain consciousness. This Teng seemed like a very dangerous woman.

The man returned with Chavo's corpse. Sand had him lay it in the detention area as well, and then climb in himself.

As he slumped against the wall, Sand felt a stab of pity for the man, relative of her father's or not.

"What's your name?" she asked, as gently as she could manage.

"Alvar," he said. "Alvar Kyashnyam."

"Well, Alvar Kyashnyam, we'll talk later, you and I. We'll have your friend to help soon enough."

He just nodded, staring hard at his feet. Sand sealed up the door and went back to the cockpit, where Tuchvala was waiting. The Wings of the Whipper was large enough that it had four seats, arranged side by side. Tuchvala was already strapped into one of the front ones, waiting for her.

"Tuchvala, that was very good. I didn't think you had it in you."

Tuchvala smiled, and unlike most of her expressions until this point, it seemed natural.

"There are plenty of things in me," she answered. "I'm a very old being, though I admit with a limited area of expertise. But I was patterned after some Maker's tohodanet, so there's a lot there that sleeps. My problem since coming here has been trying to know when and how to act; it has paralyzed me. But I think now that I'm beginning to trust you to do the right thing, to lead me where I need to go."

"Tuchvala," Sand sighed, as she cut on the underjets and gently lifted the craft up on them, "I have no idea where you need to go."

"We'll find out together,": Tuchvala replied, confidently. "This brain is doing strange things with my knowledge, shuffling it around, trying to fill in the gaps where I have lost parts of me. I'm not sure what it is filling these gaps with; there are things in me—understandings—which seem new. It's exciting."

They were clearing the canyon, now. Smoke was still trailing at the sky, and Sand was chagrined to see a petroleum-dark stain spreading on the wind, a banner kilometers long thrust into the ground right below her feet.

The radar confirmed her fears; over twenty flyers were converging on her location from the coast.

"Those are ships?" Tuchvala asked, pointing at the enhanced indicator.

"Yes. It doesn't matter, though."

"What do you mean? There doesn't seem to be any place left for us to go."

"Oh, but there is. Those flyers are all coming up from the coast. We can still go back the way we came, if we hurry."

"Back to the pueblo? Why there?"

"We were running from the Whipper. We are no longer doing that. Now I'm going to do what I should have done to start with. Introduce you to the clan councils, to the village chief. I don't know if this is what you mean by taking you where you need to go, but that's what we're doing, okay? We can't fight or elude the Reed, the lowlanders, and the pueblos; that's everybody on the damned planet. I'm a Hopi, and though I tend to forget it, that means I'm part of something bigger than myself. Like Chavo was; like Mother was."

The afterjets nearly crushed her flat when she opened them up. The Whipper's ship had a lot more thrust than her little seed-spreading vessel had.

Goodbye, my Dragonfly, she thought down to her murdered ship.

Nose following the line of the Sun, they raced west, retracing their path.

CHAPTER SEVENTEEN

"There!" Hoku said, his face drawn into its most ferocious scowl. The satellite revealed a small vehicle moving through the mountains. Below, doppler measurements spooled out information regarding the velocity of the jet.

"That's not her. That's not a Dragonfly," Homikniwa said. "That thing must be from the Reed ship. They've sent someone out to meet her."

Hoku nodded grimly. "Enough of this. I will not allow the Reed to have her. It's as simple as that."

"Hoku," Homikniwa whispered, urgently. "You can't start a war with the Reed. Not without the Tech society's approval. Your control isn't that strong; not yet."

"Strength, Homikniwa? You and I know what strength is. Strength is what I have right now, right at this moment. If I lose it, let it slip away, that will be on my head. But if I let the Reed have what they want—there will be no strength on the Fifth World. No. I have to act while I can. Come with me, Homikniwa, and don't let anyone interfere with what I do."

Kewa had been eyeing him calmly from across the Kiva, sitting near the cube terminals that, in a more traditional kiva, would have been a shrine. Only the shape of the kiva resonated with its sacred ancestor; it was still rectangular with a small antechamber. The original Sipapuni—a small hole in the floor representing the place where the Hopi had come up from the lower worlds—had been covered with an instrument console, quite deliberately. Hoku approved of that: the Tech Society knew how to keep superstition in its place. Instead of ceremony and silly songs, they stressed another very ancient use of the kiva: it was a place for people to meet and work.

Kewa approached Hoku as he and Homikniwa exited the kiva; he waved her away.

"This does not concern the alien, Kewa. I don't need your advice."

Kewa returned a skeptical look but said nothing. She nodded and hesitantly edged back towards her seat as the two men left the kiva behind.

Outside of the kiva and its faint stink of tradition, Hoku felt a little better. Waiting, watching, wondering—Hoku was not suited to such things.

I am a verb, not a noun, he thought. A verb, carrying each sentence to its conclusion through action, through motion. Nouns were self-contained, complacent, with all of the meaning they would ever have bound up within themselves. Not so, the verb: how many things could be built, burnt, or eaten? And in how many ways? A verb by itself was anything but complacent: it demanded that it be implemented. Now he, Hoku, had made the most important decision in the history of the Fifth World, and he would, by the false gods of his people, implement that decision, without hesitation.

Hoku thought this as he and Homikniwa boarded a small elevator and took it down, a hundred feet into the crumbly ridge that rose above the surrounding coastal plain. The same ridge twisted out into the ocean as a series of small islands, but in its heart was Hoku's secret place. Not a kiva, not a place of song and ceremony, life and rebirth. No, it was more like a tomb, because it held death and the promise of death.

The car opened and the two men stepped into a small room with a set of monitor cubes and a primitive panel of key-activated controls, insurance against the failure of the computer's voice-recognition capabilities. Hoku shared a little of that in common with the pueblos, who refused to use technology they could not maintain. In such an extreme form, Hoku fervently disagreed with such a policy; he would use any technology available to him, whatever its source. However, his one concession to that ancient prejudice of his ancestors was to provide less complex back-ups when possible.

Taya, of course, was already seated in front of the panel. A thin, almost emaciated woman with stringy black and grey hair, she was probably close to sixty, yet still wore her hair in the old-style coils to show that she was unmarried. Hoku would never trust someone with children, here in the belly of Masaw, the death god.

"Hello, Taya. Things have developed as I foresaw yesterday. Are these systems ready?"

"Of course, Mother-Father," she said, her voice dry as old corn-husks. Through that brittleness, Hoku could sense her eagerness. She stood taut and ready, fingers flexing and grasping into fists by her side. She had been a friend of the old woman—possibly her lover, too. What Hoku saw as his reluctant duty, Taya saw as the culmination of her life. He knew this when he chose her, just as he knew she had no descendants.

Taya busied herself at the console, chopping out a number of cryptic voice commands. When she was done, she rubbed her hands together and traced a peculiar motion with them. The wall in front of her came to life, projecting the satellite image on the wall. It encompassed perhaps a hundred kilometers square; a good chunk of the mountains, but more importantly, the grey strip of ocean in which the landing drum from the Reed ship was floating.

Taya whispered something to herself in a satisfied tone.

"What was that?" Hoku asked.

The old woman shook her head as if to clear it of reverie. She turned clear black eyes on him. "I said that I never thought I would live long enough to get a chance at this," she replied. "At the Reed. Those fuckers. Coming up from every other world, we pushed the reed down behind us, so the two-hearts could not follow. But this Reed just stays. . . . We let it stay, Hoku. Time to push it down."

Something prickled along Hoku's spine; it might have been fear. This was the Reed. Her metaphor was powerful, so powerful that even Hoku could not dismiss it as pure superstition. He was pushing down the Reed, and with it all of the aid and technology they supplied. At best, now, the Fifth World was on its own. At worst, they would be conquered. Hoku had always known that it was his fate to do this; he had never doubted it for an instant.

But he had hoped to be much more prepared.

Ah, well, it was just one ship. Surely they could destroy one ship. And then. . . . Well, that was the gamble wasn't it? Then they would have time to win over the alien craft, if they could be won. If Hoku didn't begin his war now, no matter how unprepared he was—that chance, that one real chance—would fly back down the Reed to the distant stars. To Earth, perhaps.

Hoku frowned at the monitor cube and its aerial projection the Cornbeetle Mountains; a streak of smoke trailed over them, tagged by the spectrometer as the result of burning hydrocarbons.

"What the hell is that?" He snapped at Taya.

"I don't know," she replied. "The smoke obscures any better optical."

"Homikniwa, dispatch two cadres to that spot, now. It could be the Reed flyer, downed."

"Okay," the small man replied. "Does that mean you will delay this attack?"

Hoku frowned into the screen for a moment more before replying.

"No. This could be a ruse; in fact, it probably is. What could have taken down a Reed reconnaissance craft? Not a Dragonfly, certainly. This is just to confuse us; by now they have this Sand and the alien, too.

Homikniwa took that in silently, and then—rather reluctantly, Hoku thought—turned to a console. He spoke into it briefly.

Taya interrupted Hoku's thoughts once again.

"The Prophets are targeted," she said. "The computer needs your okay."

Hoku stared at the tiny spot that was the landing drum. He narrowed his eyes, let that point become the whole world. He was Sotuknung, creation and destruction. His word would bring a rain of fire. He almost trembled with the enormity of it.

"Lavaihoya," he whispered, naming the computer by his secret name. "Lavaihoya, dispatch the Prophets."

Time trembled around them, a wind between molecules and substance. Hoku watched the spot on the screen. How long would it take for the slender rods of steel to plunge, nose first, towards their immobile enemy, winnow this way and that like so many silvery fish? Too quickly for the drum to move, that was certain, even if they saw their demise coming. Seconds.

The computer spoke into the hush.

"Prophets refuse to disengage. Lavaihoya command overridden."

"What?" Hoku and Taya shrieked in near unison.

"Cause of malfunction?" Taya gasped at the machine, visibly struggling for composure.

"Overridden," the computer repeated.

"Fuck," Hoku cursed. "How could I have not seen this?" He gripped the back of a chair with both hands and leaned forward heavily, suddenly feeling very old.

"I don't understand," Taya wailed. Hoku wanted to tell her to shut up, to let him think, but there was no point in that.

"The goddamn Reed built our satellites," he hissed at her, "They must be able to monitor and override any of our commands. We are completely crippled."

In silent confirmation of this, the screen itself suddenly went blank.

"And now we are blind," Homikniwa added, and the three of them stood staring at the flat surface of the wall.

I am a verb, Hoku insisted to himself. No regrets: move on. If he became mired in dismay, the whole Fifth World would suffer. Hoku closed his eyes, felt the grit in them, wished for a warm bottle of halia. He imagined himself on the sea, naked beneath a metallic dawn, young and strong. Invincible. Homikniwa was there, ready to stand at his side through anything.

The he opened his eyes again. Homikniwa was still there, confident, awaiting Hoku's words. He was in control. He, Hoku, was in control.

"What about the land based missiles?" Taya was asking, voice tinged with desperation. "They couldn't control them."

"No," Hoku replied, "but they could probably shoot them down with lasers. Even if they didn't, I wouldn't use nuclear weapons here on the Fifth World. Those missiles were designed to attack starships, if need be—though starships closer than the moon. I won't turn them back on ourselves."

"What about biotics?"

Hoku shrugged. "We have some plagues. But I'm willing to bet that the Reed's bioengineering capabilities are a century ahead of ours, at least in non-terraforming areas. Our own techs still don't understand a few of the subtler rock-decaying bacteria, for instance. Anything we concoct, they can probably deal with and repay us in better than kind."

"Then what are you going to do?" Asked Homikniwa. "You have effectively declared war, even if you didn't hurt them. Certainly they know by now that you attempted to attack them."

"Yes," Hoku agreed. "If they care to confirm it. It seems to me that these Reed people are scurrying rather softly, however; coming in from behind the sun, hiding behind the moon, landing on a windbrake instead of with thrusters. Perhaps they will simply choose to ignore our little faux pas."

"For the moment, perhaps," Homikniwa allowed. "But in the long term, they now know we are rebellious at heart."

"I'm sure they know that anyway. There have already been two such revolts that I know of, one on Dunstan's World and the other on Serengeti. Putting down rebellious sodbusters must be a high science with the Reed, and I'm sure they recognize the warning signs by now. But in this situation, there is an unknown quantity that makes them nervous."

"The alien ships," Taya said.

"Exactly. They've been here for twenty standard years. How can they know what little progress we have made in communicating with them? Lavaihoya, replicate that last map from memory."

The wall came back to life, resurrecting the scene as it had been moments before. Now, however, it was static, and Hoku would have to remember that.

"Homikniwa, have some ships settle in there along the coasts, and equip them with the most powerful weapons we have that will not leave contaminating radiation. If anything comes out of the mountains—anything at all—they are to bring it down if they can, annihilate it if they cannot."

Homikniwa nodded briskly, then busied himself with the task. Hoku sat in the chair and hunched over his fist, eyes on the false and enigmatic map. There were solutions, and he would find them.

CHAPTER EIGHTEEN

I know their legends. I stood in their sky—their sky—and sifted the streams of words down the long, damaged riddle of my brain. Trying to sort the data into sensible meanings. It would not sort, would not be broken down, and yet even then, I felt that there was meaning there; it just happened to be irreducible.

The legends filtered up to me every year during the "season" they name summer. Sand has explained to me why this distinction is made; because the axial tilt of their home planet is much greater than that of this world, so that dramatic differences in weather occur throughout the cycle of the planet's rotation. And summer—the hot part of the year when life is most active—summer is the time of the Kachina, when they live among human beings and tell their stories. The people of the Fifth World cluster in the pueblos and in the seashore settlements, but many, many more live far and scattered in small towns and single dwellings, tending vast kilometers of forest-to-be. For them, the kivas transmit the stories and dances which they are themselves unable to attend. And to me, above.

So I know their legends, and I know the name Sand has given me; Tuchvala, the spittle from which human beings were formed. A substance of life, a precondition for it. I also know their belief that they have moved from world to world, always enduring, always surviving.

The poetry of this struck me, even when I was a creature of vacuum and flickering light; it reminded me of the beliefs of the Makers. The Makers had a strong sense that the world on which they evolved was not the world where they belonged; that only by escaping it could they realize etadotetak, which is something like what Sand means when she says "compassion". It is deeper than compassion, however, and of all the beasts on the homeworld of the Makers, only they evolved it. To them, this was a much more important evolutionary step than their intelligence; intelligence had already come and gone on their world— twenty million years earlier—and left little behind it except a few remarkable ruins. The homeworld, with its terribly high mutation rate and its inconstant star, was, to the Makers, a place to be escaped, and it was etadotetak—not intelligence—that would allow them to do so.

Thus they sent out my sisters and me, and others like us. To change things. The legends—both Human and Maker—speak of change, of climbing to a new place.

I thought of all of this because I knew that I was changing, that the place where I had been was no longer where I belonged. I was coming to understand that life—real, organic life—recreates itself with each moment, adapts, finds new paths. I was becoming incorporated into Sand's life, and she into mine, and this kind of interaction I had never known. After all, my sisters and I had been created together and virtually identical. Only deterioration had differentiated our personalities. Sand, though, was making me alien. Many of my thoughts were becoming responses to her presence, anticipations of her responses. It was if my own single voice had become two; mine and Sand's.

Sand glanced at the moving points on her doppler screen. They were moving fast, but not fast enough.

"They want you bad, Tuchvala," she remarked.

"Why?" Tuchvala wiped at her brow, clumsily smearing the sweat still beaded there. "I had anticipated interest in me, I must admit. Your people have been probing and testing my sisters and I since we arrived at this Farm. But why this crazy violence, this persistent chase?"

"I'm not sure about that myself," Sand began, but detested the dishonesty behind her words. She began again. "No, that's not true. The truth is that all human beings do not share the same goals and motivations. My people—the Hopi—came to this planet to re-create the life we believe we were meant to live, a way of living that had become impossible on Earth. Not long after we came here, however, there was a breach amongst the children of the founders. Some became angry because they felt they had been isolated from the mainstream of human civilization and technology, consigned to do a hard and thankless job."

"Was this true?" asked Tuchvala.

"You tell me. You've been forming worlds for half a million years."

"I don't think it's the same," Tuchvala replied.

Sand shrugged. "Yeah, I guess they had a point," She admitted. "I've often felt that way myself. It all depends on whether you think the traditional ways are a satisfying way of life."

"Do you find them so?"

"Not always," Sand confessed. "But what I do find satisfying is to see sterile, black soil covered in taproot dandelions and clover, to watch the trees grow taller, to see a metric ton of grass seed float out behind me as I fly along. I don't talk about it much, and neither did my mother, but that's one way we were very much alike. I believe in the project, in making the Fifth World a fit place to live. And the traditionals believe this with all of their heart and soul. They believe terraforming is our holy, ordained purpose, and every song and story we chant accentuates the beauty of what we do. The lowlanders, though—sometimes I wonder about them. They're so bitter—sometimes I think that they would rather just flee the Fifth World and go back to Earth. They think that the project is important, too, but not with the same determination as the traditionals.

I think they might turn inward, given the chance, build their cities on the coast, where the living is easy, and let the interior fallow or green as it would. They just don't have the drive it will take to make the whole planet grow. The religion."

"So there is a conflict between your two groups, distrust. What has that to do with me? And the off-world ships?"

Sand began to speak, but something Tuchvala said clinked and rattled in her head. They were flitting over the foothills, now, and before long they would be back in pueblo territory, where the pursuing ships—certainly from Salt—would not follow. The land was misted with green that grew deeper and thicker with each kilometer. The sky was azure, arabesqued with wisps and veils of cloud from horizon to horizon.

"Tuchvala, how did you know they were from off-planet?" Sand nodded back towards their unwilling passengers.

"Are they from the starship? I didn't know that. I did know about their ship: I saw it coming, of course. They tried to hide themselves, but all of my faculties haven't fled me. I didn't know what they represented, and I was afraid that they would antagonize my sister into action. That was the reason I came down here prematurely. It may be the reason that my plans all seem so vague to me now."

"Well, they are from the Reed. They funded this project, paid for it, brought our ancestors here. In a sense, we work for them. The deal is that we carry out the terraforming project and the world becomes ours. At least, that's what our ancestors thought."

"I'm having a hard time understanding this, Sand. This is yet another human faction?"

"Tuchvala . . . we—the Hopi, whether traditional or lowlander—are like you and your sisters. We were sent out to work, generation after generation, to make this world livable. Our ancestors agreed to this, because they believed that, though it would be difficult, their descendants would live free on a fresh new world. However, those who sent us—as you say, another human group—are using us to their profit, or so many of us suspect. When we have done the work, they will take the planet from us. By force if we resist. You understand that?"

"I think so. Go on."

"The Hopi do not have the power to withstand this, but I believe that the lowlanders think that you and your sisters might. That if they can bargain with you, you could stop the Reed warships when they come."

"Oh." Tuchvala said, and she turned her head to look out at the terrain rushing by.

"Oh."

"The Reed, of course, saw this danger, and so sent a ship of their own to protect their interests."

"All on the possibility that my sisters and I would have the power they suspect—and the will and ability to use it?"

"I think. I'm not certain about any of this."

Tuchvala shook her head. "This is terrible."

"I think so. I think they are wrong, too. Why should terraforming ships have weapons anyway?"

"Oh, that's not what I meant," Tuchvala said. "We do have weapons. We have weapons that could kill every living cell on this planet. Your people—humans I mean—are right about that. What they don't know is the division that exists between my sisters and me. The balance is so fine, Sand. If my sisters decide your race is threatening them, they will kill you all. They will sterilize this planet and begin again."

"Can't you convince them? Explain to them that we have this special kind of compassion your Makers had?"

Tuchvala grimaced; Sand was unsure what emotion she meant to convey. "First of all, I'm not certain that you do. Etadotetak bound the Makers all together, it didn't tease them into factions. That is, however, beside the point, because I have etadotetak. I would gladly convince my sisters to move on, if I could. I will try, if given the chance. As I may have said, though I am perhaps the least damaged of the three, I am—was—still very confused. The Makers gave us rather explicit instructions against farming inhabited worlds. The problem is that they never allowed for the possibility that one of their uninhabited farm worlds should become peopled by aliens. Now, since my essence has been in this brain, things have begun to sort out, and I think I can see quite clearly what the Makers would have preferred in this situation. This is especially true because . . . because . . ." Tuchvala abruptly choked and fell silent.

Sand had been watching the mesas approach, listening to Tuchvala's voice rise and fall like the contoured terrain. That voice was always full of ambiguity, miscued stress and inflection, which made it difficult to read emotion into it. Sand was thus shocked when she realized that Tuchvala was crying and further, that the strange woman was bewildered by her own tears.

"Tuchvala, What . . . ?"

But the other woman only gasped when she tried to talk, frustrated by the incomprehensible spasm that obstructed her speech.

"Just stay calm," Sand said, trying to sound soothing. "Tuchvala, you're just crying; you must be upset about something. You'll stop in a moment, and then you can speak again."

Tuchvala went on crying for another few moments, reaching out her fingers to press them against the transparent windshield, like a child who did not know what chainglass was.

"What," Sand urged, when Tuchvala's sobbing subsided.

"My Makers," Tuchvala said—small, brittle words. "They must be dead."

"Listen, Tuchvala, it's been hundreds of thousands of years. I don't know how long their species lived, but . . ."

"No, no. They must all be dead. The race, the species. They will never claim this or any other world I have farmed."

"You know this?" Sand asked, gently.

"I feel it. How many worlds has your race colonized?"

"Ah . . . six. Maybe more, by now. We don't get much news from the Reed."

"Six. Six planets like this, with the same life-forms that we placed here. And your race has never encountered any other sign of the Makers? They are gone, Sand. I must face that."

Sand cut her speed back; she needed to think about sending ahead that she was coming, and she had a lot to worry about. She had a dead Whipper and his stolen ship in her possession, and that would not go lightly. But for the moment—for one moment before she released her mind to those worries—she reached over and gripped her companion's arm.

"We're both orphans, then," she said gently.

Yuyahoeva's gnarled face looked back at Sand from her screen.

Shit, she thought, the old man himself. She remembered their last exchange, just before her mother's funeral, and braced for the lash of words she knew must be coming. The other clans must have been all over him by now, to bring in his wayward grand-daughter. It's his job to deal with me and show he had no part in this.

Not for the first time, Sand found herself proven wrong.

"Sand, little granddaughter," he began, and Sand was astonished to see that the fiercely wrinkled caverns of his eyes held not anger, but deep concern. Sand knew Yuyahoeva, knew him well. He did not wear masks unless he was dancing with the Kachina. What one saw in his face was the truth. It was just that one usually saw disapproval, if one were Sand.

"Are you okay, little one?" The old man continued. His eyes edged to the right of the screen; the monitor must be just barely showing part of Tuchvala, and he was surely curious who was with her.

"I'm alright, In'na. I'm coming home."

"That's good, Sand. It's not safe for you out there. Come back here, where your clan can protect you."

"I will. But In'na, I came there before, as you must surely know. Someone set the Whipper upon me."

The hard face sharpened at the edges, obsidian showing through basalt. "I know. We don't know how this happened, yet, but we will discover the two-heart soon enough. You know that it was not Chavo himself, I hope? Your cousin loves you, Sand."

"I know. In'na, I did not kill him, but Chavo is dead."

The old man nodded his head; he was used to grief, to seeing the young die before him. Chavo was his sister's daughter's boy.

"I have his body, and those who killed him."

"The outworlders?"

"You know about that?" Sand asked.

"Not much, child. We only learned of this recently. Sand, we monitored part of your conversation with Hoku, but his references made no sense. He seemed to be speaking of an alien, of something not human."

"In'na," Sand replied, "I will explain everything when I land. I'm taking my old place near my mother's home. You will want to bring warriors to handle these captives. And come yourself, In'na. I need your strength and your advice."

The old man smiled briefly but with comforting warmth.

"Granddaughter, I would not miss this."

CHAPTER NINETEEN

Alvar felt the jet settle to earth with mixed feelings. Mixed like a drink in a blender, like sewage in a composter. Confused.

The dead man kept turning to look at him, and that was no help. He wanted to comfort Teng, but she was unconscious, though her breathing seemed regular.

When the jet stopped moving, Alvar was wondering for the tenth time whether it would be better to be a native traitor or an offworld invader. He was pretty sure it would be a toss-up.

And Teng was going to hate him when she woke up. He had let these two capture him without the slightest struggle. Alvar had never much thought about his manhood as such—the "macho" revival of '21 had passed him right by—but after three years with Teng and now this, he was certainly beginning to feel inferior. Would Teng think he had been distracted? These were the first women besides her that he had seen in three objective years, and they were both attractive enough. They could be sisters; their mouths and eyes in particular mirrored one another. One had a stocky, generous body, the other lean as a whipcord, with just enough bump here and there to make her clearly female. . . .

Alvar shook his head. Maybe Teng would be right. Maybe he was distracted, and if so, he was stupid, stupid, stupid.

As if to punctuate his guilt, the door panel suddenly slid open, and harsh light flooded his little prison, followed by a dry cloud of yellow dust. He was facing the whipcord, and behind her were a number of armed men. He didn't bother to count them. They were all dressed in linen loincloths. The woman motioned him out. Blinking, he stepped into the tableau.

A windswept mesa top fanned out about him, and for a moment the profound beauty of the place took him up and away from his predicament. His chief impression was one of vast, echoing space, a sky from boyhood dreams of sky. The mesa was a small, flat world, and he could see beyond its edge the mysterious and enticing profiles of other cliffs and buttes in the distance, islands rising from an empty green seabed. On his other hand was the city, dropping away from him or rising, depending upon which contours of the stone his gaze traced. Both geometric and jumbled, at the moment he could not imagine a place more balanced between the poles of architecture and nature.

Alvar had been confined and confined, and now he stood, stretching, tasting the kind of freedom the poor plains-ape in his genes craved. Wondering how long it could last.

He brought his attention back to his captors; something odd was happening among them, a confused murmuring. There was an old man—he looked very old—staring almost literally bug-eyed at one of the women who had captured him.

"Pela!" the old man gasped. "Pela!"

"No," the other said, stepping up almost protectively in front between the two.

"No, In'na. Can't you see how young she is? This will be a long story, grandfather, one best explained in the clan kiva, I think. Suffice to say I trust this woman. It is she that both the lowlanders and these outworlders pursue. She is important."

The old man was shaking his head. "We must check you both

for witchcraft, Sand. Two-hearts are fearsome and devious. But I think I believe you. She looks so much like Pela. . . ."

"Where is my father?" the woman interrupted. "Where is Red Jimmie?"

"He is in custody, SandGreyGirl. I'm afraid that it may have been he who activated the Whipper."

"I see."

SandGreyGirl, Alvar thought. At least I have a name to call someone.

The woman just named turned towards him. "This one is called Alvar Kyashnyam. He claims to be from Parrot Island. We should see if my father knows him."

Oh shit, Alvar thought. I can't be that unlucky. The old man had turned his eagle scrutiny upon Alvar now.

"My friend needs help," he said, trying to sound confident and fearless.

The old man challenged him with his gaze for a moment longer before nodding briefly. Several of the men came forward with a pair of stretchers. When they saw the dead body of El Diablo, several began to weep. Their silent glances at him sharpened into malicious scrutiny.

They took Teng and the dead man away, but did not let Alvar follow.

"No," the old man told him. "You come with us to the kiva."

The kiva was close and dark. Alvar was closed in by firelit faces, by the sharp scent of sage and juniper. In the shadows of the great room, mysterious bundles bunched in small recesses, the colorful feathers and carved sticks of an alter (he did not know which kind) faintly visible. The floor was stone, as were the walls, and the ceiling was some sort of reinforced concrete. The freedom of the sky was gone, and once more Alvar was a prisoner in the depths.

Captured by primitives, he thought. Were they boiling water

somewhere? Were they sizing him up for dinner? He knew better, of course, and these thoughts betrayed him to a returning, sardonic, sense of humor. Still, when the eerie chanting began, a chill stab of fear caught him through the back.

A column of light stabbed down into the darkness, from the hole in the center of the roof. It illuminated the ladder which Alvar had so recently descended at the non-to-gentle urging of his captors.

The old man and two old women came down the ladder, followed by the two women who had captured Alvar.

The light was shut off, and now only the flickering fire remained. Alvar wondered, off-handedly, how valuable the wood they were burning must be. Trees must be as scarce here as they had been near Santa Fe.

The rustling and whispering, the light, the dense smoke, and his own fatigue conspired against Alvar. When the old man began droning in slow, ponderous tones, he tried to pay attention. But it was some story, a part of the old migration myth, full of repetition and dense detail. Alvar caught his eyelids closing; he snapped them open and found that he had missed a significant part of the legend.

They began to droop again.

When he awoke, it was to a generally louder muttering, and the voice had changed. It was the woman, SandGreyGirl.

". . . . from the stars," she was saying. "My mother believed them to be Kachina."

"So they may be," whispered the old man. "Prophecies are fulfilled in strange ways. We have always known it, have we not, my children and grandchildren? That the Fifth World was created for us, just as was the Fourth? That it was made vague and incomplete, so that we must work to finish it?"

"But why should a Kachina take the form of Pela?" another, unidentified voice asked.

"I have explained that," said the woman they seemed to call——

and not call—Pela. The alien. Alvar searched her flame-revealed features, both eager and fearful to see some indication of her inhuman origin. All he could see there, however, was an attractive face, intriguing and sensuous rather than merely beautiful.

"This has been confirmed," the old man whispered gravely. "She has been tested. This body was cloned from Pela's cells."

"We could do that," someone countered. "So could the lowlanders. This does not prove her claim."

"The ojo shows that I am not lying," SandGreyGirl spoke into the assenting whispers. "I saw her ship land."

"Still, that means nothing."

"There is someone who can confirm this," SandGreyGirl said. "Ask him. Ask the Parrot-Island-Man." She gestured towards Alvar.

"Well?" asked the old man, quietly. A green light flicked on somewhere, arrowed its narrow beam in Alvar's left eye.

"Keep your eye open. Tell us if you believe that there are three starships of alien origin in orbit around our world."

Please don't ask me too much, Alvar prayed. Perhaps if he could please them, make them trust him just a little. . . .

"There are," he said. "I've seen them."

The old man's face relaxed. The green light persisted for a moment more and then mercifully retreated into the darkness.

"So. This would explain a lot," the elder commented. "A lot. And you think the lowlanders want to use these ships against the Reed."

SandGreyGirl nodded.

"That would be a worthy goal," someone else pointed out. "Let the lowlanders find a way to fight the Reed. We all know it must eventually be done."

"Oh," said the elder. "But either master would be as bad for us. If the lowlanders had such power. . . ."

"Then we should control the ships."

"These are Kachina, Movena! We do not control them."

"Please!" Alvar's heart quickened as he realized the shout came from the alien herself. Everyone else fell silent.

"This whole notion of controlling me is misguided. I have no more power than any of you. The ships in orbit—my sisters—do. But they are in poor repair. Their minds are not what they used to be. I came here to see if I thought your race was worth saving, and if you were, I hoped to help you prevent my sisters from sterilizing this world. Even I don't know how to go about that. I've either forgotten or I never knew. Now, while you people argue about which of your factions will possess me or cajole me or whatever it is you think you can do with me, your death is hanging above you heads. Your death and the death of everything you have worked for. Can you understand that?"

Alvar found that he was holding his breath; the only sound was the scrapping of bare skin and linen on stone as a few people shifted. What the hell had he and Teng come into?

Tuchvala's words hung in the air like thick, resinous smoke. Sand felt that they would choke her. Looks of indignation were fading, as the old people quickly realized that what Tuchvala had to say was more important than any breach of proper speaking order. Yuyaho-eva cleared his throat softly.

"I. . . . we're sorry, grandau. . . ." he broke off, confused. "What should I call you?" he began again.

"Sand calls me Tuchvala. That will do."

There was a murmur at that, at the sense of the name. It seemed to hold a foretelling, just as it held the past.

"Go on, then, Tuchvala."

"I don't have much more to say," Tuchvala continued, after a moment. "We are very old, my sisters and I. We came here when this world was as the universe made it. I tell you truthfully, I do not see how I can be one of your Kachina. Do Kachina become senile? For my sisters and I are that. Up there, we see a world spoiled, with no free alcohol, with too much nitrogen, too much oxygen. Down here, in the body I have now, I can see more clearly. Your danger comes not from me, or even from other human factions. It is my sisters who can destroy you all."

"And you don't know how to stop them?"

"I can only plead with them, offer my experiences as proof that you are alive and worthy of etadotetak."

"What is that?" Yuyahoeva asked of the spitting sound Tuchvala made. She explained briefly, as she had explained it to Sand.

Yuyahoeva bowed his head down.

"Perhaps we are not worthy," he said. "We are as you see us, squabbling and factional."

Tuchvala nodded affirmation. "I have seen you kill one another, and I admit that I find this conflict over me to be excessive. Still, my sisters and I have no business interfering with your lives. Our time—and the time of our Makers—is long gone. I believe them dead."

An old woman piped up, and Sand winced. It was Hano-mokuwa, Chavo's mother. Her face, even flushed with firelight, seemed drawn and pale. Her words were bitter and clipped.

"We believe that the Kachina made this world for us." She looked around dazedly.

"My son is a Kachina."

There was an embarrassed mumble of agreement from the crowd. Sand felt tears threatening to sting her eyes.

Tuchvala shrugged. "Maybe so. Maybe my Makers are just a dream I had in the long spaces between the stars. Anything seems possible to me now."

Hanomokuwa had risen to her feet as Tuchvala spoke, and she seemed to drift through the kiva like a ghost; her linen dress barely rustled. Sand gripped Tuchvala's arm protectively as her aunt approached. The old woman stopped in front of Tuchvala, slowly squatted down on her heels. Tuchvala sat impassively as the old woman reached out a finger and stroked it along her face.

"Sweet little Pela," she whispered, so that only Sand and Tuchvala could hear her clearly.

"Such a sweet thing. You knew my Chavo, didn't you? Sand, you knew him."

"I knew your son," Sand said.

"Tell me why he died, Pela. You've come back from Masaw, little one. Tell me why he died."

Sand could feel Tuchvala trembling, and she gripped her arm more tightly, hoping to reassure her. The old woman's eyes wandered glassily over their faces for another moment, and then she slowly rose.

"He knows," she muttered, and she moved towards the Parrot-Island-Man. Sand turned so that she could see his face. It was drawn into a bizarre grimace of fear and what might be remorse. Tears glistened in his eyes.

"We didn't mean too—I didn't. . . ." he mumbled.

Hanomokuwa knelt in front of the man, and he squirmed back, avoiding her gaze.

"Why did my Chavo die?" she asked him. The only other sound was that of wood popping in the fire.

The man didn't answer, though it seemed that he might like to, by the way his mouth worked silently. Hano drew back her hand, very slowly and deliberately, then brought it around in a stinging slap to the Parrot-Clan man's face. He rolled his head around with the blow, and then dropped it onto his chest, continuing to cry. Sand smothered a small spark of pity for him. He was of our Father's clan. He had helped kill Chavo.

And saved your life maybe, an unexpected thought reminded her. Because the woman, Teng, had not killed Chavo. She had killed the Whipper.

Hano calmly sat down next to Alvar, folding her stiff old legs beneath her. She sat facing him, less than a meter away, Her liquid eyes searching him mercilessly.

Yuyahoeva sighed into the silence.

"We still must decide what to do, Tuchvala. You understand that. As difficult as our struggles might be for you to understand, they are very real. The division between us and the lowlanders is difficult to lay aside. Yet, if what you say is true, perhaps we should make the effort. It would be ironic indeed if your sisters kill us while we squabble over them."

Another elder—no relation to Sand at all—spoke up.

"If you could convince your sisters to let us be, what then? Would they aid us against the Reed?"

Tuchvala stared at the man.

Yuyahoeva turned to him, and though he spoke mildly, it was clearly a rebuke. "Cousin. Haven't you been listening? This is a question for another time. For when we and our children are safe. For now, I think, we have to help this Kachina help us. We have to put her in touch with her sisters."

"How? How can we do this?"

Sand cleared her throat. Yuyahoeva looked at her expectantly.

"We need a powerful transmitter," she said. "Like the ones we use to communicate with the Kachina satellites."

Yuyahoeva nodded. "We have such a transmitter. It will be done."

A young man spoke up. His voice was flat with anger or some other fierce emotion, and Sand realized that he was a clan uncle of Chavo's.

"There is another matter," he grunted. "The matter of the lowland flyers. They have settled in a perimeter around our lands."

"But not *violated* them," Yuyahoeva pointed out. "They have not yet broken the unspoken truce."

"We should be ready in case they do," the young man snapped.

Yuyahoeva turned his ancient gaze upon the youngster.

"We already have. The warriors are preparing now."

"Then may I join their preparations?" the other man asked stiffly.

"You have no head for council," said the old man. "So you might as well. Go on."

The young man nodded bruskly and pushed towards the ladder, but stopped at its base.

"What about him?" He said, abruptly, pointing to the Parrot-Clan man. "Him and that two-heart who killed my cousin?"

Yuyahoeva fixed him with a hard stare.

"Go on, I said."

The warrior hesitated for another moment, and then went up the ladder. Light stabbed down briefly as he opened the trapdoor, then vanished.

Yuyahoeva craned his neck to look around the assembly before speaking again, as if by the touch of his gaze he could draw the all together.

"Parrot-Clan man. Come forward."

The stranger rose shakily, avoiding Hano's eyes, which followed him as he moved towards the center of the circle.

"I will do you a courtesy," Yuyahoeva told him. "I will not use the Ojo de verdad at this point. I will give you a chance to tell the truth yourself."

The man looked up, and the firelight gleamed on the tear-tracks.

"I'm sorry about the boy," he said at last. "Teng and I . . . he was trying to kill me. Teng was just defending me."

"She killed a Kachina," Yuyahoeva growled.

"I know. She doesn't know better, grandfather. She is from Earth."

"Why did she come here? Tell me."

The young man clasped his hands together and stared at them.

"My name is Alvar," he said at last. "I'm sorry, but I can't tell you any more than that. I would have to lie, and I don't want to lie to you people. I don't want to do anything else to you people. Even if you use the ojo, you will only know that I am lying. You won't know what the truth is."

"There are other ways to get that," hissed one of the elders.

"I know," Alvar replied, miserably.

"We must know what the Reed intends. You can see that, can't you?" Yuyahoeva said gently.

Alvar nodded, but said nothing.

Yuyahoeva clucked his tongue.

"As Mother-Father of this council, I suggest that we end this meeting. Our time can be better spent, if we are in agreement on certain points. Shall we help this woman who has come to us, this Tuchvala?"

"She is Kachina!" someone murmured, and a susurrus of agreement expanded into the darkness of the Kiva.

"I want to talk to the leader of the lowlanders, to Hoku. Does this seem reasonable?"

Another mutter of general agreement, though much less enthusiastic than the earlier one.

"Good. Then that is all I have to say. Ascend into the Fifth World."

Sand sat still with Tuchvala as the gathering broke up. Two guards led the prisoner, Alvar, away. When everyone else was gone, Sand came slowly to her feet.

"I hope you know what to say to your sisters, Tuchvala."

"So do I," she replied.

CHAPTER TWENTY

Yuyahoeva met Sand in the sunlight. He gently took her by the arm, and the three of them—Sand, the old man, and Tuchvala—walked towards the edge of the cliff. They stood staring at the void, at the mystery of distance. The old man rolled a cornhusk cigarette, lit it, and passed it over to Sand. She took a little puff and handed it to Tuchvala, who examined it curiously.

"Inhale through the other end, Tuchvala. Not too deeply, though."

They offered smoke to the six directions, and the wind took the blue streamers quickly away. Sand smelled rain in the air, passing near.

The old man nodded out at the vastness.

"I may have been wrong, daughter," he said at last. "I think you were right about your mother. I think the lowlanders killed her."

"Because she knew all of this," Sand said, miserably.

"She never told us," Yuyahoeva said.

"She was going to. She left me a book. She was planning to tell you, but only when she was sure you would listen."

Yuyahoeva nodded. He turned his seamed face up towards the sky.

"Sand, would you and Tuchvala come with me to my wife's house? I'd like to talk with both of you a little more."

•   •   •

Kalnimptewa was a gracious woman, about forty years old with a delicate, thin face and a shock of grey in her long hair. She smiled minutely as she set out the plate of piki and corn soup in front of Sand.

"Thank you, grandmother," Sand whispered. Her belly had forgotten hunger during the chase, but the memory was back, with a vengeance. How long since she had eaten? Before her mother died?

She dipped the roll of paper-thin blue cornbread into the broth and took a bite, savored the bread as it fell apart in her mouth. Yuyahoeva and Kalnimptewa kept their silence as the two young women wolfed down their food. When the piki was gone, the elder woman left and returned with a tray of steamed tamales and a pitcher of fruit juice. Stopping only briefly to show Tuchvala how to unwrap the savory rolls of cornmeal, Sand plunged into those too. She looked up to catch Yuyahoeva watching her with gentle amusement.

"Sorry, grandfather," she said. "It's been a long while since I've eaten."

He nodded. "You're too thin anyway. Eat all you want."

Sand did. When her stomach felt comfortably packed, she pushed the intricately patterned plate away, finished off her peach juice, and sighed. Tuchvala imitated her, almost a parody, and the other three laughed, then laughed again at her puzzled expression.

"You look so much like Pela, when she was young," Kalnimptewa remarked, her gaze traveling over Tuchvala. "It is so hard to believe you are what you say."

"I don't really know what I am anymore," Tuchvala replied, thoughtfully. "I'm not what I was."

Yuyahoeva settled back in his chair. "Fascinating," he said, wagging his head from side to side. "When a human being wears the mask of a Kachina, he becomes something different. He becomes the Kachina. I never thought to wonder what might happen to a Kachina wearing a human mask."

"Is that what I am?" Tuchvala asked. I know your stories. I don't think I am one of your spirits."

"I'm an old man," Yuyahoeva told her. "I see things the way I want. But here you come in the skin of my dead granddaughter. You come from the sky, from far away, and you are one of the creators of this world—at least as we know it. In my eyes, if you are not a Kachina, then the difference is too small to measure. Can you understand that?"

"I can," Sand interjected. "I can now." She was chagrined to find a tear trickling down her face.

"You're back with us," Kalnimptewa told her, very gently.

"This is what your mother came to understand, child," Yuyahoeva told her. "Out there alone, running . . . a Hopi without her people is only half a person. Your mother was like that, too, after she came up from the lowland school. She doubted everything, thought she was alone, all by herself. Nearly drove her crazy, Sand. Keeping her secret all those years must have been hard, too. I pity her for that."

"I don't understand what you're talking about," Tuchvala said.

"We're talking about being Hopi," Sand told her, brushing away the tear. "About belonging. The Kachina are a part of us, of what we are together. As real as stone or air. It doesn't matter that we can't touch them. But we need them. We need each other. I nearly got both of us killed, Tuchvala, because I was thinking as if I were the only person on the Fifth World."

"I still don't understand."

"Neither do I, Tuchvala. But now that I'm back here, I'm not afraid anymore."

Yuyahoeva reached over to pat her hand.

"It's okay. And it's not all your fault. I called you a two-heart that day, because you made me angry. Because I was grieving for Pela. And . . . . Because I knew, deep, that you were right about your mother."

"They killed her because of me?" Asked Tuchvala.

"I think so," Yuyahoeva reluctantly agreed. "It's hard for me to think like a lowlander, like Hoku, Tuchvala. To kill someone just because there is a small chance that they might interfere with your plans. As if one person's plans could be that important. Pela would have told us, you see, would have warned us about your coming. I suppose that when the lowlanders knew your ship had started down, they silenced her. Not your fault, Tuchvala."

"No, it's not," Sand told her, and laid her arm on the other woman's shoulder.

"But," Yuyahoeva added, "Now we can work together. Tuchvala, you can have a place here, in the mesas, if that is your wish. There must be a lot we can learn about each other. After all, we're both farmers."

"Yes," Tuchvala agreed, attempting a smile and almost making it look natural.

They sat in silence for a moment, and a cold, hard thought crept into Sand. It chilled her newfound warmth, sliced through her growing sense of harmony.

"What about my father?" she asked. "What about Red Jimmie?"

Yuyahoeva brought out his tin of tobacco, a cornhusk and a small pair of scissors and began to make a cigarette. He bent to the task intently, almost as if he hadn't heard Sand at all. She was close to repeating her question before he finally answered her.

"When there is trouble, I suspect Red Jimmie right away, Sand. I've always believed him to be an agent of the coast. But he has also served us well, better than the old woman who sent him here could have imagined. Jimmie really is a two-heart, Sand. His feet are in two different places, miles apart. It makes him sick. When the Whipper went out, as soon as I knew, I tried to call it back. The communications had been overridden. I knew it was Jimmie, then; he's too good with smart machines; he talked the Wings of the Whipper into being deaf, somehow. So we monitored his communications—caught him making a call to the coast. I sent some warriors to arrest him. He's over in the jail."

"I want to see him," Sand said, trying to keep the harshness out of her voice.

"You will. If it's any consolation, Sand, I really think he was trying to save you. If he hadn't called you out, the Whipper would have caught you both in your mother's house."

"You know about that?"

"We went back over his calls. We found some even stranger ones; coded and scrambled and in a different language. We still haven't sorted those out."

"Maybe he did try to save me. Maybe it was part of some larger scheme of his. I don't know or really care."

Yuyahoeva shrugged.

"You can see him tonight."

The jail was a squat building suffused with an antiseptic smell of disuse. It had only five cells; each the size of a good-sized room, formed from ugly red concrete with chainglass front walls.

The outworlder, Teng, occupied the one nearest the door. She was lying on a cot with a feeding tube in her arm, asleep. The next cell held the Parrot-Island man, Alvar. In the third was her father. He was folded into the corner of his cell, head resting on his knees. He looked up slowly as they came in. When his gaze crossed Tuchvala, his face seemed to drain of color.

"Jesus!" he croaked a word that meant nothing at all to Sand. "Jesus," he repeated, and then rolled over, put his face into the corner, and began to retch. The air circulation picked up a sour fetor of vomit and alcohol.

"Get her out of here!" he shrieked, between his dry heaves, grinding his face against the rough concrete. "Get . . . her . . . out of here!"

Yuyahoeva took Tuchvala gently by the arm and lead her from the building. Sand watched her father's quivering form for several sickening moments.

"She's gone," she said, trying to keep her voice flat. Was this the man who had first taken her out in a Dragonfly, first taught her to greet the sky? Or was it the man who beat her mother, who humiliated her in front of her family, who came home screaming and drunk?

And why was she thinking such silly shit? He was the latter, always the latter, and any good he had ever done was as useless and unreal as rain over the ocean.

Red Jimmie slowly turned around, wiping vainly at his face with the cuff of his beige shirt.

"It's true, then," he grated.

"True enough."

"What do you want?"

"What we all want. To know what you've been doing this whole time. To know what the lowlanders know."

Red Jimmie looked at her for a moment as if stunned. Then he threw back his head and yowled. It took Sand some time to realize that he was laughing, a horrible, insane laugh.

"They don't know shit, daughter mine. They don't know anything. Hoku and his fucking . . . ignorant plans. Everyone thinks they know it all. . . ."

He slacked off, staring at the walls of his cage.

Sand moved up close to the transparent wall. She placed her hands against it.

"Mother is dead, father. How did she die?"

Jimmie sputtered again, less like laughter this time.

"No more questions. They've all been asking me questions. Sand, they have the ojo de verdad. They have other things, too. They'll get everything they want from me, eventually, if they think of the right questions."

"I don't care about that. Who killed her? Who actually killed her?"

Jimmie lurched to his feet, lost his balance and leaned heavily against the wall. He swung his head around towards her, and she saw anger there, fury so bright it could be a star.

"Who?" he hissed, as softly as a foot on sandstone.

"Who?" he shrieked, and stumbled towards the glass. He cracked his face against it, an inch from her hand. She saw his nose spread comically against the chainglass, saw blood spurt and smear like a blooming rose. He lost balance and slid, leaving a red trail along the transparency.

"Who the fuck do you think killed her?" he snarled, as he crumpled to the floor.

"Who do you think?" he pleaded, eyes closed.

Sand nodded. Who else? And left the room.

CHAPTER TWENTY-ONE

A dust devil pirouetted down the dry streambed, laughed at Hoku and vanished. Far up the way, the line of mesas shivered through miles of heat, and a husking wind breathed up from the south.

Homikniwa had explained to Hoku once why they called the dry, harsh winds husking. How hours and days of stripping corn by hand left your hands raw and cracked, just as the southern air, bereft of moisture, could wring you out as it sought eagerly seaward. Already Hoku's lips were dry, cracking. He licked them again and watched Homikniwa, whose eyes surely saw more than his in that blurred distance.

Would that they could see above him, as well, to where the satellites rebelled.

Hoku leaned against the Bluehawk, glanced left to the troop carrier half a kilometer across the undulating plain of roach grass. Another kilometer he could not see, but there was another war craft there, and on, forming a semicircle around the pueblos.

They didn't think he would cross that imaginary line, did they?

"I don't have much choice anymore, do I Homikniwa? Our eyes in the sky no longer see for us. Surely the ship in orbit has already sent a stellar to the Reed, detailing our insubordination. In twenty years, there will be an invasion fleet big enough to put us under. If it isn't already on its way."

Homikniwa nodded. "Twenty years is a long time."

Hoku shook his head and answered without heat. He had spent his heat in his room, shouting and striking at the air behind sound-baffling walls. "We won't win with farm equipment, my friend. We can't fight starships with shovels. Twenty years won't change that."

"Maybe the aliens won't either."

"No other chance, Homikniwa. We have no other hope, and we never did. That's why I can't feel remorse."

"*I* would," said Homikniwa. "A lot of people have died for such a slim hope. There was never much reason to think the aliens could—or would—help us. You've known that all along."

Hoku stared intently at his fingernails. "No one but you would ever dare talk to me that way, Homikniwa."

The little man smiled a rare smile. "I don't know. That Tech woman laid it on you pretty thick, and that after you burned her."

Hoku nodded ruefully. "I don't know what to do about her, Homikniwa. Even my own people are starting to talk back to me."

"It's a fool that only surrounds himself with people that say what he wants to hear," Homikniwa reminded him.

"I've got you already," Hoku growled. "I don't need her, too. So young. What does she know?"

"What did you know, when the old lady took you on?"

"I knew better than to contradict her to her face."

"The old lady wasn't as smart as you are, Hoku. She always wanted to hear 'yes'. Nothing else."

Hoku spat, moistened his crackling lips. "Maybe I'm not so smart either. But I can't regret these things I've done; that would be a waste of energy. I have to move on. And I'm right, Homikniwa. Those ships are the only chance we had, ever will have. The only things that the Reed can't control or predict. You saw what happened when we tried to use our satellites. Our own satellites, even the ones we built!"

"Built with Reed components."

"Exactly. Exactly."

Hoku turned back towards the mesas. Why did they still live there? How could superstition hold them so tightly?

"Hoku. Here's one of those things you don't want to hear."

"What would that be, Homikniwa?"

"That landing drum by Wife-Tell-The-Sea-Point. That ship in orbit. Those are our enemies now. And they don't have the alien; the pueblos do."

"Yes."

"It's time for Fifth Worlders to join together, Mother-Father. Time to strike a deal with our relatives in the mesas. They no more want the Reed to take our world than we do."

"They won't accept my authority, Hom. Not now. They caught Jimmie, you know."

"I know."

"But not before he was able to open the door for us."

"What do you mean?"

"You'll see soon enough, old friend."

"Hoku. Take my advice. Get on the cube and talk to the old man. He's been trying to call you. There's been enough killing. We can still plant a field between us, the way things are. If we cross over, then nothing more can be done, and we die fighting ourselves while the Reed laughs."

Hoku closed his eyes, saw bright shapes swimming against his lids. So many roads, but he always knew which one to take. In the past, he had always been right, hadn't he?

"We won't kill anybody unless we have to. But we do this my way, Homikniwa, and though I listen to you, you must be with me."

Homikniwa reached over and gave his arm a brotherly squeeze.

"You're doing something wrong, Hoku. I can feel it deep, deep. But I'm always with you."

"Why?" Hoku asked.

"I don't have to explain, Hoku. I am what I am. What I am is loyal. Not to my clan, not to my family—they cast me out. To you, Hoku. Leave it there."

"I will," Hoku answered, gratefully.

"But I still think you are wrong here. Think about it, Hoku, before you commit."

"I have. I've been thinking for twenty years. This is the moment to act."

The two men stood there a moment longer, Homikniwa slowly shaking his head. Above, the mute sky shimmered as the sun passed midday.

CHAPTER TWENTY-TWO

Alvar feigned sleep, wishing desperately that he could see what was going on in the cell adjoining his. Through slitted eyes he could make out the woman named Sand, standing in the common chamber. She stood, facing his neighboring but unseen prisoner, body crackling with tension. She reminded him of the high-voltage fence around the arcology, back home. Something you would not dare touch.

Their words carried to him clearly enough. Alvar knew who he was in jail with, though when they brought Alvar in he had only seen the vague man-shape huddled in the cell next to his. He had no face to put with the cracked, strained voice, but he could imagine one. A drunk—bleary-eyed, soft around the mouth, black, greasy hair. A monster, a traitor to his people, a killer. . . .

He might have been Alvar, once. Red Jimmie, that was his name. From Parrot Island. Alvar knew about Parrot Island, because that was his own, fictional home. Which meant that Red Jimmie was his counterpart—the man sent here years ago by the Vilmir Foundation. The spy.

So this is what I have to look forward to, Alvar thought.

The conversation ended, and the Hopi woman turned to leave. Alvar saw her face, the flat, masklike expression, and for a fleeting instant, he wondered if there was anything he could do for her. He remembered the old woman, the mother of the boy Teng killed.

Red Jimmie's crime felt like his own, filled him with shame. Could he atone for the older man's sins, wipe that terrible look from Sand's young face?

He almost shouted as she left, to tell her that he knew things, things that might help. The impulse passed when she left his vision.

He sighed. Teng would have killed him anyway. And throwing in with these people would be stupid. They were bound to lose. How far behind could the Vilmir warships be? They had cobbled this little expedition together fast, but they must be assembling a larger fleet, too, calling ships in from Earth to Serengeti. Building new ones, despite the immense cost. If he could just bide his time for a few years, he could have it all. No point in going soft over the first woman besides Teng he had seen in three years.

Teng. He felt a guilty start. How was Teng? They had told him she would live, and he knew that she was in the cell next to him.

"Teng? Teng!" he whispered, then repeated himself more loudly.

"Well," came a voice that was not Teng's. "You must be the new boy. Welcome to the Fifth World."

It was the old man. Alvar did not want to talk to the old man.

"Speak up, boy."

"I don't know what you're talking about," Alvar snapped. Surely someone, somewhere, was listening to all of this.

"Parrot-Island man! Talk to me! How do you like the adventure of space, the romance of distant worlds?"

"Shut up! What are you trying to do?" The old man was insane. He had destroyed himself, and now he would destroy Alvar.

The voice came back to him, charged with dark derision.

"Come on, boy. I've been doing this for thirty years now. You don't think I know when I can talk and when I can't?"

"I don't know what the fuck you're babbling about."

"Don't you, muchacho?" Alvar felt a chill cut through him, as he choked back his answer. The old man had spoken in Norte, the Spanish dialect of the Western States of America. If Alvar had answered. . . . And he nearly had.

"I'm not cut out for this shit," he muttered to himself, softly, and then regretted that, too.

"The stuff—the equipment they give them to work with here is pitiful," the old man went on, still in Norte. "The computer systems are centuries behind what I learned back on Earth. No challenge at all, even after all of these years. The things I've built into them! They can't hear us unless I want, old friend."

"I am not your friend," Alvar hissed, still in Hopi.

"Oh, very good," the man said, and Alvar heard the distinct patter of applause. "You don't speak Spanish, but you understand it, eh?"

"Fuck."

"I pity you, boy. Even I was better prepared than you were."

Alvar said nothing. Perhaps he had already hung himself, perhaps not. Perhaps the old man wasn't insane; he no longer sounded so. He sounded icy-calm, clear and articulate. He might really know that there was no one listening.

"You'll find out, muchacho. That you can't ever belong here. But that's not my problem. Not my problem."

He was silent for a moment, and Alvar hoped he had stopped, but Jimmie spoke again, more softly.

"You ever been to Greece? To Oregon? Argentina?" He sighed, and Alvar could hear him shuffle closer. His head must be pressed against the wall of the cell.

"I remember once in Argentina. Me and three compadres went out to hunt Moas. Just the three of us, out on that plain, on horseback. The hunting permit cost me every dima I had, but Mary and Jesus, it was worth it. You ever ridden a horse? It's like having thunder for feet. That night, we ate Moa steaks, drank red wine. The sun went down, I've never seen a sunset like that. Kabrina—she was one of my compadres—we went out in the grass with a blanket. We fucked like crazy, and then we lay there all night, watching the stars, while Raphael played music for us on his tiplé. He wasn't jealous, you know? The best kind of friend, Raphael. I would not sleep that night, or the next. I never wanted to miss another moment of living."

The words stopped coming, replaced by a wheezy sort of sound, and Alvar realized that the man was singing. He could not pick out the words, and the tune was either unknown to him or so badly rendered that he didn't recognize it.

"Anyway," the man said, after the song trailed off and died. "Anyway, I had to sleep, didn't I? And one day I would die. That was when I decided I wouldn't die, not for a long time. A Vilmir recruiter had come to see me, months before. I found her and signed on. How else could a poor boy buy immortality?"

You weren't as poor as me, thought Alvar. I could never have afforded a hunting trip in Argentina.

"I've done my time, Parrot-Island-Man. It's over for me."

"Right," said Alvar. "Except that you're in jail. Your cover is gone, and now you've probably destroyed mine. Good luck getting your contract honored; you'll never see Earth again."

Jimmie chuckled dryly. "You don't know much. Less than them, even. They know I'm a traitor to the pueblos, but they don't understand how deep it goes. I work for the people down in Salt, that's all they know. I guess that makes me a traitor twice over, eh?"

"I guess it does," Alvar sighed.

"Hey, boy. Is your friend awake? The soldier?"

"I don't think so."

"Keep at her. Tell her to be ready."

"What do you mean?"

"Just tell her to be ready. Soon."

CHAPTER TWENTY-THREE

Night stillness had settled onto the pueblo, and Sand sat tracing her finger across her mother's table. Tuchvala was in the bathroom; Sand had showed her how to use the shower, and the sheer delight on her face had been a wonder to behold.

Sand recognized that her attitude towards Tuchvala was changing. The day before, she had been a mere symbol, fear and grief. Now—in one short day—her presence had become somehow comforting. Before, Tuchvala had been the stolen form of her mother, the threat. Now the threat hovered above the sky in a form much more alien than Tuchvala. Whatever the woman said, she was not—in a sense, never had been—whatever alien intelligence had created her. And in the brief time Sand had known her, something had taken shape between them. Sand did not know what it was, but it was quite different from the shape of her love for Pela. The angles were all different. But it was something.

Tuchvala—whose very name summarized the mystery of life and creation—was enigma and familiarity. Her thoughts seemed tantalizingly close, sometimes, but only when she spoke in the most literal manner was she entirely comprehensible. Thoughts and feelings lurked behind her brown eyes, which, as a new-born, Tuchvala had no way of expressing. And yet there was an elegance to her thought that Sand had begun to sense and appreciate.

The hushed sound of the shower ceased, and Sand was sure she heard a disappointed gasp. Water was at a premium in the pueblos, and no Household would allow the shower to stay on for long, though the water was cleaned and recirculated. Sand turned her head curiously when the bathroom door sighed open.

Tuchvala moved like a toddler, in a way, acutely aware of her body, seemingly constantly amazed by it. The shower had dried her off, as Sand had instructed it to, though her hair was still damp——a dark, ropey mass that hung to nearly her waist.

She was so lovely Sand could have wept. She had seen Pela unclothed often enough, and her thick body had always seemed host to a secret kind of beauty. Here was the secret revealed. Seeing Pela, Sand always saw the scars. The white, blistery stretch marks the marked Sand's own arrival; the transient bruises, the place where Jimmie had burned her with a sterilizer once. The thickening of early middle age, the prominent varicose veins. And yet, seeing her young, Sand realized how little difference there really was. It was only that when she was alive, her mother's little faults had masked her beauty. Sand's image of Pela was an image of hurt, rather than health——and that had been Sand's own fault.

But Tuchvala was not her mother. Tuchvala was a newborn. Sand appraised her, and thought that she had never seen a more beautiful woman. And then Tuchvala smiled, and it was if the sun had risen.

"The shower was very nice. I never imagined that flesh was so wonderful."

She carefully sat on one of the thicker rugs, leaned forward to stroke her own calves.

"I wondered if this body could feel more than need and pain. What . . . why is it that . . . it feels like this? Pain I can understand, because it warns you when something is wrong."

"I don't know."

Watching Tuchvala stroke herself Sand grinned idly. What

might it be like, to experience sensation for the first time as an adult? To feel hot water against your tired skin for the first time, to feel the hard pleasure of a good massage, the first tentative touch of a lover's tongue?

A hot flush of embarrassment reddened Sand's face. Tuchvala, blissfully unaware of any thoughts she might be arousing, was still exploring the feel of her fingers brushed against her skin. She had moved from her legs to her belly, tracing up across one breast. Sand rose quickly, crossed to the wardrobe, and selected a nightshirt. Tuchvala was watching her when she turned back around.

"You might want to put this on, Tuchvala," she said, briskly. "The household tends to let things get cool in here at night."

Tuchvala nodded, still smiling, and observing Sand's own garment, slipped the one-piece cotton shirt over her head. It hesitated briefly on her breasts and then dropped on down as she stood up.

"Thank you for showing me the shower, Sand."

Sand nodded. What had come over her? She was no prude.

"Come here, Tuchvala. I'll show you something else."

Sand indicated for Tuchvala to sit in front of her. She did so, and Sand sank down behind her, crosslegged. She reached out and laid her fingers across Tuchvala's shoulders.

"This is called a backrub," she said, beginning to knead the stiff muscles of Tuchvala's shoulders. The other woman gave a little involuntary gasp.

Pela, Sand reflected, had liked backrubs too.

Midnight was approaching when the cube pinged for Sand's attention. It startled her awake, and for the second time in two days, she awoke to find herself nested against Tuchvala. She had been giving her a massage, she remembered, and after finishing, Tuchvala leaned back against her. Sand had only closed her eyes for a moment. . . .

She gently pushed Tuchvala forward, and the woman woke with

a start, then smiled uncertainly. Sand strode muzzily across the room, shaking her head to clear out the fog.

Yuyahoeva was on the cube.

"Sand. We've found the Kachina. Tuchvala's sisters. This may be the best time for her to talk to them."

Yuyahoeva looked tired, and Sand wondered if he would survive this ordeal, ancient as he was. If any of them would.

"Okay. I'll have her there soon."

"You have about an hour while we get the laser aligned."

Sand's clothes were all too small for Tuchvala, but she hesitated before giving her one of Pela's outfits. She had distanced Tuchvala from Pela well enough to deal with her—even enough to like her a little. She feared a return of her uncertainty, of resentment. Still, she had to dress her guest, and not in the grotesque parody of clothing that she had worn up until then. She finally settled on something that she had only seen her mother wear once; Jimmie had bought it for her while seeking forgiveness, but Pela had never liked it very much. It was a traditionally-cut skirt, suitable for ceremonial garb, but it had gaudy borders of corn tassels stitched along each seam, and it was a deep, almost black, green. The matching cotton blouse was sleeveless and buttonless, and not traditional at all, patterned with black, red, and green diamonds. The green matched her skirt.

On Pela, the outfit had looked unnatural. On Tuchvala it had a certain appeal.

Sand stripped out of her own nightshirt—she had traded it for her worn jumper before Tuchvala's shower—and chose a pollen-yellow cotton body suit. Over that, a slightly unconventional pleated skirt and high-collared blouse, both black.

She combed out her hair and set it up in her maiden's coils, as Tuchvala watched curiously. A thought struck Sand, and she grinned wryly.

Tuchvala was a maiden; more so than Sand. Wielding the brush, she turned towards her companion.

When she was done, Sand mirrored one of the walls so that they could see themselves together. She whistled.

"Damn, Tuchvala. Two virgins all dressed up. We look pretty good together."

A silly remark, but Tuchvala smiled. And it was a more pleasant thing to keep in ones head when the world might be about to end. Sand's smile faded, and she ushered Tuchvala out the door.

The observatory was walking distance, and they reached it in under half an hour. It was reared up on a spit of mottled grey stone; a few lights burned down below, hinting at the town without revealing it. Above them, the stars were cold ice.

The women shed the faint outdoor chill as they entered the observatory. It was dark, but climate controlled. Sand had only been here once, though she had been to the observatory in Paso on the coast before. The telescopes in Paso were without peer, and the station could access the sky Kachina as well. The mesa observatory seemed very poor to a younger Sand. The gravity telescope was old and bulky, and,—most embarrassing of all—there was an ancient optical scope, jutting out toward the stars like some huge penis.

Now, suddenly, she saw the optical scope in perspective. If it broke now, they could fix it with the tools and parts they had on the mesa. If the gravity scope stopped working, they would have to beg Hoku for parts. And right now, they seemed to be at war with the lowlanders.

A central cube was illumined with a faint light; beyond and through it, the light limned Yuyahoeva's face, so that it appeared his features hovered, godlike, behind the toy ship. Sand approached, felt her breath quicken. Here it was.

The ship resembled a ceremonial hourglass. It was nearly featureless. Sand wasn't sure what she expected, but it must have been something more impressive, because she felt a little let down.

"It's because you can't see its size like this," said Yuyahoeva, correctly reading her reaction.

"That's me," Tuchvala whispered, shuffling forward until her hand touched the cube.

"It is? How can you tell?"

Tuchvala frowned for a moment. "Oh. I can't. It could be one of my sisters. But we were all essentially one, to start with. I still . . . how can I tell?"

"You must have been able to tell your sisters apart before."

"Yes, but by their thoughts. Little differences at first, big ones later."

"How will you distinguish them now?"

Tuchvala looked at her curiously. "It doesn't matter, Sand. Whichever I talk too, they will all hear me."

"You should do it, then," Yuyahoeva said.

Tuchvala nodded. You have a laser communicator here?"

"Yes," the old man sighed. "We have it aimed with the optical scope."

Tuchvala strode towards the panel where a young man named Nash – Sand's grandaunt's nephew's boy—was carefully adjusting the attitude of the telescope.

"I need to send a simple series of binary messages," Tuchvala told them. "They will unlock a communications link that we froze up many years ago. Otherwise, they will neither recognize me nor speak to me."

"Tell us the binary pattern," Nash said, his voice quivering slightly, so that Sand could not help smiling a bit.

"I will use the consonant "t" to indicate the absence of a pulse and the vowel "o" to indicate the presence."

"Go," whispered the young man.

"Totot'toooto. . . ." Sand began, and droned on for several moments, a look of deep concentration on her face. When she was done, she wrinkled her nose prettily.

"I think that's right. Human brains aren't very good at this sort of thing."

"No," Sand agreed.

"What happens if the signal isn't right?" Yuyahoeva asked worriedly.

"Nothing. We just won't get a response."

Nash checked the recording of Tuchvala's code, had the computer read it back to her in little flashes of light. When he was done, she nodded.

"I'll send it, then," Nash said, and spoke softly to the computer.

For a moment, Sand did not understand what had changed, but Yuyahoeva gasped, and suddenly she understood. The image of the starship in the cube was gone; the cube itself was opaque.

"What? What?" demanded Yuyahoeva. Nash frantically mouthed commands, then switched to the manual touch-board. Finally he looked up at them, fear shining brightly through his young features.

"It's dead," he groaned. "I don't know how, or why—but the computer has shut down."

"Shut down." Yuyahoeva tottered to a bench and sat unsteadily. Sand watched in astonishment. The computer was the oldest spirit of them all—it had accompanied people to the Fifth World, and though it had been changed and modified many times since, it had always been their faithful friend.

Yuyahoeva's face was hardening.

"Jimmie," he snarled.

Sand sneezed, and an instant later, Tuchvala did too.

Fifty Kilometers away, a clear note sounded from within Hoku's Bluehawk. He turned a grim smile towards Homikniwa.

"Here we go," he said.

CHAPTER TWENTY-FOUR

The night had begun to frighten me, by then. I was used to knowing where I was going, to peeling through layers of photons, neutrinos, through the very oscillating structure of space itself. I was used to being able to see.

Now I couldn't see anything, and I was denied what I most needed; myself. As much as I wished to help Sand and her people, I had additional motives for wanting to make the laser link with my sisters. I wanted to know who I was now. I feared vanishing—becoming hot water streaming on my back, Sand's fingers digging into my tight shoulders, the swirling vertigo of fatigue and sleep. I was becoming a series of events, a recording of moments. Losing the timeless clarity of real thought. I could feel that slipping away, more surly than ever I felt the mere erosion of my capacities as time decayed my hardware. And the pace was so much quicker, in this body. Images flashed and receded in my brain, masquerading as rational thought.

No wonder Sand's people valued dreams. Dreams were all they had.

The word for what I did then is sneeze. Sand taught it to me and sneezed again herself.

"Must be something in the air," she told me. I wasn't sure what she meant.

Whatever had gone wrong, they seemed to blame it on Sand's

father—on the man who had sent me away from him, back in the jail. I understand the consternation I cause, wearing this form.

But it was my form now.

I stumbled along wherever we were going, holding Sand's hand, afraid.

"What the fuck?" Teng groaned.

"Teng! Teng! It's me, Alvar!" Alvar crowded as close as he could to the wall. The lights in the jail cut off for a second time and then came back up, much dimmer.

"I know. I've been awake for awhile, Alvar. Long enough to hear you make a fool of yourself. Again."

"Hey, soldier-woman!" It was Jimmie, a peculiar ring in his voice.

"I've heard your whining shit too, spy. What do you want?"

"You hear me say it was time to be ready?"

"I'm always as ready as I can be."

"You better be real ready, now. I can help you, but you have to help me. You can't let them have me."

"Who?"

"Any of them. You have to take me off of this stinking planet."

Teng sighed. "It's in your fucking contract, okay? That was the plan all along."

"Plans can be changed, especially by soldiers. They have a bad habit of cutting plans off at the quick."

Alvar interrupted, his anger surprising even to him.

"What the fuck are you two talking about? Jesus, I still don't know what's going on. I'm sick of this shit. Teng, you talk to me. What's happening here?"

He heard Teng snort, but it was the old man who answered him.

"She doesn't know, you idiot. She may have guessed, though. There's about to be a full-blown war on this mesa. That should give us time to get away. If we're smart."

"War?"

"He must have shut down the computer somehow, Alvar," Teng interjected. "He probably knew he was going to get arrested."

"So. . . ."

"The defenses are down. Those assholes from the coast will be coming up here to get the alien, won't they, spy?"

"They still pick you killers smart."

"But not spies, it seems," Alvar sneered. "We're still in jail, or hadn't you noticed?"

"Details," hissed the old man, and a chill raced up Alvar's spine. Alvar sneezed.

The old man chuckled. "There we go," he said. "Right on time."

Alvar meant to ask what the hell Jimmie meant by that, but he sneezed again, and then the door of the jail sighed open. Six people walked in: two men armed with some kind of black pistols, the old man from the mesa-top, a younger man he did not recognize, the woman Sand, and the alien, if alien she was.

"Leave the woman in," the old man snapped. "Get Jimmie and this Parrot-Island boy." He did not look pleased.

On of the gunmen went to Jimmie's cell and Alvar heard it hiss open. He swallowed and noticed that his throat seemed a little raw. Some goddamn colona virus? He had had his shots.

Jimmie was a lot like Alvar expected, but better looking. Dried blood was smeared across his lower face. He had busted his nose and made no attempt to wipe it off.

Then they opened Alvar's cell.

"Come on, boy. The two of you have some questions to answer. Now." The old man's voice had none of the warmth in it that Alvar had come to associate with him, both on the mesa-top and in the kiva. It was terrible and cold, like the midwinter nights in the desert around Santa Fe. Alvar wanted desperately to say something, to deflect that malice from himself somehow. Instead he bowed his head and submitted without comment.

This time they weren't taken to any public kiva. In fact, they didn't go far at all. They left the jail and crossed ten meters of bare stone to another concrete building, which, like, the jail, was incongruously ugly when compared to the simple elegance of the rest of the pueblo.

Alvar noticed that Jimmie kept looking up at the sky. He was humming to himself.

The interrogation room was three meters square and supplied with straight-backed chairs. There was little else. Alvar had read medieval and early atomic romances in which torture figured prominently, but he saw no recognizable instruments of torture. Why bother when they had the ojo, as they called it here?

Jimmie went first, and there was no nonsense involved. The lights of the room were dimmed and a pair of goggles were strapped on Jimmie's face. The old man sat down in a chair facing him. He sneezed. As if by contagion, so did Sand and then the alien. Alvar felt his own nose itch.

"Red Jimmie," the old man rasped. "Did you cause the computer to shut down?"

"Yes." There was no hesitation on Jimmie's part.

The old man wrinkled his face in disgust. "Jimmie, why? She was our faithful companion from the time of our emergence here, even before. How could you do this to her?"

"She's not dead, you old fart. She's just asleep for awhile."

If the old man was relieved, he didn't show it. Instead he leaned forward, eyes intense.

"Why Jimmie?"

"I think you know, don't you? You've known I was Hoku's man for a long time."

"There's something more than Hoku in this business, Jimmie. Hoku is nothing compared to the Reed."

"If you want to know about the Reed, ask the warrior."

"I will, when she's well enough. But Jimmie, even the Reed wouldn't kill us all, wipe this planet clean. Those Kachina up there might. Do you understand that?"

The icy anger was gone from the old man's voice, thawed once more into warmth and concern.

"Spare me your superstition, old man."

"It's not superstition, you asshole!" Sand broke in angrily. Alvar thought that she would go on, but a sudden sneeze—a violent one—dispersed whatever words she might have offered. In any event, the old man held up his hand to quiet her.

"Okay, Jimmie," he said tiredly. "Let's not call them Kachina. Let's call them terraforming starships, whose job was to make this planet livable for life different from our own. Old, old ships who don't work as well as they once did. Jimmie, Tuchvala promises us that if we don't stop them, they will kill all of us, lay the Fifth World bare."

Jimmie was staring at Tuchvala. His face was working, and Alvar thought he saw the old spy squinting back tears.

"Why did you have to come?" He whispered at last. "Why? This place is no longer yours. You cost me nearly everything. May cost me everything before it's over."

Was this the same man? The self-confident smartass from the cell? Who was this Red Jimmie?

"You killed mother!" Sand screamed, a nearly incoherent screech. Her fists were balled into white-knuckled bludgeons, her lips skinned back from her teeth. "You, not Tuchvala. You!"

For a moment, Sand's voice seemed to recede from Alvar, wing up and become something different from sound. The entire world seemed to pulse with the explosive rush of her syllables.

"Jimmie. Explain it to us, Jimmie." The old man reached over and took off the goggles. There were tears there.

"It's too late," he whispered, looking at his daughter. "It's just too late."

Alvar felt a hot wind, as if he were a kid standing outside in front of the huge exhaust fans of the arcology, flying a kite. He could almost see the kite, shimmering along the wall of the room. And a sudden, profound sadness swept through him.

The old man seemed to sway—or was that the room swaying? He leaned towards Jimmie.

"Bring her back, Jimmie. Bring the computer back for us, so we aren't helpless against the ships and Hoku. We can forgive a lot, here in the pueblos."

"You can never make me one of you, though," Jimmie replied.

"You were never one of us because you were always working against us. That can change."

"No," Alvar found himself saying. His own voice sounded weird, distorted. "He can't change what he is. He's from the Reed. Like me." Mother of Jesus, what had he just said? They were all looking at him now, but their eyes were strange, as if her were a long way off and they were searching for him in some obscure place.

All but Jimmie.

Yuyahoeva sank slowly to the floor, his eyes still bright and uncomprehending. Sand sagged back too, the anger seeming to leak out of her as she bumped into the wall and slid her back against it, like a cat scratching. Alvar felt a sudden surge of emotion as he watched her, a spiraling, gut-wrenching need.

The guards were staring around, bewildered.

Someone spoke—Alvar wasn't sure who—and the words buzzed and rattled like an electrical short.

Mary! We've been 'fected! Alvar realized, suddenly, as a wave of sound and color seemed to roar up from his feet. That was why they had all been sneezing. They had all been infected with some tailored plague, the kind that the most hopeless addicts on

Earth kept in their systems all of the time. What was it carrying? What toxin was in their bodies? It could be anything. Alvar had plagued once, on something that made him happy, happy, happy. This wasn't that. This was more like the peyote he took one time, but at the same time it was more—emotional. He was not detached or godlike, noticing the little details in things. He was afraid, angry, remorseful—and he was in love with Sand. He wanted that soft woman's body—a real woman's body—crushed up against him.

Tuchvala was the one talking, some slurred dialogue that made no sense at all to Alvar anymore. Things were happening in the room, but the storm in his head made it impossible to pay attention. This could kill them, he knew. Some plagues did that, intentionally or not. Alvar did not want to die like this, flayed open to the universe, a bug with a pin through him as God and Mary thumbed through his lusts and fears.

Though his head was full of static, he did notice that Jimmie was gone.

So, apparently, did Sand. Alvar saw her go to the door, her legs jerking as she tried to control them. Alvar followed, discovered that walking felt a lot like standing on the deck of a ship in high seas—with cigarettes for legs. No wonder she was jerking. Jimmie had also engineered some kind of seismic disturbance. Yes, there was no doubt about it, the earth itself was bucking and heaving.

He saw that Sand stopped long enough to gently take a gun from one of the guards, and it suddenly occurred to him that he could do the same. That might restore some of Teng's confidence in him, if he walked in and liberated her, guns blazing. He staggered on to the door, but when he tried to repeat Sand's trick of taking a gun, the guard looked at him with a puzzled—but noticeably hostile expression. In fact, it seemed as if his mouth were expanding, his teeth grown immense, like those of a monstrous horse. Alvar had been bitten by a horse before; he retreated from the Hopi, waited until the guard's eyes spun elsewhere, and then fled out the door.

Sand hadn't gone all that far. She was standing beneath the night sky on the yellow mesa rock, swinging her head in all directions. It was mesmerizing; she just kept turning and turning. A wind ruffled the hem of her skirt, and the yellow of her body suit blazed like the most perfect color. As if the sun was out. Love at first sight. Of course he loved her.

But she had a gun, and now it was pointed at him, her fugue state broken by his presence.

"Where is he?" he thought she said. Her face was wonderful and terrible. Her grey eyes grew huge in his vision.

"I don't . . . I don't know. I'm sorry," he said, and meant it, with all of his heart.

"Who are you?" She was coming closer. "What do you want?" That was her breath he smelled.

Was he crying? He was. Why?

She was close enough to touch him now, and she did.

"What's wrong?" she asked. Her eyes were glassy, unfocused. Her hand touched him and lit fire along his cheek, fire that torched down through his skull, rushed to ignite other parts of him.

Alvar stumbled forward and kissed her. She seemed to respond almost reflexively, and the ground began to shake again. He was holding her arms, and his hands melted through the cotton bodysuit so that his fingers gripped down through her flesh to her very bones.

It was very confusing after that. Every brush of his skin against her ignited nerve cells in a way that Alvar never knew they could be fired. He had never wanted a woman so much in his life, ever, never loved one as deeply. Her face was the most exquisite thing he had ever seen, and each moment it glowed brighter. If only her expression weren't so puzzled, whenever she opened her eyes. But she didn't do that often.

At some point, he found a way to open her bodysuit at the crotch. He frantically entered her, and they were rolling and squirming on the mesa-top as lava rushed up from Alvar's feet, collecting and swelling in his groin with volcanic pressure.

Just before eruption, there was a moment of perfect clarity. He was fucking a woman he didn't know, didn't care for in the least. When he closed his eyes, it was Teng there. These thigh's did not grip the way Teng's did, the arms were not as rough. But the last time he and Teng had made love, she had actually looked at him . . . at him. This woman was looking at him, hissing, face contorted, but she didn't know who he was. She didn't care either.

Thus, when Alvar cried out, it was as much with despair as with ecstasy, and the throbbing pulses in the aftermath of his orgasm were much more like pain then pleasure. He disengaged and rolled away from the woman, disgusted, deeply depressed.

Teng was standing over him, framed by stars. For a moment he thought it might be some plague-inspired vision—but up until now he hadn't actually seen anything that wasn't there. Teng's face was as fixed as an ivory statue. Her bandaged arm hung loosely, but the other gripped a black pistol.

"So that's how it is, Alvar," she said, towering over him like the goddess she was. Her words fell on him like hail. She stared at him a moment longer, and he thought—but it could be the plague—that her whole frame was trembling, like a string on a guitar. As if something terrible were trying to escape her will.

"Today is a good day to die, Alvar, remember?" Teng raised the gun and pointed it at Alvar.

Not like this. At least when I'm sober, so I can meet death with real fear instead of confusion! Alvar struggled to speak, but his mouth was foam rubber. *I love you, Teng, I really do.* He closed his eyes.

"Let's go," another voice cried. "Oh, shit."

It was Jimmie, coming up behind Teng.

"Oh, shit. Sand I'm sorry, girl," he said.

Sand was levered up on her palms. She gathered her self quickly, however, despite her tangled and disarrayed clothing, and launched herself clumsily at Jimmie.

Teng scarcely moved. Her hand seemed to merely brush at Sand. Jimmie was screaming hoarsely and incoherently, and then Sand was on the ground. Jimmie knelt beside her.

"You're right," said Teng. "It's time to go. See you in Hell, Alvar."

With that she turned and strode away without a backwards glance, and after a moment's hesitation, Jimmie followed.

Alvar groaned and sank back down to the quaking stone, praying for the plague to end.

CHAPTER TWENTY-FIVE

Hoku watched Homikniwa sprint ahead, gun snapping first this way and then that. The speed and precision of the man was amazing. Hoku wondered where Homikniwa could have learned to move so, on a planet which had never known war. There was much that he did not know about the little man; Homikniwa had come to him long before Hoku became mother-father of the coastal communities. In those hard times, Homikniwa had been invaluable, both as a companion and as a bodyguard. When Abraham and his faction had made their move against him—fifteen years ago?—Homikniwa had been there. Alone, in the desert, it had been the two of them against six men. But those six were amateur killers, and Homikniwa was a professional. Five corpses and one frightened witness had marked the end of Hoku's struggle for succession. Only one of them had Hoku killed himself, and that had been a lucky shot. But after that Hoku knew he could kill, if need be. That one man was the only man Hoku had killed with his own hands, but when time came to arrange the death of Pela, Hoku had been able to do so without flinching. Killing was power, and Hoku understood the uses of power.

Still, he knew better than to kill too much, and to make it look accidental when he did. The Hopitu-Shinumu—whether progressive or traditional—were not used to violent death. It terrified them, and though he wanted people to be afraid of him, to respect him—he did not want them to hate him as an inhuman monster.

Red Jimmie had saved him a lot of deaths. With all of their computer defenses down and its defenders plagued into oblivion, he had thus far taken the pueblo without firing a shot. People would remember that about him. They would remember that he loved his people, even the stupid traditionals, and that he was only doing what was best for them.

Homikniwa motioned him on ahead. It was safe. Hoku, unarmed—the mother-father should not have to arm himself— moved on up into the pueblo proper.

The plague was a short-lived one: the virus itself was probably already dead in most of its human hosts, and the drug it produced would run its course in perhaps six or seven hours. That gave Hoku plenty of time to disarm the pueblo warriors, find the alien, and get down to the business of consolidating his power here. With Tuwanasavi under his control, the other pueblos would be of little difficulty; the great kivas and the rites they controlled were all here, and so were most of the clan headmen. He would allow them their traditional ways for many years—wean them slowly—but by the time he went to meet Mas—by the time he was dead, he would see them modernized, ready to face the Reed toe-to-toe. And whether he ever gained control of the alien ships or not, the Reed would at least believe he had, if he could find some way to deal with the warship in orbit.

Deep breaths, and one thing at a time. Flyers were settling everywhere, now, like bees on corn tassels. The sky was full of them.

The jail would be his first stop. Get Jimmie out, have him put the computer back to its tasks, but working for Hoku. And find the alien. Was it true, as Jimmie said, that it wore the shape of dead Pela? Or was it possible that the strain had become too much for the old traitor, that he saw his dead wife in everything? Hoku would find out, without need for middle-men. He could put his own hands to the task, and that appealed to him, after the defection of his satellites.

An hour later, Hoku had installed himself in the clan council building and was receiving reports from around the mesa. The reports were good, generally—there had still been no fighting to speak of, though one traditionals had shot himself in the foot with a Wasp. Yuyahoeva—the ostensible mother-father of Tuwanasavi—had been found and was recovering from the effects of the plague in isolation; Hoku wanted him pliable, and the drug would make him that. The woman Sand and more importantly the alien were both still unaccounted for, but Hoku did not imagine that they could have escaped the mesa while plagued. Hoku repeated this to himself over and over. How could one woman continue to stay out of his grasp?

Another disturbing problem was the absence of Red Jimmie. That meant that Hoku still did not have access to pueblo data or defensive capabilities. He must rely on information beamed to him from the coast or from space—and Hoku trusted nothing from space anymore. Still, he had a fairly tight net around the pueblo, in case this Sand did manage to summon the coherence to try and fly out again. Impatiently, he called the cube in front of him back to life, though he had silenced it only a moment before.

On his order, the cube projected a flat relief map on the wall. There was the mesa, the crooked seams of the land around it. His own flyers were ubiquitous, a swarm of red dots identified by a coded and always changing frequency. Yellow marked any pueblo flyers, and the screen showed them to be stationary, all of them. Sighing, Hoku leaned back and contemplated the shifting patterns of the red lights as they conducted search sweeps over the mesa and the rugged land near it. He had designed the pattern himself, and was slightly displeased to see that it varied a bit from his orders. Here, a flyer had deviated into another's search territory, there, one had spiraled too far across the broken cliff-side. Surely, no plagued woman could negotiate such terrain.

Then again, each man out there wanted to be the one to find Sand and the alien, to please Hoku, and so he could not blame them too much for such personal initiative. All in all, the search seemed efficient.

Where could she be? For the first time, it occurred to Hoku that the woman may not have been plagued at all; though natural immunity was out of the question, someone could have given her the same inoculation that he and his men had received.

Red Jimmie was, after all, her father. And Jimmie was missing too.

"Fuck!" Hoku softly allowed himself. Could Jimmie make a ship invisible? Almost certainly, at least in the sense that he could disable its frequency emitter.

"Give me an aerial projection from satellite data," he said, making the request sound like a curse. The image flickered and changed.

"Moving flyers in red," Hoku commanded. Immediately a number of red spots appeared on the map, located this time not by their own transmissions but by telescopes and radar two hundred kilometers above them.

Hoku studied the display intently. Was there anything . . . The image flickered out of existence. Hoku cursed, clenched his fists until the nails cut his skin.

"Still image," he hissed. "Recording of that last transmission."

The topography of the mesa reappeared. The red dots were unmoving points. Carefully, Hoku traced his search plan over, calling up a schematic of it to help him. Accounting for the many deviations, he tried to trace down every flyer. Then, in a flash of inspiration, he superimposed a still of the earlier display he had been examining, the one constructed from the identification frequencies. If there was a flyer not accounted for by that map which was present in the satellite image, he would have Jimmie. Unless Jimmie could make the craft invisible in reality, which Hoku chose not to believe possible. Or unless Jimmie had somehow slipped through the noose of Hoku's ships long ago, which also seemed unlikely. Any ships leaving the pueblo were to have been reported and then intercepted. If Jimmie was smart—and he was—he would have waited to get one of Hoku's own flyers, so he could slip out unnoticed.

To his disappointment, the number of ships in the two displays was identical. He called up a real-time map of the flyer transmissions.

Now there was one missing, he realized with growing excitement. The one whose search pattern had taken it so far off of the mesa proper. He quickly searched to assure himself that the pilot had not merely returned to his proper course, but such was not the case. A flyer was gone, headed out into the badlands south of the mesa.

What was Jimmie doing? Had he gone insane? It was possible. The strain of being an agent here in the pueblos must have been immense. And it had been Jimmie himself who had infected Pela with the deadly virus tailored for her and only her, though Jimmie himself hadn't known he was the carrier. But Jimmie could have figured that out easily enough. That and fear for his daughter might have pushed him over the edge.

"Get me Homikniwa," he growled at the unseen presence of his computer link. "And get me Kewa."

He might need the woman's advice. She seemed to understand the emotional, irrational side of human behavior better than he. Hoku reflected that most of his mistakes had been in assuming people acted as he did, rationally and with calculation. Surely Jimmie understood that his daughter was no longer in danger, now that the great secret was no longer a secret. Everyone on the Fifth World knew about the alien now, and Hoku stood to gain nothing by killing even as bothersome a pest as Sand. All Hoku wanted now was the woman in Pela's form. In fact, what he really wanted now was Sand's cooperation and Jimmie's too. If they holed up in a canyon somewhere and forced a violent confrontation, Hoku—and the Hopi people—might lose everything.

Hoku would trust this to no one else. When Homikniwa and the puzzled Kewa arrived, the three of them went immediately to the Bluehawk.

Halfway there, a voice in Hoku's ear buzzed for his attention, and he gaped as his carefully constructed theory collapsed.

CHAPTER TWENTY-SIX

Sand clawed her way along a rock face that heaved and trembled, that reached out claws to rend her, that seemed to babble. The shushing of her hands across smooth stone seemed to be a word she couldn't quite understand, but a crucial one nevertheless. Her heart was thumping out through her hands, which felt like stone themselves, and more than once she feared petrification.

She had to constantly remind herself what she was doing, that lowland warriors prowled the mesa. She should be trying to find a flyer—preferably a Dragonfly—and escape, find Tuchvala. Instead her mind just kept replaying, over and over, the crush of Alvar's body against her, the terrible need that had seized her, even though her disgust had been at least as great as her lust. The fragmented images and flashes of sensation that rushed about like ravens in her mind were more than confused, they were contradictory. Everything about the encounter had been wrong—there was nothing about Alvar she had desired, except that he had been there. When they had so frantically coupled, it hadn't been a man inside of her at all, but a woman. It had been Tuchvala moaning, grinding her into the stone. When her eyes flicked open to Alvar—a man she knew not at all—she had felt sick, and shut them tightly, though terrible colors swirled in the darkness. Now the flashes of him panting over her returned, the feel of his tongue in her mouth, and she retched, emptying what little was left of her earlier meal.

Hide! She scrambled on across the steep slope. There was a cave she knew of, if only she could reach it, stay there until this terrible thing left her brain. If it ever did. If she wasn't permanently brain damaged or even dying.

A sensation came which she only tentatively identified as a new sound, and when she looked for its source, she saw a lowland hovercraft topping the stone ridge. She froze, willing herself to become one of the yellow stone outcroppings, but in an instant the flyer had changed course. Sand darted down the slope, sliding and skidding on her butt. Her limbs refused to react properly, and she quickly lost her balance, tumbled painfully down the grade until she fetched against a projecting spur. Wildly flailing, she scrambled around it, unto the narrow ledge below. Beyond the ledge there was nothing, a sheer drop down to checkered fields streaked with the hazy trails of numerous hovercraft and cycles. Vertigo seized her, for the first time in her life, and though she was safely against the stone face, Sand felt as though she were actually teetering over the brink. The faint voice that always suggested that she jump into the void, plunge through that magical air between cliff and earth sounded like sudden, blaring music. She shivered and ran up the ledge.

Where was the hovercraft? She had lost sight of it.

The even stone broke off, suddenly, and she realized that she had gone in the wrong direction. Here was a spill channel, where rainwater traced a steep grove down the mesa. Perhaps forty feet below, she could see another shelf. Could she climb down that smooth channel? Not in this state. She turned to retrace her path, and there was the hovercraft, six meters away, waiting for her. She turned frantically back to the only route left her and was preparing to try it anyway, when her muscles wrapped her into a ball of pain.

• • •

The pain and her terrible confusion lifted at about the same time. She had some slight memory of a woman with a hypodermic and something warm that felt good against her flesh, soothed out the agony with a touch.

"That should bring them down. This will bond up with the receptors for the drug more efficiently than the drug itself."

A woman's voice, one that Sand did not recognize. When she opened her eyes she didn't know the face either. Lowlander, though.

"Good." Sand did recognize that deep, male voice. It was Hoku himself. Sand didn't know if she more flattered or terrified. Woozily she surveyed her surroundings. The shape of the cabin and the steady throb of its floor told her she was in some sort of flyer, probably one of those big hovercrafts they call Bluehawks. Alvar—her recent "lover"—sat strapped to a chair, eyes listless. I must look like that, she thought, but instead of feeling sympathy for him she wanted to vomit again. Her thoughts were becoming clearer, but in a way, that only made things worse. What had happened to them? She thought she could guess; some microbe engineered to produce psychoactive compounds. Not uncommon on Earth, she understood, but not common on the Fifth World. Such self-indulgent sensation was one of the things her ancestors fled when they left that world of lotus-eaters.

Who? Her father of course. Fresh anger cut at the clinging cobwebs left by the drug.

The fourth person in the cabin was Hoku. He stared at her with fixed eyes. The power he radiated was unmistakable, and another thrill of fear woke in her spine.

"You know what's going on, SandGreyGirl? Do you? Your father and some offworld woman have taken your friend."

What did this man want? Father with Tuchvala? That made

sense, somehow, though it shouldn't. If Jimmie worked for Hoku—and he surely did, releasing the virus and shutting down the computer so that Hoku could take the mesa—then why was he fleeing from Hoku?

"I don't know much of anything anymore," Sand sighed, wearily.

"Do you know who he is?" Hoku asked, in a way he probably thought was gentle. He pointed to Alvar.

She shook her head. "He was with the woman, the kahopi. He said he was from Parrot Island, like my Father. He said. . . ."

Alvar was staring at her, his face contorted with the effort to understand what he was hearing.

"He said . . ." she went on, and suddenly remembered. Her lips thinned into an angry line.

"He's an offworlder too. They both came here with the Reed. And so did my father."

There. The last thing Alvar had told them, just before the insanity really began. She watched Alvar; he sank into his chair with a look of utter despair.

"Yes," he muttered, to Hoku's suddenly furious glance. Hoku stood, then, crossed the cabin in four quick steps, and slapped Alvar in the face. The offworlder's head rolled back with the blow, and the red impressions of Hoku's fingers remained on his cheek.

"And Jimmie?" He growled. "Jimmie too?"

"I was supposed to replace him. The Reed always has agents on its colony worlds."

"This is *our* world," Hoku snarled. "Ours."

"He means his," Sand blurted. "That's what he means."

Hoku turned to her, and for an instant she thought he would strike her too, but instead, his face went blank of emotion.

"What do you know about me, little girl? Nothing. You know nothing. You have no idea what I have done and will do to keep this planet in Hopi hands."

"Hoku." It was the woman, who still sat near Sand.

"Hoku, there is nothing to gain by harassing these two. Sand must understand the situation clearly. Then she will see where her duty is, regardless of her feelings about us."

"He caused my mother to die!" Sand snarled at the woman, who shrank away from her a bit. "He has nothing to say that I want to hear!"

The woman seemed to master her startlement. She reached up and dabbed at Sand's forehead with a damp cloth. It felt good, despite everything.

"Listen, Sand," the woman said. My name is Kewalacheoma, from the old Snake clan. You and I, Hoku—we are all Fifth Worlders. These people that have the alien. . . ."

"Her name is Tuchvala."

"Ah. . . . Okay. These people that have Tuchvala are taking her to a landing drum north up the coast. A drum from a Vilmir Foundation starship. A Reed ship. Once they get her there, there is nothing we can do for her. Do you understand that? How can you want that?"

Sand dropped her head down. "What does it matter? While we play these stupid games, Tuchvala's sisters are preparing our doom. We had a chance, before your idiotic invasion. She was going to talk to them, try to convince them. . . ."

"What's this? What do you mean?" Hoku had a hungry look now.

Sand's head felt clearer with each instant, her anger and outrage sharper.

"Those ships in space, the ones you so stupidly think you can use for your own gain. They're alive, Hoku. Tuchvala is one of them made flesh, the only one still sane. If the whim strikes them, or if they are threatened in any way, they will destroy us all and start this planet again, from scratch. Do you understand that? That while we chase each other all over the Fifth World, Masaw is preparing an end to it?"

Hoku regarded her in shocked silence.

"She told you this?" He finally asked.

"Who else? She came down here to save us if she could, and you have chased her, threatened her. . . ."

"Sand," Hoku grated evenly. "I have been chasing you. Without your interference, we would have found your "Tuchvala" at her landing site, and she would have told us all this. I assume you used the ojo on her."

"She was telling the truth."

"I'll believe that when it's verified."

Sand lunged against her restraints. "And you have no right to my mother's body! You are the sole reason for her death."

"Her curiosity was the reason for her death. But I tell you frankly, Sand, her death was perhaps my biggest mistake, and I regret it bitterly."

"Do you. Well how nice. You and I can be mates now, Hoku. When's the wedding?"

Hoku blew out a long, slow breath and turned to Kewa.

"What can I do, Kewa? She is unreasonable. I thought she might be of some help in convincing Jimmie to come back to us, but. . . ."

He was interrupted by Alvar's harsh laugh. "It's out of his hands now. They're with Teng now. Nothing can stop Teng and nothing can change her mind. She killed your Whipper, you know."

"A Whipper?" Hoku frowned. "I didn't know about this."

Sand watched the exchange. There was pride in Alvar's voice, and also certainty. And the woman had definitely killed Chavo, despite his Kachina training. She remembered the woman's eyes, diamond hard. She remembered her, too, towering over Sand and Alvar back on the mesa. That was who had Tuchvala.

"Killed a Whipper," repeated Hoku.

"But she is wounded," Sand told him. "Chavo cut her good before she killed him."

Hoku was nodding, and Sand could almost see the calculation running behind his eyes.

"Can we catch them, Homikniwa?" he asked raising his voice. The answer came from overhead, through the comm system.

"Yes. They'll have to circle to avoid a storm, and the Bluehawk is faster. We'll catch them, I think."

"Then what?" asked Sand. Assume you overcome this woman somehow. What do you think you will do with Tuchvala?"

Hoku regarded her clinically. "Do you really believe what you said? About the danger from the ships?"

"It is true," Sand snapped. "As true as my mother's death."

"And she needs only to talk to these ships to stop them?"

"She wasn't sure. She wasn't sure she could stop them at all."

Hoku pursed his lips and nodded. He spoke once again to the unseen pilot.

"Homikniwa. Release my personal code. Launch the attack on the landing drum now."

CHAPTER TWENTY-SEVEN

Now Teng had no trouble remembering why she hated men. Alvar had tricked her, somehow, weakened her natural caution. Made her forget her pledge and her decision. Teng had never been much use as a human being, not to herself or anyone else. Always the stranger looking in a window from outside, watching other people laugh and love. For her there had only been sex and pain, and finally power. When she had the power—when she was no longer that weak little girl whose bones were so brittle and whose flesh tore so easily—then she began to appreciate the other two. Because with power, she could take sex and inflict pain—or experience it—at her leisure. Sixteen years old and a demigoddess, like black Durga herself. In the fifteen years since she had never regretted the decision; she had sacrificed nothing and gained much.

Now Alvar had her close to tears and closer to murder. Why she hadn't gutted him back on the mesa escaped her—perhaps the nagging suspicion that it was somehow her fault. After all, what man could resist one of those weak, soft things? Men liked being in control without even knowing why. Men were born with power but they never understood it. Teng was born without it and she did.

She would do now what she always did, what she should have always been doing. Her job.

"You can't fly through that," the traitor said from behind her.

"I can fly through whatever the fuck I want to," Teng told him. "If I avoid the storm, they can catch us. That isn't going to happen."

She reached up to adjust the monitoring system and felt a twinge as the dense tissue forming on her scab tore with the exertion.

"I didn't sign on for this," Jimmie snapped. "You're supposed to get me back to Earth alive."

"You aren't going back to Earth, asshole. Not on this trip, anyway. The Foundation has its central office on Plano Bello, and that's our next stop. Maybe."

Jimmie shrugged. "They can give me the immortality on Plano Bello. Makes no difference to me. But I will get back to Earth and away from these miserable colony worlds."

"Shut up. I'm sick of you."

"Without me, you'd still be back in jail, and you wouldn't have this flyer, either."

"You should have gotten a faster one. Then we wouldn't have to fly through your fucking storm."

She regarded the black horizon without fear. How high would this piece of shit climb? She should find out.

As she eased back on the stick, Jimmie swore. Behind them, the woman they called Tuchvala was asleep, tranquilized by Jimmie.

"That's really her, eh?" Teng asked. "Not very imposing."

"I know. I don't understand myself."

"You must have heard something. Try to make me understand, traitor. It could be important."

"Don't call me that."

Teng laughed. "Now isn't the time to get sensitive about your work description."

"I'm doing a job, just like you," Jimmie said, petulantly. "I work for the Vilmir Foundation; I'm no traitor to them."

"You bastard," Teng said, feeling real humor. "You aren't like me. There is no deception in what I do. I kill people. I make things happen, and I blow things up. What I don't do is tell people I'm somebody I'm not."

Alvar thought you were someone else, a little voice said. You led him to believe you could love him.

"So I could, if he loved me," she whispered. "So I don't lie."

"What are you talking about?" Jimmie asked, puzzled, and Teng realized she had just spoken her thoughts aloud. A bad habit and one that she would have burned out when they got back to Plano Bello. In three years, with this asshole. Who would she fuck on the way?

The screen suddenly showed a ship tracking them. By their exhaust, probably. Though these ships burned alcohol, the fuel was enriched with kerosene, which left a tell-tale flag of hydrocarbons behind. Another thing the storm would help out with. But of course, whoever was in the pursuing ship must know where Teng was going anyway.

"That's a Bluehawk," Jimmie said over her shoulder. "It's faster than us. And it must be . . ." he paused in consternation. "Must be Hoku himself."

Teng snorted. "Doesn't matter," she said. Their climb was leveling off as automatic controls prevented the flyer from rising above its capability to compress air. As jets, these craft were almost worthless.

"Tell me about the alien," Teng insisted.

"She claims to have been created by one of the ships. She grew the human body from cell tissue the first probe took, twenty years ago."

"Why?"

Jimmie hesitated. "She says that the ships themselves are nearly broken down, that they can't see human beings as sentient. They have come to some sort of impasse, so as one of the ships wants to sterilize the planet and the other wants to let it be. The third one could break the tie, but it is most damaged of all."

Teng frowned. "An avatar. This woman is an avatar of one of those ships. Then she does know their secrets."

"Presumably."

"And she thought she could convince the other ships somehow, by taking human form?"

"Again, presumably. To prove to them that we are sentient. They seem to have a different definition of sentient than we do."

"Ah. Well, we can riddle that out when we get to the Mixcoatl. We will be much better equipped to help her communicate with her ships than these colonists."

"I know," Jimmie said. "Else. . . ."

"Else what, traitor? Else you would have let me stay in jail?"

The old man was silent then. Teng continued. "You're right, of course. The Foundation wants as much as anybody to prevent a holocaust. Where would be the profit in that? But if she can convince them not to use their powers—whatever they may be—she can almost certainly tell us how to interface with them eventually. Or she could have told the colonists, and that would be bad."

"I know," Jimmie repeated. "I've thought all of this out."

"Sure you have, traitor. You've been thinking this through since you sent the Foundation that laser message, twenty years ago."

"Fifteen," Jimmie corrected wearily. "Fifteen. When it happened, I didn't yet have access to the observatory satellite and its comm laser."

Teng was watching the oncoming sky. It looked like boiling pitch, but she spared one incredulous glance over her shoulder.

"You must mean local years. You sent your message to Plano Bello twenty standard years ago."

Jimmie was silent for a long moment. The flyer had begun to buck against headwinds; soon they would be in hell for sure.

"Checking your math?" Teng asked sarcastically.

"No," said Jimmie. "Whoever sent the Reed that first message— it wasn't me."

The ship nosed into the pitch and began to boil along with it.

CHAPTER TWENTY-EIGHT

"Corn girl's tit! They went in!"

Hoku spared Homikniwa a startled glance. The little man rarely spoke in expletives, rarely registered real excitement at all.

"More balls than Coyote," Homikniwa continued, darting an appreciative glance at Hoku. "She must be one hell of a warrior."

"No doubt," Hoku answered dryly. What was that he felt? Jealousy? Because Homikniwa admired someone else?

He realized that Homikniwa was waiting for something.

"Can we follow them? Climb above the storm?"

"I don't think so," Homikniwa answered. "Climb above it, I mean. But shit, we know where they're going. Once she got clear of the mesa, she turned straight to the sea, to her landing drum."

That was what Hoku had let slip by him. He had been so concerned with his own situation, he hadn't checked in with the cadres at the drum. The ones he had ordered to attack it. He rectified that by commanding the shipboard computer to contact his captain there.

Captain Rosa looked bedraggled and worn. He shoved back his mop of unruly black hair nervously when he appeared on Hoku's screen.

"Captain," Hoku said, using his best "confident" voice. "What's going on down there?"

Rosa glanced away from his terminal, possibly at some sight denied Hoku, possibly to avoid eye contact.

"I . . . Not well, Mother-Father. These people have weapons we've never seen. Swarms of metal bugs that find our flyers and ignite on them. And on my men, Hoku. Pulse weapons that ruin the trackers on our missiles. We've scored some hits, but I doubt that we have hurt them; the drum looks solid, and most of it is underwater."

"You've used the submersible weapons?"

"Three dozen. As far as we can tell, none of them ever detonated. But they have taken out ten flyers, with those damned bugs and with some kind of energy beam."

Ten flyers. Hoku tried to avoid grimacing. He wanted to shout, but Rosa was no incompetent; he just had no experience fighting wars. Nor, for that matter, did Hoku.

"Captain Rosa," Hoku said, trying not to reveal his reluctance, "Pull back to a five kilometer perimeter. Stop fighting them, now. Get our men out of there. There is a flyer from the pueblos on its way there. When you have contact, I want you to bring it down. If you can get it with sonics or a lightning net, do so. If not, I want you to shoot it out of the sky, understood?" If he couldn't get his hands on the alien, then damned if the Reed would. And double-damned if Jimmie would escape him. The landing drum might be equipped with defenses proof against Hopi weapons, but the pueblo flyer would not be, no matter how good this Teng was.

But that was last ditch. Time still remained to catch the flyer before it was too late.

"Follow her, Hom."

Homikniwa grinned, and Hoku suddenly realized that his friend was relishing this.

"Just like the old days, Hoku, eh? No armies or computers. Just me and you."

Hoku laid his hand on Homikniwa's shoulder before he turned back into the cabin.

"Like the old days," he agreed.

Hoku appeared briefly in the hatchway to the cockpit.

"Kewa, see that everyone is firmly strapped in. We will be flying through rough weather soon."

"How rough?" asked the moon-faced woman who Sand had been watching tend Alvar.

"Rough," Hoku said. He began to withdraw, been then turned back to her.

"I appreciate your help and your advice, Kewa. When this is over, there may be a better place for you on my staff."

"I don't ask for any reward, Hoku, except to study the alien if we catch her."

"That and more, Kewa." Then, wryly, "If we live through this. Strap in tight." Then he closed the hatchway behind him.

Sand watched Kewa's face as she checked her restraints. The woman looked both exhilarated and frightened. Who was this woman to Hoku? His lover, perhaps?

Kewa caught her gaze. "If Hoku lets himself sound worried," she whispered, "then there must be very good reason to worry indeed."

"All his own making," Sand shot back.

"You're not the one to talk. You could have taken Tuchvala to the clan council or to the coast. Instead you kept her selfishly to yourself. Why? Because she looks like your mother?"

Sand had an angry retort for that, but it died on her lips. What was the point? And Yuyahoeva, in his own way, had told her the same thing. She had not been thinking of the people, but of herself, and of ghosts. Thinking too much about ghosts had the inevitable consequence of creating more of them. Chavo, for instance. Now maybe Tuchvala and Jimmie, everyone on this flyer, whoever had been killed back on the mesa when Hoku took control of it. All lead back to the ghost of Pela in Sand's brain.

"Sand."

It was Alvar.

"Sand. Listen to me. This would have happened anyway. No matter what you did, the Reed would have come. Teng and me, and the soldiers. You haven't any idea what they can do. Shit, neither do I, but I have my guesses. They put the revolt on Serengeti down in two days. On the coast or on your pueblos, they would have found her."

Sand did not want to speak to this man. He was like her father, in turns evil and contrite. He never stood anywhere, but always shifted from one foot to the other. Still, there were things she had to know.

"Who are you?" Sand asked, just loud enough for him to hear her over the hum of the engines. "Who are you really?"

If Alvar was trying to smile, he failed.

"An idiot. An idiot named Alvar Washington, from Earth. From the Fourth World. I thought I wanted this, Sand, but I was wrong."

"Wanted what?"

Alvar sighed, and then did manage a rueful grin. "Sand, your people were right to leave Earth. There's nothing there anymore but memory and fantasy. Anybody worth a damn came out here, long ago. Or else they're too poor. Everyone is poor on Earth, Sand."

"You thought you were worth a damn, so you came out too?"

Alvar nodded, miserably acknowledging the way she used his own words. "Yeah, that's about it. But the colonies have been planted, and the only jobs left are the ones like mine and Teng's: making sure you all stay in line. They don't tell you that when you sign up. Just that the pay is good, that there is adventure beyond your imagination, and that the ultimate reward could be to live for ten lifetimes. Sand, when you live on Earth, all you want is something real. There, everything is illusion. Can you understand that?"

"That's why you came? Why my father came?"

"I think so."

"I don't understand it."

"Because your life is real," Alvar said.

Sand bristled. "You can have my fucking 'real' life, Alvar. Hard work, an asshole for a father, my mother dead for no good reason. You want that? Take it."

"It's better than what I had," Alvar said, gently.

Sand had no retort to that, for it doused her anger suddenly and inexplicably. There was something sincere about the Fourth Worlder that almost—but not quite—made up for his despicable qualities. And there were things that interested her more than Alvar's psychological profile. She turned to Kewa.

"Will we catch the outworlder and Jimmie?" And Tuchvala?

Kewa nodded. "If they can be caught, Hoku and Homikniwa can do it. Sometimes I think they are the hero twins."

"Better not let Hoku hear you say that. He punishes deference to such superstitious ideas."

Kewa shrugged. "I know you can never like Hoku. . . ."

"He killed my mother." Not Jimmie, Sand thought suddenly, though Jimmie may have delivered the fatal tool. But Jimmie couldn't help doing things like that when men like Hoku told him to do it. Now Jimmie was trying to thwart Hoku. Shouldn't that please her, at least a little?

No. Because Jimmie was taking Tuchvala away from her, and he was working against Hoku only because someone stronger had come along to play the fool for.

Kewa was still talking, outlining all of the "good" that Hoku had done in his life. Sand let it all slip by. Her anger stayed away; what was done was done. If Hoku could get Tuchvala back from the Reed, that would be a good thing, whatever crimes he had committed against Sand and the Hopi people.

The Bluehawk dropped like a stone. Alvar shrieked and Kewa gasped, but Sand rode it out, braced herself. Then the airfoil slapped against air that would support it again, a shock that jarred her bones and teeth. A little of the Dragonfly came over her, a detachment, as the Bluehawk began to shudder, pitch and yaw wildly. Sand admired this Homikniwa, whoever he was. He was a pilot.

"Sand." It was Alvar, who looked green. "Sand. I'm sorry about . . . about back there."

"Forget it," she said. "It was both of us and neither of us." As she said it she meant it. Alvar had not raped her; her memory was clear on that count. And the fact that he wanted her to know, now that they might die, struck her as almost sweet.

Or, typically, contrite.

The Bluehawk nearly upended, and then miraculously righted itself, and Sand's excitement grew. If only she were at the stick! She had never flown a Bluehawk, never bonded with one, but she could. She felt it in her bones, along with the surge of the storm. The flailing of the flyer had become a constant motion now, and Sand settled into it. A few loose objects were hurling around the cabin; a slate-black notepad, a shirt, and tube of something. Sand felt her fear and worry thin away, evaporate.

Somewhere up ahead, Tuchvala was riding in this storm. How good a pilot was the offworlder? Good enough to save Tuchvala's life? She would have to be. Poor woman, poor new creature. She would be sick now, Sand guessed; she had been sickened by that minor bit of acrobatics Sand put the Dragonfly through; this would be far worse. If Sand were there, she would hold her, comfort her. Sand held that image, and in her mind, behind her closed eyelids, the image transformed, so that she was clinging to a vast metal flyer, shaped like an hourglass, and suns were whipping past her, flaring blue as they approached, glowing red as they receded, and a bare, bare wind began to heat her shoulders and arms. She was such a ship herself, bound to her sisters, eons crawling by. She was Sand, in love with her mother and the land that was theirs together. She was Tuchvala, being stroked by her strange new friend, held, loved.

Something broke, back in the guts of the Bluehawk. Something broke, and the fabric of the metal her chair was bolted to twisted, rippled like a sheet drying on the clothesline as a breeze came along. Sand had lost her sense of up and down—she felt by turns weightless and incredibly heavy. There was another shriek, not of metal but of human vocal cords, and a buzz, like thirty children humming the same flat little tune. Sand felt the blood sucked from her face by some unseen force, felt it balloon her feet with tightness. The sound faded out, the storm went away, and Sand softly listed into a warm, dark country.

CHAPTER TWENTY-NINE

Once, a solar flare licked us as we fell past a star. My sisters and I watched it coming, felt the outer wave fuzz our sensors. Then the pulse hit.

We were much younger then, still thinking alike for the most part. But in that moment when that electromagnetic wind blew through our minds, my sisters became as distant to me as another galaxy. Along my backbone brain, my tohodanet scrambled, and I became chaos. Sensory impressions became disjointed and mixed, others vanished entirely. My thoughts became strange, unrecognizable as my own. We would have all ended there, if our creators did not build redundancy into their designs.

My tohodanet rebuilt itself from protected memory, but because of the nature of that consciousness, images and fragments of the chaos remained. It was then that I realized how fragile our selves were, that one day that which was "us" would leak out into the great suck of entropy and never reconstitute itself.

Being human was a constant reminder of this, but the drug introduced into my system distorted that realization beyond all measure. Already afraid of becoming the sum of my limited sensory impressions, I felt my consciousness melt onto the bizarre reordering of my physical impressions, become a mere interpreter of pointless cross-circuiting. Only later did I even understand about the drug; at the time I assumed that the mesh of human brain and my tohodanet had finally become untenable, the fit broken down.

Sand would call it nightmare; my abduction by Sand's father and the woman, Teng. The ride through the storm. None of it made the least sense to me; my concerns were all inside my watery, organic brain.

It was only after the crash, as they pulled me out into the storm that lucidity began to return, and I realized I could be sane again, or what passed for that when one was human. But then, of course, my memory was clouded by pain, pain I never imagined could be felt. It was no mere reminder that my body was injured: it was the universe itself.

Teng stared up into the pounding rain and laughed. It was a non-sensical thing to do, and she realized that a little madness was stalking her reason, but she indulged it.

Lightning coiled and struck above, like a snake.

The storm had certainly been a gamble, but due to Jimmie's poor planning (she hated men) it had been necessary. The pitiful excuse for a flyer would never lift again, but with any luck she still had a chance to get back to the drum. Without their satellites, with this storm, nothing could see them. But the flyer from the drum—the one she had called for to meet her halfway—might be able to. If her pursuit had skirted the storm, that would become all the more easy. If they had not, well, they were probably down too, or flown on over her.

"What the fuck do we do now?" Jimmie hissed, shivering. "I think her leg is broken."

Teng glanced over at the "alien" who was staring at her with glazed eyes. The hallucinogen in her blood stream was probably wearing off now. Teng crouched back under the survival tent, licked a few rain-drops from her lips, tasted the blood washing down from her scalp wound. She rain her fingers up the woman's leg, experimentally.

"Yeah, it's broken," she acknowledged. She set about finding the medical kit, which contained self-stiffening strips for splinting' primitive, but effective enough. She gave the woman a broad-spectrum antibiotic, too.

"They'll get us now," Jimmie groaned. "I know Hoku too well."

"Do you," Teng said quietly. "You don't know me at all." She got up and crossed back over to the wrecked ship. The smell of alcohol was almost overpowering inside; thus far, nothing had ignited the fumes, and she moved quickly, both to avoid becoming lightheaded and the risk of explosion. She found the rifle and the handgun Jimmie had procured for her. Both were primitive affairs; the handgun was merely a pain stimulator, useful at extremely close range. The rifle was better; it fired both armor-piercing and exploding shells. Such a weapon—like the laser the "whipper" had used on her—was supposed to be illegal to colonists.

Unfortunately, she had only one magazine, with perhaps twenty rounds. Well, the ship following her could scarcely hold twenty people.

The rain was slacking a bit, which meant only that the air was no longer an opaque curtain. She remembered the radar image of the crash site, and now she saw it revealed to her somewhat-better-than-human eyes. The flyer had skipped across a flat plain and fetched up against a rugged ridge, foothills to the mountains they would have soon crossed. The flyer would be in plain sight when the storm cleared.

Well, she did not have to be. Slinging the rifle on her back, pistol at her waist, Teng began cautiously climbing up the wet stone of the hills. She found a high point with good visibility. Rain was washing constantly down into her eyes, so she unfolded a broad-brimmed hat from her belt pockets. She sat there, eyes scanning the plains and sky through the drizzle of water pouring off of her hat. She switched on the cloaker, a fine net in her clothes which would confuse her infrared image and sonar, and settled in to wait.

•   •   •

Alvar closed his eyes against the fine mist the rain had become and yearned to be in a bed. His body ached from a million bruises and shocks, from the effects of plague, and from adrenaline burn. His brain, for the same reasons, was as useful for thinking as his mother's home-made marmalade had been for toast, which was not at all. So he didn't think; he just groaned inwardly and tried to imagine himself elsewhere.

"It'll still fly," someone was saying.

Alvar found that hard to believe. The flyer had seemed to fall apart like wet fibercard, tearing at the seams. How could it still fly?

"How fast?" That was Hoku, the scary one. Actually, the little man—Homik-something-or-other—was frightening too, but in a different way. A more distant way.

"Not fast at all. There are no afterjets, just fans. But the underjets work."

Because we slid in on our goddamn side, Alvar remembered. On reflection though, landing right-side-up—sliding along the ground at high speed on underjets—might not have been such a good idea. As it was, they were all alive and relatively uninjured.

Sand was a few feet away from him, still manacled as he was with resistance cuffs. Like his, her arms sagged, lifeless and numb. She appeared to be deep in thought. Above them, the dark clouds still rolled and thundered, but the heart of the storm seemed to have passed on.

"If it will fly, we should get going, then," Hoku said. His visage seemed like a skull filled with some black flame. Like the skeletal images who danced in the halls of the arcology on the Day of the Dead.

The small man and Hoku marched Alvar and Sand back into the hovercraft. Inside, the angles seemed wrong, but without the titanic hands of the wind pulling at it, the flyer felt solid again. Kewa was already inside, a dazed look on her face. A clot of blood on her brow suggested the cause of her disorientation. Hoku stopped briefly to take her chin in his hand.

"This will be over soon," he promised her. "We'll treat that. Can you hang on?"

Kewa nodded, and a bit of clarity returned to her features.

The Bluehawk rose shakily on sputtering jets, but rise it did, and soon Alvar felt the hovercraft moving through the sky, a bird wounded but not yet dead.

Hoku watched the terrain and the radar-sonar composite intently.

"If they made it through, we'll never catch them," Homikniwa said.

"How could they have made it in that little sparrow? Bluehawks were designed to ride out storms."

"True enough," Homikniwa admitted. "But with an enhanced person like this Teng at the controls. . . ."

"Enhanced? You mean like the Kachina? Conditioned with deep hypnosis and engineered microbes?"

"More than that. Bones of chainsteel, extra organs, faster neurons. Enhanced."

"What do you know about such things, Hom?"

The little man shrugged and returned his attention to fully to flying. The flat cube pinged for their attention. It was Captain Rosa.

"Mother-Father," the man began reluctantly.

"Go. Talk," snapped Hoku. He had no time for confidence building now.

"Two flyers left the drum, some time ago. I tried to contact you."

"Did you shoot them down?"

"We got one of them. They were so fast. And they had some kind of deflection field. We were lucky to get the one we did, and that with an X-ray laser, one of the big ones."

"Idiot. A Whipper shot one down by himself."

Rosa grimaced. "They were too fast, Mother-Father," he repeated.

Hoku nodded. "When it comes back, you have to hit it. Be ready." He closed contact.

"Well," he told Homikniwa. "There's something else to worry about. How are our weapons?"

"One of the lasers still works. We have two missiles, but I have red lights on one of them. We have a laser rifle, too, and a pair of handguns."

"Wasps?"

"No, slug-throwers."

"Fine. That Teng bitch doesn't make a very good prisoner. Better if she dies, I think."

Homikniwa nodded. "I agree"

They swept over eight kilometers in silence. Then Homikniwa pointed solemnly at the screen.

"That's it," he whispered. "That's them."

Even at this distance—still too far away for visual contact—the reconstructed image their instruments gave them was one of a badly damaged ship.

"At least it isn't strung out all across the landscape," Homikniwa offered. "They may still be alive."

Moments later, the ship itself came into view, a crumpled silver and blue toy against the Cornbeetle Foothills. Homikniwa began descending.

"I have two people down there," he said after a moment. "Two live people anyway."

"That's one missing," Hoku observed.

"It's her," Homikniwa said, with quiet certainty. "The warrior. Hiding somewhere."

"Where?"

"In those hills. That's where I would be."

Hoku stared intently at the folded black stone that was growing close with each moment, searching.

"Why can't the infrared pick her out?"

"She could be wearing some kind of screen. She had her offworld clothes, you know. I'm sure the traditionals took her weapons, but they might not have noticed a screen woven into her clothes."

"Or, like me, they never heard of one," Hoku said, shooting his old friend a suspicious glance.

"Just trust me, Hoku," Hom said.

The ship hove closer, and one of the infrared figures suddenly began moving. Hoku squinted through the viewport.

"That must be Jimmie," he said. "Shoot him."

"Not right now," Homikniwa said. "I don't want her to know where the laser ports are."

"She could be dead," Hoku hissed in frustration.

"If Jimmie lived, then Teng certainly did, Hoku."

"She was wounded."

"Makes no difference."

Hoku considered that for a moment and nodded. Homikniwa was usually right about such things, and he had to trust somebody besides himself.

They settled to the ground thirty meters from the ruined ship.

"Maybe she isn't armed," Hoku suggested. "She hasn't fired on the ship. Oh!" Hoku mentally chastised himself. Of course not. She wanted their ship. She would fire on them, when they came out of the craft.

"Right," Homikniwa confirmed, seeing the realization dawn on Hoku's face.

"What, then?" He could see the woman, slumped beneath the awning of a survival shelter. So close, but the ground was too rough to move the hovercraft any closer. They would have to walk out there and get her.

Hoku made his decision quickly.

"Kewa and I will get the woman. You keep your eye on the hills and shoot her with the laser if she fires at us. Surely she will miss her first shot."

Homikniwa looked grim. "No, I wouldn't count on that. Kewa and I should go. You man the laser."

Hoku felt a brief irritation. Homikniwa had been gently countermanding his orders and discarding his suggestions for the past hour. But then he saw the sense of the suggestion. Certainly Homikniwa was quicker than he, more adept at surviving injury. Kewa, though, with her head wound. . . .

"Take one of the rifles," Hoku said, by way of assent. Homikniwa stood, nodded confirmation. He opened a locker and lifted out a tough-looking weapon. He already had a sidearm.

"Keep your eyes up there," he told Hoku, pointing at the highest reach of the first ridge. Then he went back.

Hoku saw Homikniwa and Kewa after they exited the Bluehawk. Homikniwa was moving quickly, not quite running, and Kewa stumbled after him. She seemed better, and Hoku felt a bit relieved; maybe she didn't have a concussion after all. Ten more steps and they would have the alien. Hoku could deal with Jimmie later. For now, they just had to get out of here, before the Reed flyer showed up.

There was no sound at all, but a red rose bloomed on Kewa's back, and she spun around like a child playing "whirlwind". Her eyes were very wide, the one glimpse he had of them. Then she was lying on her face in the dirt.

Homikniwa was moving faster than a human being ought to move. A score of bright green spears stabbed out from him toward the ridge as he sped across the ground, leapt over a two-meter high shelf of stone, and vanished.

Hoku gaped, comprehension suddenly inserting itself into his forebrain. Where the fuck had those shots come from? He hadn't seen!

But Homikniwa had been shooting at a specific target; Hoku had seen the bursts. Furiously, Hoku thumbed the gun sight around and fired a missile towards where Hom's shots had been aimed. The Bluehawk seemed to gasp with its release, and Hoku watched the white trail bridge the distance to the mountain. There was the briefest of pauses, and then a blue-white flash that left spots before his eyes. A few seconds later, the sharp roar of the explosion shuddered the Bluehawk.

Hoku watched the ridge, now obscured by drifting smoke, blinking furiously at the afterimage of the detonation.

For a few moments, nothing, and then a sharp report, as of someone clapping boards together, right by his ear. He jumped, startled. There was a pockmark on the windshield, right in front of his face. It would have gone right between his eyes, had the shield been anything less than chainglass.

What was this creature?

And where was Homikniwa?

Frustrated, targetless, Hoku waited with his thumb on the laser contact.

CHAPTER THIRTY

Teng squeezed off two more shots at the man in the flyer before she gave up. She hadn't been certain that the colonials would use chainglass for everything, but it appeared that they did. Still, whoever was there was rattled; the missile had come nowhere near her, and the jabs from the laser were sufficiently uninformed that they posed no threat either. Not so the little man on the ground, whose aim had been uncannily accurate. Teng wondered if he were another of these "Kachina". If so, he would be a problem, but not one she couldn't handle. The last time she had been too concerned about Alvar to concentrate. This time, there would be no such distraction. Wherever Alvar was, he was no longer any concern of hers.

Bullshit, said an irritating little voice. At least she hadn't spoken out loud this time.

Where was he? Teng wished for a pair of broad-spectrum goggles. Her own "natural" sight had some enhancements—she could see a bit further down the red end of the spectrum than the unenhanced, could see more detail at greater distances. But she couldn't see the heat tail her foe was leaving—if he was moving at all.

She glimpsed him an instant later, darting from the shelter of a rock, traversing an open slope with improbable speed. She squeezed off two of the explosive rounds, almost instantly regretted it as the eruptions clouded the area with dense grey dust. She had assumed that the storm wet things down, but she didn't know this area. Or this planet, for that matter.

Well, he would be closer, soon. Teng searched about for a defensible position, found it in a ledge of stone a few meters away.

While she waited, Teng thought through her long-term plans. If the peacekeeper flyer had made it through the colonials' defensive perimeter—and Teng had few doubts about that—the reinforcements would be here soon. What then? Retrieve the alien, she supposed, and Jimmie if possible. But then again, what did Teng want with the alien? She found it unlikely in the extreme that the alien would be of any use to the Vilmir Foundation. The real challenge was the alien ships themselves. The Vilmir Foundation wanted them of course, for the technology they might contain. Yet the possibility that they could learn something from the ships paled before the dangers they represented. The ships had made one attempt to contact the colonials, by sending down this bizarre clone. Why couldn't they do it again, after Teng left, with or without the alien woman? Teng had no idea how long it would be before a real pacification force managed to get here, but she supposed it would be some time; Vilmir resources were spread thin, and despite the importance of the alien ships, it would take many years for a real expedition to get funded, built, and sent, especially after the recent revolt on Serengeti.

The other great risk was that Jimmie was right, that the ships posed a danger to the colonists themselves. If the Fifth World were destroyed, the long-term investment of the Foundation would be in shambles. Teng had already fought in one stock-market war, and had no particular wish to fight in another.

Yes, counting on the alien woman was a risk the Fifth Worlders had to take because it was their only choice. Teng, however, was rapidly coming to see another. She was a warrior, and she wanted to fight. It was the only thing she was good at, that much was clear to her now.

A rock clattered down-slope. A ruse or an actual stumble on her opponent's part? It didn't matter. She was death, and the man was coming to meet her. Teng took several deep breaths, preparing. She checked her weapon. Thirteen rounds left, and it only took one.

Fuck Alvar, anyway. Sure, he had been plagued; that meant only that he had done what he really wanted. Maybe he really had loved her, when she was the only woman available, but now . . . she would have had to leave him anyway. What was the point? He was right and she was wrong. His life was here, now, and it was best that the break be clean. Very clean.

She caught the motion in her peripheral vision and dove without hesitation. Green light licked at her ear, and the wet stone behind her hissed and spit. She rolled, firing twice, using explosive rounds—and that was the end of those. She flicked the magazine to armor-piercing as she came to her feet, running straight into the new cloud. Her wounds hurt mightily, but they would not bleed; a day or so was all her system needed to throw up dikes around such surface cuts. She could wish for a little less stiffness, but everything had a price.

Another laser burst scored across her shoulder, and the concealment web sputtered, most likely broken now. She would have to end this fast, then: now the man in the flyer would be able to see her. In fact, the one glance she spared to the plain showed her the flyer slowly lifting. She needed the laser, now.

She spun down behind a rock as the barrel of her enemy's rifle appeared again, and she squeezed off two more rounds; they struck bright sparks on stone, both of them. If she gave the man time, he would pin her down. He was only six or seven meters away. It was now or never.

Teng leaped up like a panther, the rifle pumping steadily in her hand. She covered the distance in no time at all, following her bullets. She suppressed an urge to howl, and a fierce joy bubbled in her blood as adrenaline that was better than adrenaline lit her up.

When she came over the ridge, he was moving, and her first two shots missed. The third caught him clean in the belly, and the fight should have been over. Instead, he launched himself at her, leg stabbing out a sidekick. She fired once more before the blow hit her, reasonably assuming any physical attack he landed was less dangerous than the laser. Blood spurted in the center of his chest.

The kick punched into her like a steel piston. She felt her hardened ribs break, and one tore into her lung. The impact lifted her up and back, and the rifle spun from her hands as she twisted to break her fall against the rocks. The little man followed her; his face was a mask, set and certain. He still had the laser, but he did not point the barrel at her, instead swung it down on her like a club. She deflected it with a rising block and countered with her own kick, striking him a glancing blow. He fell back, landed roughly against the stone. They watched each other then, both lying there. Teng noticed that he wasn't bleeding very much.

"Who are you?" she gasped painfully. Her punctured lung felt as if it had collapsed, and breathing was painful.

The little man rose shakily to his feet.

"Leave these people alone. Just get the fuck out of here and leave them alone." He spoke in English, not the local language.

"Who are you?" she repeated, rising to her feet also, watching him for any move. She still had the pain pistol, but he had a sidearm as well. Who would be quicker? And if what she suspected was true, the pain pistol might not hurt him at all.

"Escobar Jemez, of the colonial Peacekeepers, at your service," he said, mockingly.

A wave of nausea swept through Teng, but she kept her focus. She would have to move soon.

"Bullshit," she said. "How can that be?"

"You think the Foundation just sent one traitor here? You know better than that."

"You sent that message. Not Jimmie: you."

"I shouldn't have done it. I knew that even then. This place isn't for the Reed. They have no claim on this place."

"Fuck you," Teng gasped. "They bought and paid for this planet. You too."

"That's the way you see things," Jemez said. "I don't see them that way. I've been here twenty-five years."

He didn't look that old. Had he been rejuvenated once, already? Paid in advance?

"You went native," Teng observed. "How touching."

He went for his pistol, and Teng jumped. They came together in a flurry of blows. Fists like rocks slammed into Teng, but she felt her own punches land, too. She got a fistful of hair and yanked his head back, felt the knife-edge of her hand deflected from his throat. Something clattered near their feet, and she twisted, managed to throw him a meter or so. Her hand found the gun without the assistance of her eyes, and she brought it up into his belly as he closed again. Fired, once, twice, three times.

These bullets were not armor piercing: they did not slide cleanly through his body, but mushroomed, kicking him backwards. He hit the rocks, curled around his belly, so that she could see the caverns that had been torn from his back. Teng scrambled away; he might still get up. She pointed the pistol at his head and carefully pulled the trigger.

The hammer clicked on an empty chamber.

No matter. Jemez looked up at her with glazed eyes, but the light in them was fading. Or was that the light she saw growing dimmer? It was very hard to breathe, now. She cast about, looking for her rifle.

Green light stabbed within a meter of her. She had forgotten the fucking flyer. If he had another missile . . . But she couldn't even run from the laser.

The flyer puffed then, and the trail of a missile screamed out of it. Teng watched it, ready to meet death, but the trail sang over her head. She threw herself down, and even to her protected ears, the detonation was deafening. Above her, lasers flickered.

She turned her head, and there, coming over the ridge, was a peacekeeper flyer, listing. A dark smudge showed where it had taken a direct hit.

The colonial flyer dropped out of the air, however, underjets flaming. It limped away, back down toward the plain.

"Shu!" said the voice in her ear. Who was that? Vraslav?

"Come get me," she hissed. "Ignore them. Come get me."

Figures were scrambling out of the burning flyer, which had managed to land. Two men, a woman—one of them was Alvar.

Something broke in Teng, something besides her modified parts.

"Just come get me," she repeated.

For the second time, Sand felt the Bluehawk jar to earth. She felt the heat seeping up through the floor and knew that the underjets were burning. Outside, she could see Kewa's body, and beyond that the shelter where Jimmie and Tuchvala lay.

The hatchway to the cockpit swung open, and a grim faced Hoku came through it. He unfastened Alvar's straps and then her own.

"Go," he said harshly. "Get out. We're on fire."

Sand scrambled out as best she could without using her arms, which were still cuffed and numb. Alvar followed, even more clumsily, and then Hoku, pistol in hand. The three of them rushed away from the burning Bluehawk; flames were fluttering underneath it as if it were being roasted.

"Take our cuffs off, Hoku," she gasped. "I'll help if I can."

He ignored her. He was stock-still looking up at the mountain. A haze of smoke drifted there, but it did not entirely obscure the unfamiliar flyer as it dipped down.

"For Masaw's children!" Sand shrieked. "Uncuff me!"

Instead, Hoku took up a marksman's stance with the pistol and waited. Sand thought about rushing him, but there was no point; she could accomplish nothing. Instead she ran over to where Tuchvala and Jimmie lay.

Tuchvala looked asleep, and there were splints on her leg. Jimmie watched her coming. He looked hurt, but Sand couldn't tell how bad.

"Sand. . . ." he began, but her kick in his ribs cut him short and set him to coughing.

"Uncuff me, you murdering bastard," she screamed. Jimmie scrambled back from her, crabwise.

"Uncuff me!" she repeated.

"Wait!" Jimmie howled as she kicked him again, this time in the arm he raised to defend himself.

"Wait. I will."

Sand stopped and stood panting as her father jerkily climbed to his feet. She kept him impaled with her stare, and it seemed to draw him to her, though the reluctance was plain in his eyes. He reached up and fingered the cuffs, and suddenly Sand could feel her arms again. She shook the cuffs of and Jimmie backed up. He walked off a few meters and sat back down. Sand watched him go, then turned to Tuchvala.

Tuchvala was breathing regularly. Sand knelt and stroked her face, very gently.

"Tuchvala?" she said. Her mother's face twitched, her eyes opened.

"Sand? Sand, what's happening?"

Sand gasped, realized that she was crying. She took Tuchvala in her arms and hugged her, pressed the bitterness of her tears against the other woman's cheek.

"It's good to see you, Tuchvala," she said.

"Sand," Tuchvala sighed, clinging back.

The moment seemed to last forever, but Sand knew she could afford very little time. Reluctantly, she turned back towards Hoku and the mountain.

Hoku was still standing there, waiting. The Reed flyer had risen again, hovering over the erstwhile battlefield. Sand watched it, made ready to die. They would not get Tuchvala away from her again, not while she lived.

But the flyer turned its nose away from them, and with a distant whine, disappeared west over the hills. Hoku howled and fired three shots after it, then began running over the rough ground, favoring his right leg.

Feeling weak and unsure of what was happening, Sand sat back down. Alvar was leaning against a stone, watching Hoku dwindle in the distance. Jimmie still sat where he had retreated to, his back to them.

"Are you okay, Tuchvala?" Sand asked.

"I think so, Sand," the woman answered. "But I don't understand what's happening."

Sand expelled a harsh little laugh. "I don't either, my friend. I only know we're together again." She reached over and squeezed Tuchvala's hand.

"Teng, what are you doing?" she heard Alvar mutter. Wearily, Sand stood and walked over to where he was, and without a word, freed him of his cuffs. He looked at her with surprise.

"Thanks," he said, with real gratitude. Sand nodded. The Bluehawk was burning merrily, now, thick smoke billowing out of its interior.

"We should move away from that," Sand said.

Tuchvala was incapable of walking, but she and Alvar together managed to carry her another hundred paces from the burning craft. Jimmie did not follow, but he watched Sand with eyes she was unwilling to meet. Why? She was justified in hating him.

But at the moment, for some reason, she did not.

"Can you puzzle any of this out?" She asked Alvar, when they again slumped down to the desert floor. He shrugged, but looked thoughtful.

"Maybe," he said, after a long moment. "If I know Teng, maybe."

"Well?"

"I think she's going to do something extreme, Sand. I think she's decided to fuck it all.

"Meaning?"

Alvar looked up to the sky. The clouds were clearing rapidly, hastening east to bring rain to the pueblos. Sand wondered briefly how many days Pela had been dead: she had lost track. Could that be her mother up there, wearing her mask of cotton?

"She's going to attack the ships," Alvar said quietly.

CHAPTER THIRTY-ONE

Hoku found Homikniwa in the rocks, painted red with his own blood. He was still breathing, and his eyes, though fogged with approaching death, flickered with recognition when Hoku scrambled down towards him.

"Ah, no," Hoku hissed. "Hom!"

Homikniwa shifted his head feebly.

"I'm sorry, Hoku," he said. Blood frothed on his lips. "It's just been too long. Forgotten too much."

How could Homikniwa still be alive at all? Hoku counted at least five bullet holes in the little man.

"It's okay, Hom," he said. "I. . . ." He reached down to his friend. Homikniwa's blood felt sticky, like syrup. Hoku had never actually had another person's blood on his skin. Now, he was smeared in it as he raised Homikniwa's head to hold it.

"There's more, Hoku. It was me that. . . . The Reed planted me here, long ago, to spy on you. I did bad things at first, evil things. I was a two-heart, Hoku. Two-hearts are real."

Hoku stared down at what was left of his friend.

"You're like her, aren't you?" Hoku asked.

"Not anymore. Hoku, I betrayed the Fifth World, long ago. But it's my home now. These are my people. Believe that Hoku. I want to be buried a Hopi."

"Of course you are Hopi, Hom. The best of us, that's you."

Homikniwa coughed again.

"You can stop the Reed, Hoku." His voice was draining out of him, his eyes were already dull.

"But you have to cooperate with the traditionals. Do you understand? I can't see you anymore, brother. Can you hear me?"

"I hear you, brother. I hear you, ibaba."

A dry wind bustled about them, stealing off the lingering smell of rain and explosives. A clean, husking wind. Homikniwa continued to mumble, and Hoku made soothing sounds as the world rotated into night, as the stars lit. By the time the little Moon rose, Homikniwa was speaking no longer, but Hoku continued to talk to him. The wind died down, but Hoku had inhaled it. It swirled within him now, and for the first time in his adult life, Hoku had no plans, no schemes, nothing he could conceive of doing, but to sing softly, to sing the song of the Sipapuni that he had tried so hard to forget, to beg the Kachina to come and take one of their own.

"That is very bad," Tuchvala said, breaking the silence that followed Alvar's pronouncement.

"If she attacks my sisters, there will be no stopping them. They will kill us all."

Alvar felt the chill of coming night, but could think of no way to stave it off, nothing to say. He could not even imagine a whole world wiped clean, but the picture Tuchvala painted seemed real enough. She believed it, Sand believed it. What choice did Alvar have?

"This is my fault," he muttered.

"What? What language is that?" Sand asked him. She seemed calm, bereft of the fire that had seemed so intrinsic to her from the moment they met.

"It's called Norte. It's what we speak back home."

"Where is that?"

"I was born in Santa Fe," Alvar answered. An ugly place, he added to himself. An *ugly* place I miss more than the memory of God.

"On Earth? That's on Earth."

"Yes. What I said was, 'this is my fault'."

"Is it?" Sand asked mildly. You summoned Tuchvala's sisters here, then commed the Reed to come and get them? You arranged for Hoku to have my father kill my mother, and then you somehow put the idea in my head that I should hall Tuchvala all over the Fifth World like she was my toy and I some selfish child? No offense, Alvar, but you don't seem capable of all that."

"No," Alvar answered. "No, I'm not capable of anything grandiose. But Teng is my fault. I think when she saw us . . . ah, you remember . . . I think that drove her over the edge. Otherwise, she would have just taken Tuchvala and gone." He raised his hands and added hastily, "I know that isn't what any of you wanted. But it couldn't be as bad as having the whole world destroyed."

Tuchvala cut in. "He's right. It would be better. I wonder . . ." she trailed off, then turned back to Alvar. "What kind of weapons does she have? Could she win? Could she destroy my sisters and me?"

Alvar shook his head. "When she was saner, she didn't even want to try. I don't know. If anyone can beat anything, it would be Teng. But we came in one little ship, cobbled together. Against those three monsters in orbit—ah, no offense—I don't see what she can do. But then, I'm sure she didn't show me all of the weapons, either."

Tuchvala shrugged. "I suppose we will see. If I could talk to my sisters first, that would be good. Sand, can we contact your people? Or even Hoku's?"

"I don't know. Hoku's gone insane, too. But I would guess any transceivers were in the Bluehawk. I suppose Hoku's men will come looking for him, eventually, but unless the computers are back on line, we don't have much of a chance."

Sand caught movement from the corner of her eye. It was Jimmie, shuffling up behind them. His gaze slipped about, unwilling to
touch any of theirs. He reached into his jacket and removed a black,
translucent cube. He laid it near Sand, then walked off, slowly, ten
meters or so.

It was a transceiver.

Sand picked up the cube, felt the weight of it. She spoke the
code for the council chamber in Tuwanasavi. It glowed and cleared,
to reveal a longish man in the garb of Hoku's lieutenants.

"This is SandGreyGirl of the Sand clan," she said. "How is your
day, ibaba?"

The man frowned and addressed her stiffly.

"What does this concern?"

"Your chief and the rest of us are in the desert west of the pueblos, at the feet of the Cornbeetle mountains. I suggest you send a
flyer to get us."

"If the mother-father is there, I would like to speak to him."

"He's off hunting," Sand said. "Come get us. I'll leave this on so
you can have a signal."

She broke visual contact and set the cube down. It began ping-
ing for attention almost immediately, and she lifted it again and
threw it as far as she could.

Hoku paused over the corpse of Kewa for a long moment, unsure
what to feel. Here was a woman he hardly knew, and he had killed her
on a gamble. He had killed her. He once believed he was up to that;
he had planned deaths all of his life. He had had Pela killed, and never
flinched; he was as insulated from her death as he was from the vacuum and cold of deep space. Even when he realized that the woman
need not have died, he was able to justify his decision, move on.

Now Homikniwa, whom he loved, was dead. Kewa, whom he
could have loved lay at his feet, her glassy eyes fixed on mystery. His

Bluehawk was still burning, and in the unsteady light her shadow shivered about her like a ghost.

This is what comes of trying to make order out of chaos, Hoku thought. The hero twins did that—made the world orderly and sane—and he had always supposed, deep down, that he and Hom were the hero twins. But no, he was Coyote, who only thought he could bring order. Coyote, more often tricking himself than anyone else, but bringing disaster to all.

Part of him sneered at that thought. What was a coyote? No Fifth Worlder had ever seen one. But now he had a picture to go with the old stories, and the picture was of himself. Not the happy trickster, but the jealous destroyer. Was that it? Had he always been jealous of those with close clan and kin, of the pueblos?

Part of him rejected that, too. It was just that his vision had been so clear. What hope did the pueblos have against something like the Reed, against creatures like Homikniwa and Teng? Probably about as much chance as he and his lowlanders, in retrospect, which meant none at all. But he had had to try! Now the alien woman—this Tuchvala was here, in his grasp. He could see her with the others, huddled beneath the stars. They had watched him impassively when he returned, carrying Hom's body.

Well, he had her. What now? He went over to ask.

No one spoke to him when he joined the circle. He didn't expect them to. Hoku turned to Sand, respectfully not meeting her eyes.

"I had my reasons, all of you," he said at last. "Looking back, maybe I was wrong. But I saw the Reed coming—for us, or worse, for our children, and I saw us helpless. Helpless. I don't want forgiveness from any of you; forgiveness wouldn't help any of us. Sand, I owe you a clan debt, and someday, one way or another, you may collect that. I don't know. I killed your mother."

Sand just watched him, her face tired and unreadable. Hoku went on. "Jimmie didn't know. He would never have done it. We infected him with a virus, but it was a virus which could only kill Pela. When he touched her, or kissed her. . . ."

"I kissed her!" The anguished cry was barely human. Jimmie was on his feet, and for one moment, Hoku thought he had a gun in his hand, or a knife, that he would fling himself at Hoku. But instead, he just stood there, shuddering, weeping.

"Sit down, father," Sand said quietly. "Sit down and listen to what Hoku has to say."

"I killed her, not Jimmie," Hoku repeated. Jimmie sat down, gasping for breath. What could Hoku ever do for him? What was done was done.

"My friend is dead," Hoku went on. "Before he died, he told me what he has always told me; that the Hopi should be one people."

"The pueblos will never follow you, conquered or free," Sand told him, without heat.

Hoku shrugged. "True. I don't care about that. I don't know what to do at all, SandGreyGirl. I've schemed and chased and killed to get this woman, this Tuchvala."

He turned towards the woman. She was beautiful. Had Pela been so beautiful? Hoku had never met her. He never would.

"Tuchvala. I am Hoku, from the lowlands. You have been the prize in a game I thought that I understood. I have to know now; was it worth it? Do these deaths mean anything? Can you save us?"

The woman looked back at him with—sadness? Concern? She spoke slowly, as if making absolutely certain he would understand.

"I came here to save you," she said. "I don't know that I can. I understand what you fear from the Reed—now—but I did not come here to save you from them. I came here to save you from myself, from my sisters."

And as Hoku listened, she told her story, a story of stars and time, of age and madness. And Hoku believed; this was no mystical vision, no religious nonsense. This was metal and energy and fact. He had seen those ships, through the telescopes.

"The pueblos revere you as a Kachina," he whispered, when she was done. "I have never admitted belief in them, never given credence to such superstition, save perhaps when I was very young. It doesn't matter anymore, does it? Whatever I call you, whatever you are named, you are the same thing. Tuchvala, all of you. My life has always been lived for this world, the Fifth World—believe that or don't. Tell me what to do now, and we will do it."

In the distance, there was a sound like wind. The flyers were coming at last.

CHAPTER THIRTY-TWO

"There," the man said. The binary code had been sent to my sisters, and a string of signals answered. They were listening. From now on, they would listen to me speak in the language of human beings; it was apparent that this was the easiest course, since I could no longer send or comprehend in our own language, and human speech organs could not produce the sounds of the language of the Makers.

The others sat around me, more quietly than I ever knew human beings could be. Despite the throbbing pain in my leg, the tension of what I was about to attempt, I felt at ease. These people comforted me in a way I had never been comforted, despite my short time amongst them, despite the fact that some of them had been intent upon my capture or demise since I came to be on the Fifth World. Perhaps—I had to consider this—perhaps something of Pela's tohodanet still lived in me, mixed with mine. In many of my dreams, I am a mother, Sand is my child. Perhaps Pela is the only reason I never became insane, though it is clear tom me that I should have. Whatever the reason, live or die, I had found a place I never imagined existed before.

"Sister," I began.

The voice that came back to me was one of the many voices of the Hopi computer, and still, when I heard it, it became the voice of my otherself, my mother and my sister. I knew it in an instant.

"Hello," it said. "So you have accomplished this much, at least."

"Yes."

"I recognize your voice," my sister said. Of course she did. She had listened to me learn to talk. I hoped that it would make things easier.

"How is the situation up there?" I asked, cautiously.

"Our sisters have not changed, though Hatedotik (The name sounded like sputtering to me, but I understood who she meant) has become more agitated, because the outsystem ship has been conducting odd maneuvers. She is also aware of you, now. I could not keep the information from her, and she had more sentience left than I thought."

"She can hear us now, of course," I said.

"Of course, as can Odatatek, for what that may be worth. You remember that what we speak of here is an analogue of the three of us, not merely "my" voice."

"I understand that. I *am* you, remember?"

"Of course. Tell us what you have learned."

I drew a breath. Could I be truthful? Maybe. And maybe they would not know if I lied.

"As we suspected," I told her, "these people are intelligent, like the Makers."

"But not the Makers," she answered.

"No, of course not. But they have worked hard, made this planet a home. They are worthy to keep it."

"You have yet to convince me of that."

"They understand etadotetak," I told her, carefully attempting to render the hissing clicks of the Maker's language.

"You mean etadotetak?" my sister corrected me.

"Yes."

"They understand it. But do they possess it?"

"They are willing to kill and die that others might survive."

"There is more to etadotetak than that."

"True," I said, "But how to quantify such a thing?"

I recognized my emotion as fear, now. I had indeed changed. How much of what I said would my sisters even understand?

"Listen," I continued, urgently. "I am you. You know that. There is no cause to re-seed this planet. It is already seeded. And the Makers are dead, anyway. They. . . ."

"What? From what evidence do you draw such a ridiculous conclusion?" There was, of course, no human inflection in the voice, but I suddenly recognized Hatedotik's impatience. My sisters had drawn more tightly together. They saw the starship as a threat, and they were re-integrating. Combining their madnesses.

"The three of you, listen to me! The Makers must be extinct. These people have colonized many of the other farms, and never have the Makers returned to dispute or claim them. Never, in all of the millennia. We formed these worlds so that the Makers could live upon them, didn't we? Where are they?"

My sisters think with great speed. There was no pause, no chance for me to marshal other arguments.

"This is not important, unless these creatures themselves killed the Makers, which we consider a distinct possibility."

I had not thought of that, and the prospect appalled me. The humans in the room were shaking their heads violently, no—but I knew them by now, knew that they would deny such a thing even if it were true. Or they might not know what had occurred; there were so many factions among them, so much done secretly, by only a few. . . .

"That doesn't make sense," I decided. "As evinced from what we have experienced, these people do not have the technical power to destroy the Makers. Their weapons are too crude, their means too limited."

"The Makers have etadotetak," my sister said. "Perhaps they allowed these creatures to populate some of their worlds."

"Listen to yourself!" I cried, seizing upon that. "Perhaps that is so! And if the Makers made such a decision, how can we do likewise?"

"But I think your first guess is more probable," she answered. "I think the Makers are dead."

"Then this world should belong to these people. They are sufficiently similar to the Makers."

"We weren't built to decide that. We were built to maintain these worlds in a particular way. Not so the Makers could settle them, as you claim. That was a secondary consideration. We were built to do this because the Makers had etadotetak."

She had said it; what I had been unable to voice, what I had forgotten when I made this human body. Who had remembered it? Hatedotik? Odadatek?

"Sisters, listen. We are very, very, old. Older than our brains and systems were really meant to function. You know that: that's why I was created. Because in this body, in this brain, I could become whole, undamaged, sane. I am that, or very nearly so. Of all of us, I am the most like a Maker. That is the truth. I am the only one capable of comprehending etadotetak. Consider your last statement, sisters, because it is crucial. We were designed to modify planets so that they bore life. Not just so that the Makers could have habitable worlds, but so that there would be more life. They had etadotetak, not just for their race, but for the universe. They would not object to a modification of that life to suit the needs of another race. That is all that has happened here. The Makers' plan had been fulfilled."

"The Creator!" Croaked Yuyahoeva, from behind me, before even my sisters could react. "Elder sisters, listen to me! I am Yuyahoeva of the Sand clan, mother-father of the pueblo of Tawanasavi! We know that this world was created, not for us, but just so that it would be! But the creator—and Masaw, the caretaker of this world—he indulged our existence here. You have heard this! You sister tells me that you have heard our songs, our legends, our faith. We understand that this world is not ours, but that we have been allowed to live upon it. The hero twins were given leave to change it, to make it suitable for us. But every moment of every year, we send our thanks to you and your Makers. You know this, if you have listened to us." The old man panted off into silence, but the other Hopis in the room—Hoku included—sounded gentle agreement to the words he had spoken.

This time, there was a silence, and in that silence, my sisters could exchange a hundred billion thoughts. They had ceased to reckon with us, I knew that, though my friends thought my sisters were merely mulling over a response. They had heard all they were going to hear. Our fate, I thought, was already decided.

"We consider that a convincing argument," my sister said, finally. "But the human ship in orbit has just fired energy weapons at us. Apparently, their sense of etadotetak is not as finely tuned as you claim."

Teng was a goddess again. The little man had hurt her, shaken her. How could she have known that there was a rogue peacekeeper on this miserable planet? But now her torn lung had a temporary inflation, and a half-liter of medical miracles had her feeling fine. With the help of her comrades' covering fire, she had brushed aside the defenses around the drum as if they were flies. Nothing had impeded the drum's assent into space, and the single pitiful nuclear weapon the Fifth-Worlders sent climbing after her had been easy to stop. Now the drum was back with its mother, and Teng sat poised behind some of the deadliest weapons known to humanity.

"Strap in." she snapped, over the intercom, and ten seconds later she kindled the drive and opened it to a full gravity. Coiled compensators whined to cope with the stress as she increased the feed, and she sagged back in her couch as her weight doubled. One pass, that was all she would get; she would not float about while the alien ships marshaled themselves; she would whip by them, one at a time, and when she was past they would be debris. After that, who gave a shit?

Already the first one was within weapons range. She clenched her teeth, happier than she had been in some time. She targeted and cut on the particle beam, launched a half-score of her smartest missiles. She watched the beams punch out at the alien ship, checked the spectrometer when nothing dramatic happened. Nothing; no sign of vaporized metal, nothing.

Three of the hydrogen bombs detonated, but too far from their target. Nothing.

"Fuck!" She howled. In moments, she would be past this one, and she hadn't scratched it. What could withstand the beam? Maybe some kind of charged field. Lasers, then.

She flicked on the forward x-ray lasers. Was her enemy responding at all? Seconds ticked by.

The cube crackled and lit of its own accord. Someone with a code.

Alvar, of course. His face was wild with fear—she had always loved that expression on him, the first few times they fucked, when he thought she might kill or cripple him.

"Teng! Teng! What the fuck are you doing? Teng! They'll destroy this world!"

"Fuck you, Alvar." Her attention was on the ship. It was spinning on its axis, faster than she imagined might be possible for a craft of such mass. It was pointing its drive at her! And, she noticed, the X-Ray lasers were having an effect. They had boiled perhaps a millimeter of her opponent's hull into space.

"Teng, calm down." Alvar was desperately trying to calm himself, she knew. She spared him a glance.

"I am, calm, Alvar. I'm not human, remember?" But his face

made her ache, like she hadn't since she was a child. Ache! That, she would not have. She adjusted her course a bit and launched two more bombs. Of course, at this acceleration (climbing now past four gravities) she would get to the ship long before the weapons did. And there was one other weapon, one which would almost certainly be effective.

"Teng. I love you, Teng."

A sudden calm settled over Teng Shu, a calm such as she had never known in her entire life. It was sweet, sweeter than anything. It was like swimming in the cool waters of the Kelbab River, but it soaked all the way through. She could see the open mouth of the alien drive, a hole that nearly eclipsed the ship itself. It would not quite make it; she would reach the monster before it was fully turned. Her lung had collapsed again under the pressure of acceleration, and even her heart was reaching its limit, as the blood's uphill climb to her brain became too steep. But she was lucid, sharp. She saw everything.

"It's okay, Alvar," she managed to whisper, through her skinned-back teeth.

"Today is a good day to die."

And then she saw the brightest light she had ever seen.

There should be a sound, Alvar thought. There should be trumpets, drums, an explosion.

There wasn't though. The telescope showed them very clearly, at a speed they could comprehend, the visual of what happened; but it happened in utter silence. There was the Mixcoatl, his home for three years. It was aimed dead on at the alien ship, which was turning with incredible speed to meet the attack. Teng and her crew were less than a hundred kilometers away when a perfect white light stabbed out from the alien craft. Actually, "stabbed" was wrong, because it wasn't there, and then it was, even on this slow rendering. The Mixcoatl was not caught full; it just brushed the drive, or whatever it was. But it was suddenly gone, replaced by a white-hot tongue of flame.

Jimmie was shaking his head. "She got close enough. Son-of-a-bitch. At those speeds. . . ."

The molten jet of plasma that had been the Mixcoatl skinned up the side of the alien ship, which suddenly light up like a red candle, dull save for that one brilliant streak. The drive stayed on.

"Jesus! Jimmie leapt to the telescope, and nobody stopped him; they were staring at the image, the column of light and its dull, glowing apex. It didn't seem to be moving, despite the drive.

"Where the fuck is that thing going?" Jimmie asked no one, but then he began giving the computer pointed commands. A new display appeared some kind of gravitic map that made no sense to Alvar at all.

It's not going anywhere! Alvar thought, and then: Teng!

But of course the ship was moving. Its drive was on. The Hopi telescope must have had orders to track it, wherever it went, so it didn't appear to be moving. If the ship was coming down, into the planet's gravity well. . . . then it would be here very, very soon.

But after a long moment, Jimmie visibly relaxed.

"Fucking drive is barely on. And it's headed out."

"What if it explodes?"

Tuchvala was blinking at tears like an owl. She was crying for the ship. What about Teng? Why wasn't he crying?

"No," she said. "The drive can't explode. It would just go out. She must be . . . that would have killed her, but the drive is still on. . . ."

"What will they do?" Sand asked, softly, taking Tuchvala's arm. Alvar thought they looked more like sisters than ever.

"What will the other two do?"

Tuchvala shook her head. I don't know. She buried her face against Sand's shoulder.

Alvar looked back at the image, which the tech had just had re-set for a wider angle. The wreath of gas that had been the Mixcoatl was barely visible, far behind the dead, fleeing ship.

"I do love you, Teng," he murmured.

CHAPTER THIRTY-THREE

"The ships are moving," Jimmie whispered. "The other two are moving."

"No. Oh, no." Tuchvala gasped, disengaging herself from Sand. Sand let her go reluctantly. She felt unreal, as if in a fever. It seemed that everything had happened so long ago, so far away. Her mother, Tuchvala, the Whipper—and most of all, the terrible, slow dream that was unfolding before them on the cube. The battle of Kachina.

Unreal.

Hoku pounced from his chair. "We have some weapons. We may yet . . ."

Yuyahoeva waved him down. "No. What can we do that the Reed ship did not? Tuchvala, speak to your sisters."

Hoku looked ready to dispute the old man, but the gleam in his eye wavered. He slowly nodded his head.

"But they will kill us, now," he said. No one disagreed.

Tuchvala stepped a little closer to the cube.

"Sister? Sister?" Her voice seemed small.

"Tektakdek. Tektakdek." The voice was as uninflected as before.

"Tektakdek is me," Tuchvala told them, eyes wide. "Sisters."

"You sound different, Tektakdek, now that you are dead." No irony, no anger, just syllables.

"Listen to me," Tuchvala began, but the voice cut over her.

"Tektakdek, tell us what to do."

Tuchvala was silent then, her face changing with each instant, as if she were experimenting with her muscles to find the ones that would properly show her feelings.

"You two are moving," Tuchvala said at last. "What are you going to do?"

"I think. . . ." the voice didn't trail off; it just stopped, and then started an instant later.

"Don't we have a planet to seed?"

"No," Tuchvala said. "The time for planting is long past."

"Tektakdek. There were human people on that ship, weren't there? The one that killed you?"

"There were."

"That was etadotetak, wasn't it?"

"Yes, sister, it was. That was sacrifice, one of the six legs of etado-tetak."

"You did this also. The humans on the ship, and you."

Tuchvala hesitated before answering. "Yes. We are all like the Makers. We have pleased them."

"Perhaps they will come some day, and tell us they are pleased," the voice said.

"Perhaps so. Sisters, are you still moving?"

"Yes. We are moving to a higher orbit."

"Why are you doing that?" Tuchvala looked concerned. What would her sisters do from a higher orbit? What could they unleash upon the Fifth World?

"Tektakdek. I thought you said we should sleep for a time, as when we are in the spaces between the farms. Didn't you tell us that?"

"I may have, sister," Tuchvala told the voice. "That would be a good idea. I, also, shall sleep."

"We will sleep," the voice answered.

"Dream well, sisters," Tuchvala said, and they did not speak again.

They tracked the ships for another day, neither sleeping nor eating. The two craft went out far, where the atmosphere was very, very thin. And there they went to sleep.

CHAPTER THIRTY-FOUR

That is my story. If I had been wise enough, I would have known from the beginning that my own death was the answer. After all, Hatedotik and Odatatek couldn't really think without what was left in me. There was no possibility of adjudication without Tektakdek; even the fierce certainty of Hatedotik was only the shadow of her in my own backbonebrain; without my will and life, its voice was feeble and indecisive. My death was always the answer. Did I—my other self—realize that, in the moments before the Reed warship lit me up like a prayer candle? Probably; brief moments were once an eternity to me.

Now I age and grow old, watch the children grow. I learn what it means to be human, and even more, what it means to be Well-Behaved. To be Hopi. We gave my old self a funeral; though there was no body of course. Sand and I went together to watch the clouds, to try to pick out which one was Pela, and a few days later, which one was me. We were never certain, but I think it made Sand feel better, and I myself felt some easing of sadness.

Was I a Kachina? The older I become, the more reasonable it seems. My human brain cannot comprehend the hundreds of thousands of years I once lived, condenses them into mystery—the same mystery I have been shown in the sunset and in growing things. Perhaps I was a Kachina, once. But now I am a woman, and for me that is most sufficient.

EPILOGUE

2445 A.D.

Sand found Jimmie on the fourth day. He had moved his farmhouse to a ridge overlooking the vast bowl where Tuchvala had landed, four years before. Jimmie himself was rocking back and forth on a stone slab, watching the stars wink open in the blue velveteen sky.

"Hello father," she said, as she walked up to him. She thought her voice sounded rough, decided there was nothing she could do about it. Tenderness did not easily cut through pain, and she had little enough tenderness for Jimmie anyway.

"Sand. Hello." He continued rocking, not looking at her. "Would you like some corn coffee?"

"You got corn growing out here already?"

"Yes. Big cornbrake down in the bottom there, see? Where the Kachina landed."

Sand squinted a bit. Sure enough, she could see a dark patch of the tough plant, spreading across the crater floor.

"Good work," she said. "Pela would like to know her land is blooming."

"I know," Jimmie said. "See her smiling?" He pointed up at the purple sky. "That faint star," he told her. "She only really shines when she smiles. Kind of like you, Sand."

"Well, I am her daughter," Sand agreed. Then, after a moment: "and yours. Your daughter too."

A long, strained silence fell between them, Jimmie suddenly taking an interest in the ground near his feet. But after a while, he answered her.

"That's good to know, Sand."

She just nodded. She took him up on the offer of the coffee; it was good enough, a little bitter. He had probably boiled it too long.

"Remember," Jimmie asked—almost as if he were asking Pela, up there in the sky—"Remember that time the three of us flew out here? The first time you ever flew in a Dragonfly?"

Sand shifted uncomfortably.

"I remember. I do remember that."

"That's a fine new one you have."

"Yes it is. It can carry five hundred more kilos than the other one, too. I seeded that back stretch, near the mountains, while I was looking for you."

"What with?" He started rolling up a cornhusk cigarette.

She forced a little laugh. "Taproot dandelions. What else would grow there? Two years, maybe some fire clover."

Jimmie nodded. "Maybe. Maybe three." Another uncomfortable silence, until Jimmie had the cigarette going. Then he half turned to her, offering her a smoke. She took it, delicately, between thumb and forefinger.

"What's going on down there?" He asked, as she kissed the four winds, the sky and the earth with her smoky breath.

She shrugged. "A lot, I guess. My cousin Tali just had twins. Big news, in the pueblos. Twin boys."

"I can see her uncle bragging, now. Insufferable. I never liked him much," Jimmie confided.

"You never liked anybody much," Sand said, then wished she hadn't.

"Yuyahoeva died a while back. We tried to find you, but you were hiding out somewhere."

"Just as well," Jimmie said, taking back the smoke. "Just as well. I hate funerals."

"Me too. Maybe I got that from you."

"Maybe. If you got anything from me, it was probably some kinda hate."

Sand considered a reply, but nothing seemed appropriate. Instead she went on. "The elections finally settled out, down in the lowlands. Hoku came out pretty well, the bastard."

"He always will," Jimmie said. "But people are watching him, now. It won't be like it was before."

"No. After the truce, things just started breaking up. A lot of the lowlanders came home. Some of them complain about tradition, but it's better than it was, I guess. And the lowland council has real power again. And the Kachina thing—well, they had a referendum on that. Started an independent counsel, lowlanders and pueblos alike. Guess I'm sort of on it. The offworlder, too. Alvar."

"A politician," Jimmie said, smiling a bit. "Shoulda known that's what you'd come to, one day."

"Oh, no. I'm strictly an advisor. But we've decided to move ahead. Hoku was right about that. The Reed will come, probably sooner than later. Tuchvala thinks it might be possible to use her sisters, somehow. But as yet, we don't know."

Jimmie flinched a bit on hearing Tuchvala's name.

"She's not mother, dad," she said.

"I still can't stand to see her, Sand. You either, really. It's too hard."

"Selfish to the last," Sand remarked, a last taste of acid on her tongue.

"Yep."

Sand stood and dusted of her pants. "None of that's what I came here to say, father. You should come down to the pueblo. They can cure it, you know. There's still time. They can have you well in a couple of days, and you can come right back out here and hide."

Jimmie stubbed out the cigarette. "You happy with her?" He asked.

"Yes," Sand told him. "The two of us are thinking about marrying Kaso's boy for a year or two, maybe have some kids. You could be a grandfather."

Jimmie shook his head as if nodding affirmation. "One time, I thought I was gonna live forever," he said. "For that, your mother suffered and died. There it is."

He stood up, too, and after a moment, offered his hand.

"Thanks for coming out, daughter. Don't reckon I'll probably see you again."

She took his hand and squeezed it, hard.

"Bye, dad," she told him, turned and walked back towards her Dragonfly. She looked back once. He was staring back up at the sky, at Pela where she was smiling.

ABOUT THE AUTHOR

Greg Keyes was born in 1963 in Meridian, Mississippi. When his father took a job on the Navajo reservation in Arizona, Keyes was exposed at an early age to the cultures and stories of the Native Southwest, which would continue to influence him for years to come. He earned a bachelor's degree in anthropology from Mississippi State University and a master's degree from the University of Georgia. While pursuing a PhD at UGA, he wrote several novels, including *The Waterborn* and its sequel, *The Blackgod*. He followed these with the Age of Unreason books, the epic fantasy series Kingdoms of Thorn and Bone, and tie-in novels for numerous franchises, including Star Wars, Babylon 5, the Elder Scrolls, and Planet of the Apes. Keyes lives in Savannah, Georgia, with his wife, Nell; son, Archer; and daughter, Nellah.

EBOOKS BY GREG KEYES

FROM OPEN ROAD MEDIA

Available wherever ebooks are sold

OPEN ROAD

INTEGRATED MEDIA

Open Road Integrated Media is a digital publisher and multimedia content company. Open Road creates connections between authors and their audiences by marketing its ebooks through a new proprietary online platform, which uses premium video content and social media.

Videos, Archival Documents, and New Releases

Sign up for the Open Road Media newsletter and get news delivered straight to your inbox.

Sign up now at
www.openroadmedia.com/newsletters

FIND OUT MORE AT
WWW.OPENROADMEDIA.COM

FOLLOW US:
@openroadmedia and
Facebook.com/OpenRoadMedia

CPSIA information can be obtained at www.ICGtesting.com
Printed in the USA
BVOW05s1219200415

396400BV00001B/1/P